Reasons not to miss th

"Readers of your story .... of health and life philosophy, which will carry them to new heights of understanding—perhaps giving them the most definitive look at personal life responsibility they have ever had."

Dr. M.T. Morter, Jr., Founder and Developer
of Morter HealthSystem, author of *The Soul Purpose*
and numerous other books.

"Dr. Murdock is a born storyteller who sees the lighter side of life as well as the trials that we all go through."

Harriet Austin, the beloved writing teacher and
inspiration for the *Harriet Austin Writers Conference.*

"I look for good stories that teach me something; Dr. Murdock's entertaining and thought-provoking book is found treasure."

Genie Smith Bernstein, 2006 recipient of the
Carrie McCray Literary Award.

"Jim Murdock's story provides strong argument that what affects the soul also affects the body and that forgiveness of self and others holds the key to a healing that we might just call miraculous. This book might just save your life."

G. Richard Hoard, author of *Alone Among the Living*,
University of Georgia Press, 1994 and
The Race Before Us, Nancy Ann Publishing, 2006.

"The author of this book introduces a bold new way of writing a novel. Hold onto your hat and rev up your funny bone as a rogue narrator takes you behind the scenes of this story."

Patricia Bell-Scott, teacher at the University of Georgia
and author of *Life Notes* and *Flat-Footed Truths.*

THE BLANKENSCHIPF CURSE

by

Jim Murdock

Copyright © 2006 by Jim Murdock

ISBN 0-7414-3812-7

Published by:

INFINITY
PUBLISHING.COM

1094 New DeHaven Street, Suite 100
West Conshohocken, PA 19428-2713
Info@buybooksontheweb.com
www.buybooksontheweb.com
Toll-free (877) BUY BOOK
Local Phone (610) 941-9999
Fax (610) 941-9959

Printed in the United States of America

Printed on Recycled Paper

Published April 2007

To Andrea

Her love has sustained me
over the years. She has given
me two wonderful sons.
I admire her courage under
great mental and physical
stress.

Acknowledgements

A novel is never the work of one person. There are always those who urge, encourage and make contributions along the way. My special thanks to the following people.

My wife, Andrea, who continued to support me even when fighting for her life.

My sons, Mike and Matt, who amaze me with their patience and inner strength.

Jerry Tewmey, my friend of many years who is the best story teller I've ever heard.

The members of the "White Car Gang," my special writing group who worked very hard to make me a better writer: Harriette Austin, Genie Bernstein, Dac Crossley and Pat Bell-Scott.

To my mother and father, and six brothers and sisters who love me.

To Doctors W.B. Bean and M.T. Morter and the rest of my "teachers" over a lifetime.

God, the source of all things, including my ideas and inspiration for writing this book.

CHAPTER ONE

Reuben (Rube) Winters was only five years old when the first unusual event in his life took place, at least the first one he could remember. His parents, Calvin and Betty, took their handsome son to the First United Methodist Church in Winder, Georgia on a beautiful Sunday morning in late May, 1973.

The church had been built twenty years earlier to replace the original wood frame building. A concrete path sliced through the lawn in front of the tall brick, steepled building with white columns. Ornate doors opened to a marbled vestibule leading to the nave of the church. Between the vestibule and side doors, carpeted staircases led to the balcony.

When the communion service began, they dragged Rube along to the altar railing, in front of the entire congregation. They bowed their heads in reverent prayer and let go of his hands.

Rube grabbed the spindles which supported the railing and wondered if his head would fit between them. He pressed his head against the spindles, and found the widest space allowed by the curve in the wood. He forced his head through the opening and worked his head up and down much like a dog scratching fleas. Bored, he tried to draw his head out, but his ears caught on the spindles. He panicked a little but knew that given time he could work his head out of the opening.

There was no time. Preacher Lee approached with the bread, and the associate pastor followed with the wine. Rube's father reached to take the small wafer as the pastor stared down with a puzzled look on his face.

Seminary school and fifteen years of ministering in the North Georgia Conference had not prepared the preacher for such a situation. How could he handle Rube's entrapment and maintain the solemnity of an important Christian ritual?

Rube's father dropped his wafer, grabbed his son by the back of his shirt and pulled. His mother, Betty, uttered a loud gasp heard over the collective sucking in of breath of those watching.

Rube must have felt like his ears were being torn off. He yelled in pain, and began to cry. His mother took his legs and tugged with all her might, trying to end this debacle, knowing that her bridge club members were watching in amusement. The preacher worked Rube's head from the other side of the railing, trying to find the best spot for the retraction. He wanted to do this quickly so he could restore order to the ceremony. A few titters of laughter rose from the younger church members.

His father and mother's urgency did not help young Rube. The skin behind his ears was soon rubbed raw from the pulling and he pleaded with them to stop.

Rube's mother climbed over the railing to help the preacher's efforts and ripped her best Sunday dress down the back. The congregation lost interest in the sacrament. Some laughed aloud, others snickered, and one local jokester unkindly shouted, "Grease him up!"

The associate pastor was standing there, wringing his hands.

The members who had been at the altar railing were still there and didn't know whether to remain or go back to their seats. Some were kneeling, others stood to see what was going on. Old Lady Gilbert felt faint and sat down in the front row next to Lexsy Johnson who prayed loudly for the Lord to surround the boy with his love and protection, and prevent the preacher from pulling Rube's head clean off.

Ben Sumner, a carpenter, sitting five rows back on the right side of the church, knew what to do. He left his pew, walked to the altar, and yanked on the spindle until it broke. Mother, father, preachers, and congregation rejoiced. Rube had been freed from captivity! Hallelujah!

The church members began applauding as his mother, closely followed by his father, picked him up and carried him quickly up the aisle and out of the church.

Those closest to the aisle congratulated the carpenter as he made his way back to his seat. God had used a carpenter at least once before.

The preacher brushed the hair out of his eyes, straightened his robe, and wiped the foolish grin from his face. When he regained control of himself, he said, "The Lord works in mysterious ways." There was an "Amen!" and muffled laughter.

Preacher Lee continued, "We will have our communion next Sunday. Let us pray. Dear Lord, please bless young Rube and his family. Turn this embarrassing moment into a blessing for them, and a blessing for us all. As we experience the sorrows and tribulations of each day, and as we get our heads caught in the spindles of life, remind us that you are always there, ready to break the spindles and set us free, just as you did for young Rube. Amen." The congregation enthusiastically replied, "A--men!!"

The people filed out and shook hands with the preacher. They were smiling and happy, delighted to have attended church that morning. Old Man Kharr exclaimed that he'd stayed awake the entire time. Bunny Claxton said the service was more fun than when the last preacher stumbled from the dais and fell face down in front of the congregation.

Rube's blunder caused the most life and enthusiasm Preacher Lee had seen since he had taken over the church five years ago. He asked Old Lady Gilbert how she was fairing. She replied, "I'll be fine as soon as I get home and have a big glass of ice tea with half a lemon squeezed into it."

As carpenter Sumner passed by, he promised to come by next week and replace the spindle.

After the incident, everyone knew Rube, and gave him a warm hello with a smile or at least a grin, and patted him on the head.

In fact, the church was no longer the formal, stuffy place it had been before. Somehow, that single event had released a pent up fear among the congregation of making a mistake, doing something wrong, stepping over an imaginary line that had been established by the founders of the church some fifty three years ago.

Betty Winters took her son to the family chiropractor, Bill Glasson, on Monday. He found and corrected two misalignments in Rube's neck from the twisting and pulling.

Rube shuddered the next time he took communion and made certain his head remained above the railing. When he looked down at the newly replaced spindle, the bones behind his ears ached.

Preacher Lee always grinned when he saw Rube at the altar. Of all the children, Rube was his favorite. That pleased Rube. Nevertheless, he dreaded Communion Sundays.

Inside Information

Shhhh. Please don't tell anyone that I've done this, especially Jim Murdock or the National Writer's Groups.

None of them would understand and it might bring bodily harm to me from the author, and I could lose my job as a narrator. After all, my job is to narrate, not commentate.

Being the narrator, there's certain information in the author's mind that I'm privy to. That's the only way it can work. Well, I'm supposed to keep that secret, but I just can't do it. After all, you're the reader and paid no telling how much for this book.

You will notice that this excerpt has not been assigned a chapter number or even a page number. That's because it's not part of the book. So, once you read it, please tear it out and throw it away. I'll feel a lot safer if you do that.

This is about a secret that Rube has. He's never told anyone about it, and probably never will. I just happened to find out about it when I took on the job of narrating this fine piece of literary work.

Rube has a cousin by the name of Caresse Lafayette. Her father is Lee "Tear Drop" Lafayette, a truck driver from Louisiana, who married Rose Fontaine, Rube's mother's sister. He carried her off to his home state and they had Caresse who grew up to be quite a looker. She was three years older than Rube, and he only saw her this one time.

Rube was fifteen years old when Caresse and her family came to Winder for a visit. There were only three bedrooms, and Rube's room had twin beds.

That's all I'm gonna say about Rube and his cousin at this time. In fact, I've probably already said too much. I just felt like you had the right to know. Maybe it'll help you understand the main character better.

If you have questions about any of this, you may contact the person whose name is on the cover of the book. He may or may not admit to knowing anything about it. But, please don't mention me, or let on that I revealed this secret to you.

Narrator

CHAPTER TWO

Rube went to Winder High School, a plain public school like a hundred other high schools built in Georgia during the nineteen seventies. The flat brick and glass building had school offices in the center. The cafeteria sat behind the offices and overlooked an open green space. Two corridors with classrooms extended down each side, with a gymnasium that stood tall on the north end of the campus.

In high school Rube was taller than average with a full head of blond hair. He was quiet, but popular, and breezed through his classes. A good athlete, he played football, baseball, and basketball where he was captain of the team. He would've had no trouble getting dates, but most of the time was too bashful to ask.

His life had been good, and yet, something was not right. He couldn't put his finger on exactly what was wrong, but things kept happening to him and others who were with him. At first he thought these things were merely a coincidence, but eventually, he knew there was more to it.

In the spring of his junior year at Winder High School, an event took place which reinforced his belief that he was cursed in some way. He had never had an official date with a girl, although he had taken part in numerous group functions when girls were present. He had no problem talking to them, and they liked his thick blond hair and his easy lope down the hall. Some of them giggled and blushed when he passed them by. He had fantasized about girls in his class and youth group, but never found the courage to actually ask them out. It became clear to the girls, even before Rube knew it, that he had eyes only for Amy Buchanan in his English class.

Amy had perfectly combed, dark brown hair to her shoulders. Her eyes were a lighter shade of brown and sparkled when she smiled. The most attractive part of Amy was her full lips. Many times in class Rube stared at those lips like the best thing in the world would be to kiss them. When she caught Rube looking, his cheeks turned red and he turned away, thankful she could not read his mind.

Amy was not among the "in" group at school and as far as he could tell, she didn't date other boys. That was surprising to him and he wondered why.

One day Rube saw Amy in the cafeteria. She was with other students, but he could tell that she was really alone.

Rube was sharing a table with his two best friends, Cal Munson and Will Sanderson. They teased him terribly about Amy and dared him to talk to her. Rube walked over and asked if she minded if he joined her. She smiled and Rube sat down.

Amy wore lavender and Rube caught a scent when she turned to him. They talked about the writing assignment due Tuesday, mutual friends, and where she lived. "Out in the country," she said, and described the crossroads near her home.

Rube asked if she'd like to go to the movies on Saturday night. Her smile faded and a dark shade fell over her eyes.

"Yes, but first I'll have to find out if it's okay with my father," she replied.

The next day in class she smiled at Rube across the room. After class she told him of her father's approval and gave him more specific directions.

Rube said, "Great. I'll pick you up at six o'clock so we can be in Athens for the seven thirty movie. Is that okay?"

On Saturday, dressed in his best khakis and Polo shirt, Rube wheeled his dad's Chevy Blazer on to the dirt and gravel of Johnson road. He found the mailbox with her family's name, Buchanan, and parked next to a steep embankment that sloped down to the shoulder. He got out and walked past the seventy nine Dodge pickup parked in the driveway.

It was an old farm house with a long wooden porch and a swing on the far end. A pair of muddy boots stood by the door. Rube was winded by the time he climbed the hill and reached the porch steps. He saw a chain tied to a support post and heard a low growl from under the porch. Rube cleared the steps in two jumps, and plastered himself against the front of the house. The chain stopped the Rotweiler's snapping teeth just short of his leg. He reached as far as he could and banged on the door. Feeling like raw meat dangling in front of a shark, and hearing no action, he banged again.

The door opened. "Get outta here Wild Thang! Don't you mind him none, Son. That's my old man's pet."

Wild Thang slunk off the porch, cutting his eyes back at Rube, slobber dripping from his mouth.

A frail woman wearing a plain dress with a flowered apron around the waist, invited him in. She was in her forties, but looked older, especially her eyes, and had a large bruise on her right temple.

He noticed the calluses on her right hand as she motioned him into the small, dark hallway.

As they entered the living room, Rube saw a television set on the opposite wall, and he immediately turned his head to one side as the stale smell of cigarette smoke assaulted his nostrils. On the screen was a wrestling match. One of the contestants had been hit with a metal folding chair and blood streamed down his face. Facing the television was a large reclining chair. The glare from the screen provided the only light and reflected off the head of the bald man sitting there.

As they drew near, Rube saw a huge hand resting on the right arm of the recliner. There was the snorting, gurgling sound of a man fast asleep.

Mrs. Buchanan touched the arm and said softly, "Wendall, Amy's date is here."

The man aroused with a start and blurted, "What the hell...! Woman, why are you...? Where's my beer?"

Mrs. Buchanan scurried to the kitchen, and the man finally looked at Rube. Wendall Buchanan had a large, bulbous nose which protruded from a pockmarked face, with dark, deep-set eyes. Only the pupils were visible as their brightness penetrated the dark. The eyebrows, dark and bushy with specks of gray, had apparently never been trimmed. Mister Buchanan didn't

9

bother to rise or even offer his hand. In a nicotine voice he said, "Sit down, Boy." They watched the conclusion of the match as Dusty Rhodes jumped off the top turnbuckle, landing with his elbow across the throat of his opponent, then rolled over on top of him for the easy win.

"What are you doin' here, Boy?"

"I came to take Amy to a movie, Sir."

"Let me tell you somethin', Boy. If you touch one hair on her head, even look at her the wrong way, you'll never live to graduate. You hear me?"

"Yes, Sir."

"Now, I want her back in this house by ten thirty, untouched, in good condition. Do you hear me?"

"Yes, Sir."

Just then, Amy entered the room, followed by her mother. In the soft light. Amy was a very pretty girl. There was a touch of lipstick on those beautiful lips and a slight blush to her cheeks. Her mother had made Amy's dress of small, brightly colored flowers on a white background that gathered under her rounded breasts. The sleeves were puffed out, but not exaggerated. She wore a pink ribbon in her hair, and white, pointed slippers with low heels.

Rube rose and wanted to rush over and greet her, but felt Mr. Buchanan's eyes glaring holes in him.

Amy, sensing his hesitancy, came over and offered her hand, saying, "Hello."

Rube mumbled something about how pretty she was.

Amy kissed her father on the forehead, telling him goodbye. "I love you, Daddy."

A hint of softness came over Mr. Buchanan's face as he looked at his daughter. Amy was the only person or thing in this world that meant anything to Wendall. That confused and comforted his wife.

Rube knew that he was taking responsibility for protecting her for a short period of time, and that nothing must happen.

On the television, Dusty Rhodes said, "I've had many a fistes on my noggin! I'm just a po' white boy, son of a plumber."

As the young couple left the living room, Wendall said, "Hey, Boy, remember what I said. Ten thirty. No later."

"Yes, Sir," Rube replied.

Rube turned around in the driveway and headed down Johnson Road toward Highway 78. Dark clouds gathered far to the west. He thought how lucky those people would be to get rain.

He offered Amy a piece of Juicy Fruit. She slid closer to his side of the Blazer, and touched his hand as she removed the gum from the pack.

She smiled, and laughed at times as they talked about school and some of the silly things their friends did.

Finally, Rube said, "Your father is not very friendly, is he?"

"No. He was beat as a child and never got over it. I worry about my mother." Amy's eyes went wet with tears and Rube changed the talk to basketball.

They drove down Atlanta Highway to the shopping center and parked the car. Amy waited for Rube to open the door for her. She held his hand as they walked through the parking lot.

He bought tickets, and they picked up popcorn, cokes and Jujubes as they went through the lobby.

The movie was *Risky Business*. Rube put his arm across the back of Amy's seat as the film played and rested his hand on her shoulder. She leaned closer. Rube swallowed a Jujube whole when Tom Cruise started dancing on screen in his underwear.

Rube and Amy stayed through the credits. "Thanks for bringing me," she whispered.

The movie was over at nine-thirty and Rube felt comfortable because that gave them a whole hour to get to Amy's house.

They strolled around the shopping center before going outside. The weather had turned to thunder and lightening mixed with a few drops of rain.

"Let's make a run for the car," said Amy. They dodged raindrops and were out of breath from running between the cars and laughing.

Rube opened the door and brushed against Amy as she got into the car. He shivered being so close to her.

They headed west on Highway 78 and had passed the Athens city limits sign when there was a major cloudburst. The windshield wipers lost their battle with the downpour and Rube pulled over to wait out the worst of the storm.

Amy slid next to Rube, and as he put his arm around her, he felt her shiver from the cold, damp rain. He held her closer. She looked up at him and said, "I've waited a long time for you to ask me out."

"I'm sorry. I'm a slow learner. Ask my math teacher."

As they gazed into each other's eyes, it seemed only natural that their lips should meet as well. Amy was not a loose girl, but she yearned for Rube like he yearned for her. Rube tingled at the taste of Amy.

"I've wanted to do that for a long time."

"I know," she said.

Their lips met again, and this time lingered. As it ended, his eye caught the digital clock on the dashboard as the numbers changed to 10:05. He broke the embrace and started the car. "We've got to go!"

She sighed, "Yes, we do."

The rain had let up slightly as they pulled onto the highway.

It was ten twenty-five when they turned onto Johnson Road, and by the time they reached Amy's house and pulled to the side of the road, next to the embankment, it was exactly ten-thirty.

Amy could tell Rube was very nervous. She leaned over and kissed him on the cheek when they came to a stop. He wanted to kiss her back in the worst way, but there was no time to lose. He said, "Your dad is going to be furious if we wait an extra minute."

Rube waded around the front of the car to open the door for Amy. She stepped out, then up the hill from the car. Rube slammed the door and Amy shrieked as the slippery red mud gave way under her feet. She slid by him, clawing at the slimy clay without success. He reached and slipped down behind her, his weight pushing her under the car.

"Rube, help me!" she cried as Rube tried to regain his footing. He slipped again and fell facedown. He reached under the car and grabbed Amy by the front of her dress, ripping the buttons loose.

"Don't! You're hurting me," she screamed.

Rube slipped his arm around her waist, braced himself against the car and pulled her out. Exhausted, they lay there for a moment. Rube then got to his knees and helped Amy grab hold of the door handle. They pulled to their feet, holding onto each other.

Amy sobbed and Rube tried to quiet her with apologies. They clung to the vehicle and worked their way around the front until they found solid ground. Rube kept saying, "I'm sorry. I'm sorry."

Rube was a mess with his khakis and shirt covered with red mud. Amy's hair was matted with red clay. Her flowery dress looked like it had been dyed red, and the front had torn to show red welts between her breasts. The right breast was visible, but quickly covered. The pink ribbon dangled from a single strand of hair. There was a large grease spot on her face, extending into her hair and left ear. She had lost both shoes under the Blazer.

Amy was sobbing and shaking beyond control.

Rube was horrified. "Amy, I know your dad is going to kill me!"

She just sobbed louder.

Rube wrapped his arm around her, trying to keep her warm as they slowly made their way up the driveway, past the pickup, to the front porch.

It's my fault. Tell your father it's all my fault," Rube repeated. The muddy water sloshed over his shoes. He should have warned Amy about his curse.

When they got to the house, Rube asked, "What about Wild Thang?"

"Oh, he's all right as long as you're with me. I'm sorry I didn't tell you about him before," said Amy.

As they climbed onto the front porch, he noticed a glimmer of light from the door leading into the living room. He suspected that Wendall had fallen asleep watching a re-run of "Crime and Punishment" or some such program.

He hurriedly said goodbye to Amy as she opened the door and went inside.

He quickly stepped off the porch and made a dead run for the Blazer.

The front porch light came on as the car's engine turned over. Wendall bellowed from the house. Rube heard a shotgun blast and buckshot zing over the top of the Blazer. He gunned the car down the slippery road and cursed his curse. He wondered if he would ever find out how to stop these things from happening to him.

Another date with Amy was impossible. He was sure her father wanted to hit him over the head with a folding chair like Dusty Rhodes, and body slam him to the canvas or whatever surface Rube happened to be standing on.

He worried the rest of the weekend and waited by Amy's locker Monday morning before class.

"I want to apologize for what happened, Amy. You were wonderful and I had a great time except for the mud. Is your dad still angry?"

"I explained to him what happened, but he has this terrible temper. He told me we couldn't see each other. I'm really sorry."

Rube stayed away from dating other girls at Winder High. He kept busy with school work, sports, and other excuses. He only wanted Amy, and if her father said no, he'd settle for dreaming about her at night.

He never told anyone about that night because he was afraid it might hurt Amy. But, now he understood why she didn't date nor take an active part in school activities.

CHAPTER THREE

In the summer before starting his senior year, Uncle Billy invited Rube to fly out to Dallas, Texas for a three week visit.

Uncle Billy was his father's older brother and Rube's favorite uncle. He was a genuinely nice man who treated everyone with kindness and respect, and fun to be around. Whatever was said to him, he always replied, "That's wonderful, just wonderful!" Rube wondered what Billy would say if someone told him that his grandmother had dropped dead of a heart attack. He suspected, "That's wonderful, just wonderful!"

Rube had never flown before, and was a little anxious as his father drove him to the Atlanta airport. He had not told his parents about the suspected curse.

He was afraid they might think he was foolish, and maybe he was. He wondered if the curse would be on the plane.

They checked his bags outside the South Terminal, and signed in at gate 16. His father hugged him and said, "Goodbye, Son. Give Billy my best."

"Thanks for bringing me. I'll write you and Mom."

Rube sat in the terminal and watched the people go by, especially the girls, while he waited for his number to be called. The girls in short skirts and tight blouses reminded him of Amy. He also thought of Cousin Caresse Lafayette, but quickly jammed it deep into his memory.

Only the announcement by the flight attendant brought him out of his reverie, "We are now boarding flight 714 to Dallas, Texas. Those with seat numbers 80 thru 100 please come forward at this time."

Rube was assigned seat 91G and found it next to the window. Great, he thought, I'll be able to watch them load the plane. He put his suitcase in the compartment above and slid in.

He looked up to see a very heavyset woman coming down the aisle. She wore a print dress faded from hundreds of washings and a straw hat pinned to her hair. She held her old tan valise in front, but her hips still banged each passenger as she made her way to 91F. Somehow she fit her hips in, but her right shoulder and arm hung half way into Rube's lap. Her blond, curly hair, red lips and broad smile coaxed nods and smiles from otherwise sullen passengers.

"Moochie Dunlop," she said. "I'm seeing my sister in Dallas. She manages a fitness center, and says I can lose weight on her machines while watching television."

The airplane must have tilted down in the rear and listed to the side to accommodate Moochie's weight. Rube's ears popped as they ascended to thirty thousand feet.

Moochie took a box of chocolate covered pralines from her bag and offered them to Rube.

"No thanks. I'm trying to stay in shape for football."

"Why, Lord-a-mercy, Honey. Chocolate's good for you. It'll put some weight on your skinny self. Make you able to stand up against them boys trying to knock your head off."

"Okay, I'll try one. Thanks."

Moochie had settled in and begun the in-flight magazine's crossword puzzle when Rube decided he needed to visit the lavatory in the worst way.

"Ms. Moochie, I hate to bother you, but I have to go to the bathroom."

She looked at him like---you've got to be kidding! Then, softening, she smiled slightly and said, "Sure, Sweety."

Moochie braced herself on the armrests and tried to get up. Rube would have climbed over, but was at a loss to figure out how.

"Let me put my hand on your shoulder, Sweetie."

The extra pressure increased Rube's need. He wiggled past her without being personal, and made it to the lavatory in the rear of the passenger compartment.

The room was small and all stainless steel, making it look like the inside of a can. Rube unzipped and began as the airplane hit a pocket of turbulence. He was knocked off his feet and peed on the mirror, the sink, the walls and everything else in the small compartment. He finally ended up on his back, peeing straight up in the air.

When the plane settled down, he heard the muffled sound of the pilot announcing, "This is your pilot. Please don't be alarmed. We just ran through a bit of turbulence. Everything is fine now. Please return to your seats and fasten your seatbelts if you have not already done so. The seatbelt light will go off when the air is more stable."

Rube was glad the pilot thought things were fine. He was not aware of the desperate situation in the rear of his plane, nor did he know about the curse.

The stewardess knocked on the bathroom door, "How are we doing in there?"

Her eyes widened when she heard his reply from the vent at the bottom of the door, "Yes. Yes. I'm fine. No problem."

He emptied the paper towel holder, and cleaned the mirror, sink and walls. He slipped his pants off and soaked them in the sink. They would look better wet all over than in one large spot.

Several people were waiting when Rube came out. They saw his pants and tittered.

Rube's face was sunburn red as he made his way back to Moochie's side. She looked up, groaned, and began to extract herself from the seat. She said, "My goodness, Son. You really did have to go, didn't you?" She glanced down and said, "Lordy!"

He wedged past Moochie, sat down and stared out the window, trying to figure out why the good Lord had given him his curse.

His thoughts were interrupted when the flight attendant came by with refreshments. Moochie had to turn sideways and lean into Rube for the cart to pass. A scent of Musk oil passed between them.

"Can I have two or three extra bags of peanuts, Honey? I don't want to waste away to nothing before we reach our destination," said Moochie.

Rube's pants were dry by the time the pilot came on the intercom and announced their arrival in Dallas.

Moochie and Rube were the last ones off the plane, Moochie not wanting to hold up the other passengers as she walked the narrow aisle. Rube let Moochie take the stairs ahead of him. If he went first and she slipped and fell, his cursed life would be over.

"Take care, Honey." Moochie said in the terminal. "I hope your bladder problem improves."

Rube blushed, "Thanks, Ms. Moochie. Good luck getting in shape."

They waved goodbye, thinking this would be the last time they saw each other.

Uncle Billy and his children, David and Ellie, met Rube at the arrival gate. He had been looking forward to seeing his cousins again. David was a year younger than Rube and Ellie was the same age. He had been close to them before Uncle Billy was transferred to the Dallas plant of the Prime Meat Packing Company.

"How was your flight?" asked David.

Rube said, "Smooth as silk," not wanting to go into the gory details.

Uncle Billy sensed that something had gone wrong, but said nothing.

Billy was a small man, five-six with a slight build. His dark brown hair was thin on top, with gray showing in the sideburns that grew to the middle of his ears. His nose was bent slightly to the left from being hit with a basketball in his youth. He walked with a limp because his right leg was a bit shorter than his left.

He did an outstanding job as the manager of the meat packing plant. The people who worked for Billy loved him.

This was due in part to Billy always telling them what a wonderful job they were doing, just wonderful. The encouragement made them work harder.

Neither Ellie nor David had the curse. It had skipped over them like a recessive gene and landed on Rube with both feet. Uncle Billy carried the curse and that comforted Rube.

Stories about Uncle Billy abounded in the family. There was the time he pulled into a full service station for gas, soon after he had moved to Dallas. The service man put the pump on automatic and stood by watching the numbers roll. Billy asked him if he could lubricate his truck and change the oil.

"I'd be glad to," said the man. "You'll have to pull her into the garage."

Uncle Billy said, "That's wonderful, just wonderful," as the man moved across the island to pump gas for another customer.

Billy started his truck, put it in gear, and pulled away as the service man yelled, "Stop!"

It was too late. The hose pulled away from the pump, and gasoline sprayed over Billy's truck and the service man. Uncle Billy got out and put both hands over the opening, trying to stop the flow. The gas kept coming.

The service man warned the other drivers. "Don't start your cars, and whatever you do, don't light a match. Please don't light a match!"

A mechanic inside the station shut off the pump and the gasoline slowed to a trickle. Uncle Billy ran to each car and apologized for the mishap.

The service man managed to get Billy settled down. "There's no real damage and no one's been hurt. Pay me for what I've lost and we'll be square."

They both reeked of gasoline. The man said, "I'll clean this mess and go home and change. Come back this afternoon to have your truck serviced."

"That's wonderful, just wonderful," said Uncle Billy.

Being the manager at Prime Meat Packing was a serious responsibility. Billy went on to the plant and headed for the bathroom to wash his hands and face. He went through his regular work routine and things went fine except for people asking about the gas fumes. Uncle Billy was accustomed to the smell. "What fumes? I don't smell anything."

That evening at home, his wife, Lucille, said, "There's a scent of gas in the house. Do we have a leak?"

"No, Dear. Must be the stove."

"That's right. How was your day?"

"Wonderful. Just wonderful!"

Uncle Billy's only flaw was his craving for alcohol. He'd had the problem since high school. Billy was a religious man who tried to live by the Good Book, but could not resist the temptation of alcohol. He had bottles hidden around the house and emptied one almost every night.

Aunt Lucille accepted this about him. She was always there to dry him out, and in some cases bail him out.

Sometimes she tied him in bed to keep him from going to the liquor store for more whiskey. After each incident, she carried on as though nothing had happened. They never talked about Billy's drinking. That's just how it was.

No matter how drunk he had been the night before, Billy rose early the next morning and dressed in his sear-sucker suit with his straw hat and bow tie in place. He'd add a splash of Mennen after shave to his cheeks and be off to work.

One morning after a long night of drinking, he told Lucille, "Dear, that potted meat you left in the refrigerator was delicious, just wonderful!"

After he went to work, Lucille found that Billy had eaten a bowl of cat food she was trying to keep fresh.

Another time he brushed his teeth with a dab of *Brylcream* hairdressing.

The family always enjoyed hearing about, and Uncle Billy enjoyed telling about these incidents. While Uncle Billy never referred to himself as cursed, Rube knew.

If Aunt Lucille let him out of the house or he started drinking before he got home, he usually went to the Longhorn Bar and Grill on Elm Street. The Longhorn was the local hangout for off-duty policemen, and being a friendly sort, Uncle Billy got to know many of them by name.

One afternoon, Uncle Billy stopped at the Longhorn to have one drink. At eleven thirty that evening he told the bartender, "I had enough. I need a freath of bresh air."

He stumbled out of the bar and got into the first car he bumped into. Unfortunately it was a police car.

He fell against the wheel causing the horn to blow. No one was in the parking lot to stop him and the keys were dangling from the ignition. Billy started the car, dropped the gear shift into drive, and pulled onto Elm. The cars he met blinked their lights and blew their horns. He acknowledged his error and managed to turn on the car's lights.

Billy turned right on the Main Street through downtown Dallas. He decided a cigarette would sober him up a bit. He fumbled for the cigarette lighter and instead turned on the siren and flashing lights. "That's wonderful," he said. "Just wonderful."

His ride was exciting while it lasted. He rolled down the window and waved to people as he drove by. Cars pulled to the side and allowed him to pass when he sped through an intersection.

He thought to himself, Dallas is a great place to live, all the people are so nice!

Suddenly, he noticed a police car behind him. Its lights flashed and siren blasted. There was another police car behind that car, and another coming down the side street to Billy's right. One of the police cars pulled beside him, and an officer demanded that Billy stop.

The officer sounded upset, so Uncle Billy obliged by turning into the lot of a nearby convenience store. Police cars surrounded him and officers jumped out with weapons drawn, and hunkered down in the shooting position. "Get out of the car! Hands behind your head! Get out now!"

Uncle Billy did what they said in no great hurry. "Howdy, boys. Wasn't that a kicker?"

Squinting into the lights, he thought he recognized two of the officers. "Carl, it that you? Ronnie, my old drinkin' buddy. How ya doin'? What are you doin' out here?"

Ronnie held Billy's arms and handcuffed him. Carl escorted Billy to a car and locked him in the back behind a wire mesh screen.

"My hat," said Billy. "Don't forget my hat."

The officers were ticked off at Uncle Billy, and embarrassed because of their relationship. After they cooled off a bit, they realized he meant no harm. He was just drunk. But, they couldn't back down. It would make the department look bad.

Uncle Billy spent the night in the drunk tank and was charged with grand theft auto and hindering a police officer in doing his duty. The next morning he was sober and ready to go to work. The police allowed him one telephone call.

He called Lucille. "Good morning, Dear. I'm in the city jail and they won't let me go to my job."

"Billy, you're a born worry. Just sit tight. I'll call your secretary. Then, I'll be down to take care of this silliness."

Billy's arraignment was scheduled for eleven o'clock that morning before Judge Wilbanks who was a member of their church. Lucille arrived early and watched as her husband shuffled in, weighted down with leg chains and handcuffs. He waved to Lucille the best he could under the circumstances and flashed a weak grin. While he waited for his case to be called, Billy chatted with the officer who had been assigned to see that this "dangerous criminal" did not escape.

Lucille was too far away to hear what they were saying, but knew that by the time the case was heard, the officer would be on Billy's side. She liked having Billy for a husband. She just didn't like other people knowing.

Billy and the officer went before the judge. "Good morning, Judge," said Billy. "How's Evelyn and the kids?"

The judge uttered, "Fine," then asked the officer for the charges and an explanation of what happened. The officer complied, adding that the officer whose car was stolen regretted that he had left the keys in the ignition.

There were a few chuckles from the people there to see their loved ones arraigned.

Judge Wilbanks asked if Uncle Billy had anyone to represent him.

"Yes, Your Honor. I think you've met my wife, Lucille."

She rose and came forward. "My Billy had no intention of stealing that police car. If he had wanted to steal that car, would he have turned on the lights and siren and driven through the middle of Dallas? He has a problem with drink as you can plainly see, but he's not a thief."

"Officer Conner, do you have anything else to add?"

"No, Sir, except that I know Billy is a good man."

The judge said, "In my opinion, there is insufficient evidence to show that this man intended to steal the car or purposely hinder an officer in doing his duty. It appears that the officer had other things on his mind besides doing his duty. Therefore, the charges are hereby dropped.

"My advice to the police department is to always take your keys with you, especially when you go into a bar. If you later wish to file charges of public intoxication, the court will listen."

Judge Wilbanks then turned to Billy and gave him a stern lecture about the dangers of drunk driving. "What if you had run over a child or hit an ambulance? If you ever appear in my courtroom again, I'll put you under the jail."

By this time Uncle Billy was crying and apologizing, "I'm sorry, Your Honor. I'm sorry. I'm sorry."

After the policeman removed the cuffs and chains, Uncle Billy went looking for Lucille who led him out of the courtroom.

The very next Saturday, Billy was at the Longhorn. He tried to make conversation with a couple of the officers who were at his hearing, but they were cold to him. Billy promised not to donate to the Police Officers Association that year.

When closing time came, Billy told the bartender, "Joseff, I guess I'll be headin' home before I get drunk."

Joe said, "You may have waited a smidgen too long, Billy. Either walk or call a taxi. The judge don't want you drinking and driving."

Billy liked the bartender and he sure didn't want to face Judge Wilbanks again. He lived seven blocks from the Longhorn and he set out at a brisk pace, staggering back and forth across the width of the sidewalk. The few people he met stepped off the sidewalk to let him pass. He tipped his straw hat and said, "Isn't it a lovely evening?"

He passed four teenage boys who were laughing and talking loudly. They ran behind Billy and hit him on the back of the head. The blow sent him sprawling on the sidewalk. They dragged him behind a bush and stripped him of his jacket, trousers, and shirt.

A young woman in a passing car saw the attack and called the police from a pay telephone. When the police arrived, the culprits were gone. They found Uncle Billy leaning against a tree in his under-shorts, socks and shoes.

His straw hat was cocked to one side to avoid the big knot on his head. Blood trickled from his left nostril and there was a cut under his chin from falling to the sidewalk.

The policemen took Billy to the downtown station and called Aunt Lucille to retrieve him. Unfortunately, a news photographer was at the station when Billy entered. He snapped a picture of Billy in his straw hat, shorts, and shoes. Billy gave a brief statement to the photographer as an officer led him down the corridor to a cell. "Tell the people of Dallas I think they are wonderful, just wonderful."

An investigator tried to get a description of the teens, but Billy had no clue as to what they looked like.

The police decided not to charge him with public drunkenness, mainly to avoid being embarrassed in court again. Besides, they were worried about the knot on his head.

Lucille arrived with clothes for Billy and drove him to the emergency room. The doctor said his wounds were not serious and put two stitches in his chin. "Watch for dizziness or disorientation for the next few days. If there is a problem call me right away."

"Billy has those symptoms from cocktail hour until sunrise," said Lucille.

"Call me if they disappear," smiled the doctor.

Billy was up bright and cheery the next morning. He dressed as though he was meeting the President of the United States. The only problem was that his straw hat did not fit properly. He had to tilt it forward and to the left.

Everyone at work wanted to know what had happened to him. "It was terrible, just terrible," he said. "I was minding my own business when I was attacked by a jealous husband. He was six feet four if he was an inch, and weighed two hundred and fifty pounds. We fought hard and mean for hours until I finally dropped him. He's in St. Michael's getting religion and buckets of plasma. I hope I didn't hurt him too bad."

The truth came out that afternoon when the newspaper with his photograph hit the stands. Billy's secretary cut out the article and picture and posted them on Billy's office door. The employees loved it.

When a man from corporate headquarters in Houston came to Dallas to review Billy's performance, he could not find a worker in the plant who spoke badly of him. Production had risen twenty percent since the incident.

Long before Rube arrived in Dallas, Billy knew what he must do. As he looked back on his life, he decided that the curse worked in different ways. It would visit him sober like at the service station, or lead him to drink, which was a curse of another kind. Who knew what course it would take in his nephew's life. Billy had to reveal the family secret to Rube and prepare him for what might lie ahead.

CHAPTER FOUR

Rube had settled into the guest bedroom, and was getting used to the hubbub of Uncle Billy's family.

One night at supper Uncle Billy was unusually quiet. After the Texas Ranger's game was over, and Rube was getting ready for bed, he heard a knock on the door. He opened it and found his uncle there with two fruit jars of ice tea. He handed one to Rube.

Billy walked over and sat on one of the wingback chairs near the far wall. "Sit down, Son. I need to tell you something." Rube had never seen him so serious.

Rube plopped down in an adjacent chair and leaned forward. "What is it, Uncle Billy? What's wrong? Are Mom and Dad okay?"

Billy looked surprised. "Oh yes, they're fine. I didn't mean to scare you. Nothing's wrong, really. It's just something I have to tell you: I've been trying to find the words all day."

Rube threw one pajamaed leg across the arm of the chair. "Is it about the curse?"

"Why, yes. How did you know?"

"I had a few clues, like getting my head stuck in the spindles at church, knocking my first date down in the mud, and getting shot at, among other things." Uncle Billy's eyes widened. "Shot at! I should have told you sooner."

"Don't worry. His aim was high. I understand you suffer from the same problem."

"Yep. Sure do. Now, relax and drink your tea while I tell you the story told to me by my grandmother, Willadean Winters, your great grandmother. She had noticed unusual things happening to me like the time I got my tongue stuck to a cross-cut saw blade in the dead of winter. She warned me not to tell anyone about it, including the family, unless I knew they had the same problem. Said she was ashamed and didn't want to worry anyone else.

"They lived in the mountains of North Carolina before the family migrated to North Georgia. She was a girl of sixteen when it happened. Her best friend, Imogene Blankenschipf, had her eye on the most handsome young man in the hollow, and a reputation for being a gypsy. The man was Ned Winters, your great grandfather. Fact, here's his picture." Billy reached for a family picture on the dresser. "He's the one on the left side, front row, with blond hair and a black hat slung behind his shoulders. Does he remind you of anyone?"

Rube took the picture and studied it. He smiled. "If you gave him a bath and combed his hair, he'd look a lot like me."

"A spittin' image if you ask me," said Billy. "Well, Sir. If what Imogene intimated to Willadean was true, they were a lot more than just acquainted. They'd spent time together in the hayloft at Imogene's place." Uncle Billy winked.

"One Saturday night Willadean and Imogene went to a barn raisin' dance together. Ned was at the dance too, and Imogene sidled up to him with her 'come hither' smile. The fiddles and guitars were hot that night. Ned was a good dancer, but Imogene was better. In the midst of the Virginia Reel, Imogene twirled when Ned didn't intend for her to. Well, Sir, that got his goat. He didn't want no girl to lead him around and tell him what to do. He walked off the floor and left her standin' there, big as life. Imogene was fit to be tied.

"Later, while Willadean and Imogene were having punch, who walks up but Ned? He flirted with Willadean and asked her to dance. Ned and Willadean fell in love that night on the dance floor. They were married two months later."

Rube finished his tea and wiped his mouth on his pajama sleeve. "That's a good story, Uncle Billy, but what does it have to do with me?"

Uncle Billy picked up his tea and took a sip. "I'm gettin' to that part. On the day of Willadean and Ned's wedding, a letter was found inside the screen door at Willadean's house. I have it right here, and I'm gonna read it to you." He reached into his pocket, pulled out a worn envelope, and removed a yellowed paper written in pencil. "Here's what it says:

'Dear Willadean,

You were my best friend. We finished the sixth grade together. I thought we would be friends forever.

But, you stole the only person in this world that I'll ever love. And, it was all because I twirled when I shouldn't have. Does that sound fair to you?

I never told you or anyone else this because I didn't want to be different, but now you need to know. I have special powers which have been passed down to me through generations. I now feel compelled to use those powers. It's a matter of family pride, at least that's what my Aunt Louise tells me. I like you, so I'm only going to cast a wee spell on you. Since it was mostly Ned's fault, some of the male members of your family will have to suffer more. The oldest male in each generation of your family will be cursed. The hard part for them will be that they won't know which events in their lives are part of the curse.

Your own spell will be that you have to dip snuff the rest of your life. We'll see how that sets with Ned. That will help even us out after you stole my man.

Oh, I almost forgot. There's only one way to lift the curse. The answer can be found in the Bible.

Happy honeymoon,

Imogene"

Uncle Billy carefully re-folded the paper and tucked it back in the envelope. "Well, now you know."

Rube laughed. "Uncle Billy, you're kidding me. Right? I mean, there's no such thing as someone having power over you, especially future generations. That's ridiculous."

"That was my first reaction too, My Boy. I've thought about it a lot. Fact is, I don't know. I do know that the power of suggestion is strong. Maybe that's what we're dealing with here. A suggestion gets planted, takes root and grows. Makes you wonder if everything that happens after that is part of the curse.

Maybe it's in our genes like them scientists talk about. Who knows? I've learned to accept whatever life brings and deal with it, even enjoy it. Whatever happens is wonderful. See?"

"I see what you mean. Guess I'll have to do the same. Anyway, thanks for telling me. By the way, did Great Grandmother Willadean dip snuff?"

"'Til the day she died. Tried it two weeks after the wedding just to prove Imogene wrong, and was never able to lay it down. She also read the Bible every night."

They stood and hugged. Uncle Billy handed the envelope to Rube.

"By the way, Imogene had a baby boy six months later. She named him Ned. Your grandfather was born three months after that."

CHAPTER FIVE

Gathering around the supper table was a major event at Uncle Billy and Aunt Lucille's house. When ready, Aunt Lucille would call out "Supper time!" She was a good cook and made cornbread from a recipe that had been handed down for generations. Billy said he'd be hard pressed to find a finer meal than Lucille's corn bread and a bowl of navy beans, though that night there was also thick slices of smoked ham and a bowl of beet salad. A resident pitcher of iced, sweet tea sat on the table. Billy drank his from a quart fruit jar with a long handled spoon in it, not wanting to wait for a second glass.

"Why do you have a spoon in your tea?" asked Rube.

"So if the ice melts on top, I can stir it up, My Boy."

Billy gave the blessing as the family held hands around the table. He thanked God for his wife, the children, the house, his job, their church, the preacher, and the food and hands that prepared it. If he was really hungry he simply said, "Thank you Lord for supper." He always waited for an "Amen" from those around the table.

Billy held the spoon with his index finger as he drank. He didn't want lemon in his tea, claiming it made his lips pucker so he couldn't get the full-flavored taste of the tea.

Ellie and Rube compared high schools over the meal, and David was asking his mother about staying over at a friend's house that coming weekend when Billy stopped the conversation.

"Quiet! Do you kids hear that?" In the silence was creaking from the house cooling after the heat of the day.

"I hear something," Ellie said.

Uncle Billy leaned back in his chair. "Must be that Nazi I have chained under the house. He makes noise every time he gets thirsty."

"Daddy! You've been pulling that trick on us since we were little," said David.

"After supper I'll go down with water and cat food. You'd think he'd be quieter after all these years."

Billy turned to Rube. "After I came home from World War Two, I hated all Germans until my mother told me I was half German from her side of the family. I had to change my hating to only Nazis, the worst excuse for a human being that ever crawled this earth. There's a lesson for you."

Ellie and David cleared the plates and Aunt Lucille brought out bowls of peach cobbler for dessert.

"Tell us a war story," Ellie pleaded.

"War is horrible, just horrible, and doesn't make a good story," said Uncle Billy, waiting to be coaxed.

"Come, now, Billy," said Aunt Lucille. "How about a little bitty one for our guest?"

"That's different. I went into the Army and my recruiting officer, who was a friend of my daddy's, warned me not to volunteer for anything and keep my mouth shut. What he didn't tell me was that keeping my mouth shut included whistling.

"It was 1943 and I volunteered right out of high school. They sent me down to Fort Stewart for my basic training, then to Fort Bragg for paratrooper school. My outfit was the Eighty-second Airborne Division. We were in formation on the dock at Fort Dix, New Jersey, Yankee country, waiting to board the ship that would carry us to England. The men were getting bored what with having to stand for hours and nothing to do. I started whistling to break the monotony. *You are my sunshine, my only sunshine. You make me happy when skies are gray.* Some of my buddies hummed along.

"Sergeant Wilcox was in charge of our unit. When he heard the faint strains of 'You are my Sunshine,' his ears perked up. He began to strut in front of our ranks, looking at each man as he passed, tapping a swagger stick in his hand.

"I hadn't noticed him coming, being caught in the mood of the tune. When he got in front of me, he stopped. 'Looks like we got us a G.D. canary in our outfit,' he said, loud enough for everyone to hear. 'Winters, this ain't no talent contest. We're off to fight the Krauts, not tuck them into bed and sing lullabies. You're in the Army, not enjoying a picnic in the hills of North Georgia. Shape up or I'm gonna rope you behind the boat and make you swim to England.'

"From then on, my nickname was 'Canary.' Here I was, a big tough fighting man with grenades and machine guns and pistols and they called me 'Canary.' I didn't like it.

"On D-day, June 6, 1944, my unit was dropped behind the German lines at Normandy. My parachute was tangled in a tree and I had to cut the lines so I could fall to the ground. The other men I had dropped with were nowhere to be seen. If I fired my weapon, the Germans would hear and capture me, and do all kinds of terrible things. I sat and thought a bit, then the answer came: whistle like a canary. I did and my buddies found me. After that, I liked my nickname very much. There's a lesson for you."

Aunt Lucille always tried to maintain a semblance of order at the table, but she enjoyed the banter between Uncle Billy and the children. Ellie, David and Rube would give a low growl and bark like a dog if anyone reached across their plate. She would say, "Stop it, David!" But, she couldn't help but grin as she said it.

During the second week Rube was in Dallas, Uncle Billy came home from work with news that a very important client would come for dinner on Friday night. The man, Mr. Bennett, was president of a large distribution company in Chicago. If Uncle Billy impressed Mr. Bennett and landed the account, it would be a large feather in his straw hat and perhaps earn him a raise.

Uncle Billy was concerned that something might happen to insult this very important man. He gave Ellie, David and Rube as stern a warning as he could muster. "Sit up straight. Say yes sir, no sir and please. Politeness and respect all the way."

Each day that week the children were given a list of chores to do in the house and yard before they were allowed to go to the swimming pool or meet their friends. By Friday, the house and yard were spotless.

On the appointed evening Uncle Billy and Mr. Bennett arrived at six thirty. Lucille and the young people met them at the front door, dressed in their best clothes. She'd had her hair done and was very pretty in a dark green dress whose hem hung four inches below her knees. Ellie switched from the tomboy that Rube knew, and had pulled her medium brown hair back on both sides with light blue hair clips that showed off her eyes. She wore a white blouse with light blue stripes and a matching, pleated skirt. Rube and David wore dark suits with white shirts, and clip-on ties that Aunt Lucille had bought for them earlier in the week.

Mr. Bennett was very proper and reserved in his banker's suit with red power tie. He looked like he would rather be anywhere else. He was a Northerner, and uneasy about being invited for a Southern family supper. Mr. Bennett would have been more comfortable at the Ritz Carlton downtown.

He had heard stories and jokes about Southerners and knew they had to be exaggerated and untrue. His friends in Chicago warned him that a seven-course meal in the South was a possum and a six-pack of beer. What if chitlins and collard greens were served? How could he politely say no?

Billy made the introductions, and the family and Mr. Bennett visited in the living room. Aunt Lucille excused herself to make final preparations for the meal. Rube, David and Ellie sat straight up on the couch with their feet flat on the floor, saying "Yes, Sir" and "No, Sir," if they were asked a question.

Mr. Bennett had his thick, dark hair slicked back with a potion known only to Northerners, and a heavy beard in spite of being close-shaved. His eyes were shades of gray. In spite of his somber demeanor, the corners of his eyes crinkled up occasionally like he was about to smile. His hands were strong and not confined to office work, but well manicured. He used them freely as he told Uncle Billy about his company, and what they did to make sure the food they sent to their customers remained fresh. Their reputation depended upon the quality of their meat and other food products.

Aunt Lucille called them into the dining room, escorting Mr. Bennett to his place next to Billy at the head of the table. The young people waited for Billy's cue to take a seat. There was a glass of iced, sweet tea at each place, and water in case the guest didn't like tea. As Mr. Bennett sat down, he noticed the quart fruit jar at Billy's place. There was a quizzical look on his face followed by a fleeting smile.

In the middle of the well-set table were platters and bowls filled with roast beef, milk gravy, green beans, cob corn, mashed potatoes, cornbread, biscuits, and honey dew melon.

Billy asked everyone to bow their heads and thanked God for his family and home, Mr. Bennett and his family. Then he thanked Him for the food, and asked Him to bless their bodies to His service. Mr. Bennett said, "Amen," at the end of the prayer, regardless of his own faith.

Billy passed the roast beef to Mr. Bennett. Lucille and the young people each picked up a dish, helped themselves, and passed it on.

Mr. Bennett's fear of Southern food was quickly dismissed. He dug into the food as though he had been picking short cotton all day. The sweet tea was especially appreciated and he remarked how good it was. Lucille refilled his glass from a large pitcher and left it on the table in front of him.

Ellie helped her mother clear the plates when the eating was done. They brought in freshly made banana pudding for dessert, with whipping cream and a mazzard cherry on top.

Mr. Bennett asked Billy about the sanitation procedures at the plant. Uncle Billy leaned back in his chair to answer as he always did and one of the legs slipped on the dining room floor. His chair continued its backward motion. Billy grabbed at the curtains to break his fall and pulled them down. His feet flew up trying to correct his balance as he went down. Unfortunately, they struck the end of the table, knocking his bowl of banana pudding up in the air so that it landed upside down on Lucille's linen tablecloth.

Uncle Billy rose sputtering, "I'll be damned! That was wonderful, just wonderful!"

Aunt Lucille was mortified, unsure of what to do next, when Mr. Bennett burst out laughing. He had held it as long as he could, but now there was no holding back. He slapped his knee, got up to help Billy, but was laughing so hard he fell into the side of his chair, and slid to the floor with his knees bent under him. He couldn't get up because of his laughter. Tears rolled down his cheeks as he slapped the floor with both hands.

Billy was caught in the humor of the situation. He tried to help Mr. Bennett and was pulled down along side him. Each attempt at speech was interrupted by another spasm of laughing. The youngsters were laughing out loud and Aunt Lucille was covering a grin.

The men finally got to their feet and Uncle Billy declared, "This calls for a celebration!" He brought out a hidden fifth of Old Hickory and filled their glasses with whiskey.

Mr. Bennett and Billy took a meaningful swallow of the alcohol. Billy leaned back and told the story about how he got his nickname. Mr. Bennett had been in the First Division and landed on Omaha Beach on the first day of the invasion. He had been wounded and was the only survivor of his squad. Mr. Bennett told of how he'd had his own nickname. He spent so much time peeling potatoes on KP duty that his platoon members called him "Tater."

The grandfather clock in the hallway struck twelve. Mr. Bennett rose with a slight wobble and announced, "Thank you for a fine evening but I must leave you, my fine Southern friends, before Billy gets too snockered."

Everyone, especially Uncle Billy, hated to see him go. They talked like they had known each other for thirty years. Uncle Billy put his arm around Ben, and said, "Don't call no cab. I'll drive you to the hotel."

Aunt Lucille whispered in David's ear, and he volunteered to drive Mr. Bennett into town. Another appearance in front of the judge was narrowly avoided.

A week later, word came from the home office. Mr. Bennett had called the president of Prime Meat Packing Company, and said he would be buying most of his meat from them. People in the company asked Uncle Billy what he had done to sell that tough and demanding customer. He said, "I turned on my Southern charm and he fell for it."

Rube's three weeks were soon finished and he had to return to Georgia. For Uncle Billy and Aunt Lucille, his departure was like sending a son off to the military or college. Ellie and David knew they would miss Rube and the kidding and laughter they shared.

David and Ellie readied the car to drive Rube to the Dallas/Fort Worth Airport for his flight back to Georgia.

Uncle Billy pulled Rube aside.

"Son, it's been special having you here. Things happen in life, good and bad. My advice is not to fight them. Sit back, relax, and enjoy whatever comes your way. Many times life is not under your control. Let God do the worrying. Do your best in all situations and the outcome will take care of itself.

"Life has been very good to me in spite of the troubles I've experienced. I've made things harder by drinking the way I do. Don't ever let the bottle get the best of you."

He grabbed Rube and hugged him. "I love you, Rube. Come back real soon."

Since the revelation of the Blankenschipf curse, Rube felt a special kinship with Uncle Billy. They both knew they were afflicted in the same, strange way. Living with that demon formed a bond that defied explanation and could never be broken.

"I love you too, Uncle Billy. I have really enjoyed my visit with you and the family. This trip has been wonderful, just wonderful."

"That's the attitude," Billy said.

Inside Information

Well, now. I'm back again. I stood it as long as I could. But, now it's time to bring you up to date. I hope you don't mind if I use my regular voice. I get so tired of using my formal voice which I am forced to do by the author. What a tyrant. Please, please don't tell him I said that. If you do, he'll run my ass through his paper shredder.

You probably wonder how I got this printed in the book. It wasn't easy, but I got my cousin, Herschel, to do it. He works for the company that's printing this book for the publisher. The publisher is a scrooge. He tried to keep the number of pages down to save money. I asked Herschel to perforate these pages so it would be easy for you to remove them. He said he couldn't do that. I'll just have to trust you to rip them out. If you don't, my career as a narrator will be over, and Herschel's days as a printer's assistant will be reduced to the low, single digits.

Rube's mother told him she got a letter from her sister, Rose. Caresse got married right after they got back to Louisiana. She met this Italian boy, Antonio Colosimo, who was visiting his aunt. They got married and nine months later she gave birth to a towheaded boy. The author has not allowed Rube to even mention Caresse's name. Can you believe that?

Imogene Blankenschipf never got married and passed the family name on to her son, Ned.

Just tuck this information in the back of your mind. It might come in handy later.

Narrator

CHAPTER SIX

Rube was a flanker back and received honorable mention on the all region football team, in spite of the curse raising its' ugly head during the game with Commerce. The offensive coordinator called Rube's special play which was a reverse, with him taking the handoff from the quarterback. At the snap Rube had a sudden sneezing attack though pollen season was long over. One of Commerce's linebackers blitzed through the line, sliced between Rube and the quarterback, stole the ball, and scored an easy touchdown. No one blamed Rube for the breakdown, except Rube.

Basketball began immediately after football. He was the point guard and felt an added responsibility to know all the plays and lead the team. By Christmas break the team was three and one, with their only loss to Oconee County. At least basketball went well.

He never saw Amy at the games, and knew that her father would never consent to bring her.

The youth group at the First Methodist Church planned a ski trip to North Carolina for January seventh. Rube's best friend, Will Sanderson, said the trip would break the routine of home, school and basketball. Rube signed up. He had never been skiing before, but sliding down a hill sounded easy and fun.

A light snow fell as the church bus left Winder and headed north. Heavy snow was predicted for Kentucky, Tennessee, North Carolina, South Carolina and Northern Georgia. The prediction came true and the bus chugged through a snowfall carried by a forty mile per hour wind.

Associate Pastor Ronnie Gaston steered the bus through the storm guided by prayer when possible. Large flakes hit the windshield and were wiped away for the next batch. Adam Vanderpool, the youth director, moved from the back of the bus where he had been leading a sing-along, to the front and helped Gaston navigate the disappearing road. Tense hours of driving passed before the church group reached the parking lot beside the resort.

The next morning the students were awake by seven o'clock and met at the cafeteria on the ground floor for breakfast. Rube was excited and a little scared. He had watched the downhill events of the Winter Olympic Games, and wanted to swoosh down the slopes with his scarf flapping in the wind. He'd go slower than the Olympians and have two poles to hold him up. How hard could it be?

The students went to the rental shop for boots and skis. A poster announced that those who wanted skiing lessons should report to the beginners slope at nine o'clock. The cost was fifteen dollars for a thirty minute session.

Mr. Vanderpool urged everyone to take a lesson. Instructors would teach them how to fall and slow down by using a technique called snowplowing. Rube decided against the lesson. Fifteen dollars was a lot of money after paying forty dollars for the boots and skis. Besides he was a good athlete and could learn on his own.

Rube put on his boots in the shop and walked outside where he slipped his toes into the bracket on the middle of the skis. He stepped down hard for the latch to catch the back of the boot and hold it in place.

He headed for the beginners slope for a practice run. Rube slipped and fell a couple of times, but was doing well when he reached the tow rope. He held on to the rope and was jerked along as he struggled to keep the skis even.

The exit at the top was unspectacular. Rube spread his feet far apart for stability. The result was little control over the skis, and he made wide turns if he turned at all. He looked like a protractor going down the hill. Other beginners scrambled far from his wide, scythe-like maneuvers.

Finally, Will said, "Hey, Pal, are you ready for the big time?"

"Sure, why not? I've been around the ski slopes all my life," said Rube in jest.

They slipped and shuffled to the chair lift for the expert hill. When their turn came, they moved into position in front of the next chair. Will sat down and the chair swung back as Rube sat into open space. He was about to hit the ground when the chair swung forward and he caught it with both elbows to be dragged twenty yards until the operator stopped the machine. Rube dropped to the ground, removed his skis, and walked back to wait for the next lift.

Rube arrived at the top on his second try and watched the other skiers get off the lift and casually go down the hill. The experienced ones stood up straight with their skis close together. They moved from one side of the trail to the other, making a quick jump and turn just before reaching the tree line. Rube decided his scythe technique was not appropriate for the big slope. Besides, there were girls around. He would use his skis like the pros, and stop on the way down to rest and check out the girls.

He pointed his skis to one side of the trail and moved out cautiously. Rube picked up speed as he proceeded. When he reached the other side, he did a quick jump and turn like the experienced skiers. The right ski turned, but the left one kept going straight. He fell on his right side and slid until he came to rest against a poplar tree.

A girl from another group came over to see if she could help. She grinned as she made a quick turn, and dug the edge of her skis into the snow, stopping only inches from Rube's head.

"Turn sideways and bring your skis together." she advised. "Place your pole underneath you on the right side and pull yourself up."

He rose to his feet. "Thanks. One of my skis must have caught on a root."

"Are you a beginner?" she asked.

"Not since I was younger," lied Rube. "I've been around the ski slopes all my life."

She swished away, leaving the scent of spring flowers. Not now, he thought, please no curse now. He had exaggerated some, but she was too pretty to tell her the truth. He'd try again and this time he wouldn't zigzag so there would be no need to turn.

Rube pushed off with his skis together and began his descent. Not knowing how to turn made him unable to slow down. He rapidly picked up speed and barely kept his balance. Rube skied as best he could. When another skier came close, he shouted, "Playing through!" Rube had no idea about ski etiquette.

The other members of his church group finished their lesson and waited in the lift line at the bottom of the advanced slope. Melissa Daniels, a schoolmate of Rube's, saw him coming straight down the hill.

"What a great skier," she said. "Look how fast he's going. He must be a professional."

"He looks familiar," said Cal Munson, standing next to her.

Rube sped toward the bottom of the slope and Melissa saw he was in trouble. "It's Rube! Somebody help him!" He headed straight for Cal and Melissa, and reverted to his earlier cry, "Playing through!" Those standing in line tried to run, but Rube was faster. He skied across the tips of an older woman's skis making her fall in panic, and continued toward the lodge parking lot.

Melissa slipped her skis off and ran behind Rube. There were two rows of ski racks about five feet apart by the side of the building. Cal saw a disaster about to happen and chased after Melissa. Rube passed through the racks unscathed. Skiers in the area scattered.

A five-foot drop-off separated the lodge from the paved parking lot. Fortunately for Rube, there was a large, bushy clump of shrubs to the right of his path. He turned slightly and dove headfirst into the bushes. Rube lay in the broken shrubbery unable to move, exhausted from having every muscle working at maximum intensity and the fear in his head.

Melissa screamed, "He's dead!" as she and Cal ran to help, along with Will. As they approached, Rube crawled out from under the greenery, his face beet red. What would his friends think if he told them his curse had made him do such foolishness?

When Will saw that his friend was okay, he smiled and said, "I thought you told me before you went up to the big one that you'd been around the ski slopes all your life."

Melissa kissed Rube on the cheek and he regained his composure. "Did I say ski slopes? I meant bushes. I've been around bushes all my life."

Will laughed and chucked him on the shoulder. "I have an idea. Why don't you take some lessons after lunch?"

In the cafeteria, Rube met the girl who had helped him earlier.

"Interesting form," she said. "Unique in its daring if not execution."

"I'm trying a new technique. There's still a few bugs to be worked out."

"Let me know when you're ready to share. I'll see you around." She flipped her ponytail and walked away.

That evening he saw her again in the lounge. She had freed her long, blond hair and it glistened in the light. Her eyes were sky blue and there was a hint of a smile on her lips as she talked to her friends. Her face glowed with wind tan from the day of skiing.

Rube walked to her table. "I've been rude by not introducing myself. I'm Rube Winters."

She stood. "I'm Kristy-with-a-K Free. Nice to meet a fellow skier."

"I have a confession. Today is the first I've been on a set of bed slats with turned up toes."

"You mastered the slope like the son of Jean-Claude Killy," she teased. "By the way, I met a boy on the slopes today who looks a lot like you, in fact I thought it was you when I approached. His technique is similar to yours, and he was lying on his back. Said his name was Ned, and he is from Athens. Do you know him?"

"No, can't say that I do. I need to meet him so we can hold each other up."

Rube asked her to dance and they moved on to the small dance floor. An unseen DJ dropped Phil Collins' *Something in the Air Tonight* on the turntable. Rube took Kristy in his arms and held his breath. He had never felt this way dancing with a girl. Strangely, there was the smell of plums in the air. Kristy laid her head on his shoulder as they moved around the floor.

"You're a better dancer than you are skier."

"Not having those sticks on my feet helps."

The song ended too soon. Rube and Kristy bought cups of hot chocolate and stepped outside to the large wooden deck. The weather front of the previous evening had passed, leaving a night sky sparkling with stars. A full moon lit the deck with a soft glow.

They sat on the bench attached to the railing around the deck. Kristy told Rube that she was a senior at the high school in Conyers, Georgia, and had traveled to the resort with a Baptist youth group. Her mother and father were born and raised in Gaylord, Michigan. Since she was five years old, they had taken her on ski trips to Aspen, Colorado and Boyne Mountain near Gaylord.

In the background they could hear the faint sound of R.E.M. playing "Fall on Me." They finished their hot chocolate and Kristy stepped on the bench to sit on top of the railing.

"Do you always wear tennis shoes for winter sports?" she asked.

"I'm not up on proper ski attire. I like the boots you're wearing."

"I got them for Christmas from my mom. They're wool-lined and the zipper in front makes them easy to put on."

Rube reached down to look at the boots and raised her leg. Kristy tilted backward and began to fall, pulling him with her as she grabbed the back of his sweater. They fell five feet into the snow piled around the porch. The snow broke their fall, but Kristy was miffed.

She rolled on top of Rube, put her hands around his neck, and said playfully, "I'm going to choke you for doing that." Rube reached between her arms and embraced Kristy. Their lips met.

"Rube Winters, you're crazy. You lured me outside and now you're trying to take advantage."

Rube was dizzy from the scent of plums.

"Accidents happen when I'm around. I can't help it."

"My hair is tangled and my clothes are wet. I can't go back into the lounge like this."

"Let's go for a walk, then I'll see you to your room." Rube and Kristy hiked around the lodge and then down the road leading to the main highway. They talked about their lives and what happened on the slopes.

At her door, Rube kissed her good night.

"I'm not certain you didn't plan this," she said as she wrote her telephone number on the back of his ski lift receipt. "Promise me you'll call."

The next day Rube skied until noon. He saw Kristy on the trails, and she gave him more tips about how to fall and turn. Will saw that Rube had changed. Love had struck in the cold winter snow. He was envious of his friend's luck.

Rube tried to join the singing and banter on the bus trip back home, but mostly stared out the window, thinking about Kristy.

Inside Information

It's me again. I hope I'm not interfering with your enjoyment of the book, but I feel the need to keep you informed about the undercurrents swirling below the surface. The author is too strait-laced to let you in on these things, but I think it's your right. Besides, I enjoy the freedom of being my real self. Throw off the traces and let her rip if you get my point. It gives me a high if you want to know the truth.

Herschel says hello. He's also enjoying the rush of endorphins that you get from putting your job on the line.

Aunt Rose keeps Rube's mother informed about Caresse.

I don't know if I told you last time, but Caresse named her little blond headed boy, Ruben. Said she just liked the name. Well sir, right after the birth, the young Mr. Colosimo headed back to the Big Apple. Said these southern women were too wild for him. The truth is, he was worn out. His nerves were frazzled. The boy was confused.

Ned Blankenschipf, III, grew up in Athens, Georgia. He worked for his dad, a private investigator. Did a lot of work for insurance companies, suspicious husbands or wives and such. A master of disguise and deception, he fit into any group or situation.

He had also been indoctrinated in the family traditions. He felt honor bound to carry them out.

Narrator

CHAPTER SEVEN

Rube dated Kristy through spring, but only occasionally because Conyers was thirty-three miles from Winder. Basketball season was over and Rube started baseball practice. Kristy was on the girl's softball team. Weekend dates had to be arranged around their games.

Besides the physical attraction, Rube experienced an unknown ease with Kristy. His parents were immediately taken by her and how gracious she was when visiting their modest home for Sunday dinner.

Rube drove the family Blazer to meet Kristy's parents on a Sunday in March. They lived a mile from the center of town in a large stucco house, the wide front yard was planted with flowers and a weeping willow tree. Kristy and her father met him at the door.

"He's the boy I told you about," she said. "The one training for the Olympic Ski Team."

"The new techniques," said Andy Free, Kristy's father. "We'll have to hear about them."

Rube blushed.

"This is my little brother, Dennis. He's ten."

"Happy to meet you, said Rube and stooped to shake his hand.

Dennis tossed his light brown hair to one side and declared, "I'm almost eleven."

Kristy's home overwhelmed Rube by its size and rich furnishings. The living room had cream-colored leather couches facing a floor-to-ceiling fireplace and Oriental rugs. The dining room was bigger than any room in Rube's house, with a long walnut table and matching chairs to seat twelve. There was also Mr. Free's study full of old books and a television room. Upstairs were the bedrooms. In the back yard was a swimming pool, and table and chairs under a covered patio.

Kristy's mother, Wilma, joined them in the living room. Dennis stuck by Rube's side. If Rube crossed his arms, so did the boy. When Rube put his finger to his chin, Dennis did likewise. Kristy encouraged Dennis to go to his room without success. Rube crossed his eyes, pushed his ears out, and stuck his tongue out to the side. Dennis tried to do the same, but his giggling interrupted his concentration.

"My sister likes you," the boy blurted out. "Are you going to marry her?"

"Dennis!" snapped Kristy. "I'm gonna feed your hamster to the dog if you don't behave." She grabbed for her brother as he fled the room.

"Kristy, dear, he's only a child," Wilma said.

"He won't grow up to be an adult if I have any say in the matter," said Kristy. "Rube, let's go see the rest of the house and family."

She led Rube up the stairway to the second floor and the master bedroom. In front of the curtains leading to the balcony was an iron-wrought cage with a parrot as big as a kitten. The bird had a bright patch of blue above a curved black beak. The blue narrowed over the top of his head, then spread to cover both wings, running all the way to the tip of his long tail. There was a white patch on each side of his face and he had a vibrant yellow chest. Long claws wrapped around the wooden perch. The bird was haughty and knew himself to be strikingly beautiful.

"Rube, this is Pretty Boy."

Rube tapped his finger on the cage and said, "Hello, Pretty Boy." The large beak attacked Rube's finger and struck metal.

"Gawk! I love you!" said the bird.

"We bought Pretty Boy last year from a pet shop in Aspen. It was love at first sight. Now he's like a member of the family. He goes everywhere with us."

"Can he ski?" Rube asked.

"No, but he's learning. Pretty Boy gets out of his cage once a day to fly around the bedroom. Then we put in his food and he returns. Males are so easy to train." She grinned.

They rejoined the Frees downstairs and soon left for a pool party with Kristy's friends. Rube enjoyed being around her family and they liked him in spite of his lower economic status.

On Monday Rube talked to Amy at school. There was still a great attraction between them, but they could not go out because of her father's restrictions.

"How's your mother doing?" asked Rube.

"Not very good. She's depressed much of the time. Daddy has a terrible temper and I'm afraid he's hurting her."

"Isn't there something you can do? Turn him in to the police?"

"He'd blame Mom. All I can do is try to keep peace."

"If I can help, let me know."

At the end of their senior year Amy told Rube she wanted to become a nurse. This compelled Rube to make his own career decision. He thought of Dr. Bill Glasson, the family chiropractor who had helped him with spinal and other health problems. Dr. Glasson's family lived nearby and Rube was friends with their son, Nathan, and daughter, Betty, neither of whom wanted to become a doctor of chiropractic.

Whenever Rube was injured playing sports, he went to see Dr. Glasson. He took time to talk with Rube about life and getting an education. Dr. Glasson cared about his patients. He liked sports and attended many of Nathan's and Rube's sporting events. Rube took Dr. Glasson's example seriously and decided to study chiropractic.

Rube graduated from Winder High School with honors and was accepted at the University of Georgia, Athens.

He took pre-med courses of chemistry, biology, anatomy, physics, psychology, and English, and planned to have enough credits in two years to apply to Life University in Marietta, Georgia.

Kristy also moved to Athens and entered the University for a degree in special education. She joined a sorority, but Rube decided against a fraternity because he would be changing schools. They were serious about their studies and many times their dates consisted of study sessions at the library.

Kristy invited Rube to go with her family to Aspen on their annual ski vacation during the Christmas holidays.

Rube accepted, though his mother was disappointed he would be away. They left the day after Christmas and stayed a full week. Kristy's father had rented a three-bedroom condominium with big glass windows that stared at the frozen mountains.

Rube was happy that he only had to pay for his rented equipment and the ski lift. By the end of the week he was a decent skier. He marveled at how far he had come from his first attempt in North Carolina.

In the spring of their second year at the University, Rube and Kristy decided to get married. Rube was in love and enjoyed the scent and feeling of sitting next to Kristy even in the musty old library.

Kristy and her mother made plans for the wedding which was to take place on August fifteenth. Rube wanted a small wedding, but the day was hers. If she wanted big, that was fine with Rube.

Kelvin Johnson, Kristy's preacher, would administer the wedding ceremony at the Conyers First Baptist Church, with Rube's preacher, Ralph Lee, saying an opening prayer. They met with Preacher Johnson the week before the wedding.

The church was a beautiful, old red brick structure over eighty years old. Preacher Johnson welcomed the young couple into his study for a talk about the commitment they were making. He asked of their plans for the future.

"We'll live in Marietta. I'm enrolled at Life University and Kristy will transfer to Kennesaw State College to finish her degree. We'll both work part-time."

"Do you intend to have children?"

"Not until after we finish our education," said Rube.

"Are there any impediments in your lives to interfere with the success of your marriage? Bringing them out now will make for a better union."

"I can't think of one. Can you, Rube?" asked Kristy.

"Reverend, there is something I'm concerned about. I don't know quite how to say it, but I have this curse. Accidents happen to me and I can't stop them. I never know when the curse is working, only that when it does, a feeling of dread comes over me." He bowed his head and massaged his temples like he was trying to rub away the memories of the curse. Kristy's eyes narrowed.

Pastor Johnson's eyes widened, but he still managed to be solicitous. "There is no such thing as a curse. Perhaps you're too serious for your own good. Every man makes mistakes."

"What are you talking about, Rube?" asked Kristy. "Don't you want to marry me?"

"Of course I do, but you should know about my curse. Remember when we met at the ski resort?"

"Oh, that was just an accident. Wasn't it? Besides, you were better in Aspen."

"You've blown simple clumsiness out of proportion," the preacher said. "Don't let this superstition interfere with your wedding or your life."

"I'll try." He thought, I don't dare tell them the story of Imogene Blankenschipf.

Rube's father, Calvin, was the best man. His friends from high school, Will Sanderson, Claude Stanfield, and Cal Manson, along with his present roommate, Wade Carlton were the ushers.

Of course all of Rube's family was invited, including Ellie, David, Aunt Lucille and Uncle Billy. He missed them and looked forward to seeing them again. Uncle Billy promised to control his drinking.

The day before the wedding, Rube drove to the Atlanta airport to pick up his uncle's family. He waited at gate nine for the flight from Dallas, in front of the exit for a good view of the people as they came off the plane.

The first passenger was Moochie Dunlop. She pulled a large suitcase on rollers and carried a shopping bag full of snacks, a package of chocolate covered pralines sticking out of the top. Moochie recognized him and yelped, "Rube! The boy who wet his pants! Lordy, it's been a long time since I seen you."

She dropped her bag and pulled Rube into her massive bosom. Moochie let go after a few suffocating minutes and he regained his breath. "How have you been?" he asked. "And your sister?"

"She's fine. She tries to get me in shape every time I visit Dallas, but so far I've kept my figure."

Rube bent over to help her with the bag she had dropped. "I see you still carry pralines."

"These are a special kind I order from California. They're low calorie. What brings you to the airport?"

"I'm waiting for my Uncle Billy and his family. They're coming to attend my wedding."

"Your wedding! I never got my invitation," she teased.

"I didn't know your address, Ms. Moochie."

"Why, everyone in Conyers knows me."

"That's where we're having the wedding, tomorrow at the First Baptist Church at two o'clock. We'd love to join us."

"I'll wear my nicest dress, Honey. Count on me being there. Now I must be going home. See you."

Ellie rushed Rube as Moochie walked away. He gave his cousin a hug, lifting her off the floor.

"Rube, you've grown since we last saw you."

"Six feet two and one hundred eighty-five pounds. What's not muscle is brains."

He shook David's hand and Aunt Lucille grabbed him around the neck. "You've let your hair grow too long for a married man."

"Yes, Ma'am," said Rube. "Under orders from my bride to be. Uncle Billy! It's so good to see all of you."

He and Uncle Billy tried to shake hands and hug at the same time, knocking Uncle Billy's new Stetson hat to the floor.

"My fault," said Rube. They both bent over to pick up the hat and bumped heads. They laughed and gave each other a knowing look. Rube caught the faint smell of whiskey on Billy.

"Where's your straw hat?" Rube asked.

"I decided to modernize myself. What do you think?"

"Very nice, but I like your old hat better."

"You're like my workers. I wore my new hat to the plant and the employees had a fit. The next day I went back to my old one to keep them happy. How's life been treating you?"

"No complaints. I'm going to school and studying hard."

"That's wonderful, just wonderful," said Uncle Billy.

At the South Terminal baggage claim area, David spotted their flight number over claim area two. They joined the crowd waiting for their luggage.

Rube heard Moochie from the other end of the return rack. "There's my suitcase."

Bodies bumped and fell as Moochie made her way to collect her belongings from the moving belt. There were shouts of "Watch out!" and a few swear words. A man next to Rube remarked, "We're being attacked by aliens from the fat planet. They're trying to flab us to death."

Moochie pulled her suitcase through the crowd to her other belongings. She glanced into the bag to make sure the pralines were safe.

While Rube watched Moochie, Uncle Billy spotted their luggage and moved closer. The suitcases were high on the rack and he reached over another bag to grab his. He worked his hand down between the suitcases to grip the handle.

Billy was snatched off his feet onto the moving belt. Ellie grabbed her father by the leg and tried to hold him back. Instead, the belt pulled her along and she began to knock into other passengers.

"Someone stop this damned machine," she pleaded.

Rube jumped on the moving belt, made his way to Uncle Billy, and lifted the suitcase, freeing his hand. Uncle Billy and Ellie slid off the ramp to the floor.

Rube rushed to their side. "Are you hurt? Ellie, are you all right?"

Uncle Billy said, "I'm wonderful, just wonderful." His knuckles were skinned and his wrist was swollen. Ellie had some scrapes and scratches on her left leg, but otherwise was fine.

An airline official offered to call a doctor. Uncle Billy explained what had happened, and assured him medical assistance was not required. "A little accident is all," said Uncle Billy.

Moochie jerked Uncle Billy's bag from the belt on its' return trip, and dropped it on the foot of a robust man who complained, "Damn, Woman, watch what you're doing." Moochie gave him a fierce look that caused him to slink away.

On their way to Winder, they stopped at the College Pharmacy for an ice pack and wrap for Uncle Billy's wrist. They had a good laugh when they told Rube's parents about the airport. Even with the problems, Rube was comforted having Uncle Billy and his family with him. Tomorrow was his wedding day. He shook off a feeling of dread and hoped everything would go as planned.

CHAPTER EIGHT

Rube awoke early on his wedding day. Confusing thoughts had played on his mind throughout the night. He really loved Kristy and felt guilty that thoughts of Amy kept entering his mind. She had been his first love, but now those feelings had to be set aside. Most upsetting were his memories of Cousin Caresse. Was that love or another feeling just as powerful? No one must ever know about that.

Would the Blankenschipf curse be present at the wedding? He wondered.

His mother, Betty, and Aunt Lucille prepared a large breakfast of eggs, grits, gravy, biscuits, jelly, sorghum molasses, orange juice and coffee for the family.

When Rube arrived at the table, David asked, "Are you nervous, Rube?"

"Of course not. This is only the most important day of my life. Everything's under control," boasted Rube.

"Then why is your fly open?"

Rube corrected the problem. "Just a small glitch," he said.

Uncle Billy sat at one end of the table with a bit of shaving cream clinging to one ear. His wrist was a little sore. Ellie was fine. They talked of Rube's visit to Dallas and Mr. Bennett's visit.

Remembering the story Uncle Billy used to tell, Rube asked, "How's the Nazi, Uncle Billy?"

"He's fine. Still acts up every now and then. Rattles his chain and makes noise." They all laughed as he continued, "Rube, I want you to know that the Nazi's feelings were hurt that he didn't receive an invitation to the wedding."

"Oh, I'm sorry about that. I couldn't have him disrupt the wedding by dragging his chains down the aisle. Besides, who would want to sit next to him?"

"You have a point there, my boy. I'll give him your regrets when I get back to Dallas."

The young people winced as Calvin said, "Billy, would you please give our blessing?"

"Yes, but first we must hold hands." He proceeded to bless the family, naming each member; the President, the Vice President, the Congress, the Supreme Court, the State of Georgia, the Flag, American soldiers all over the world, the peacemakers of the world, Kristy's family, the church where they would be married, the preachers, and everyone in the wedding party.

When he got through, Ellie said, "Daddy! You forgot to bless the food!"

"Okay, bless the food. Amen."

David piped in with, "I hate to say it Daddy, but you also forgot the table cloth and silverware."

They laughed and began devouring the lukewarm food.

Cal Munson picked Rube up at twelve-thirty. When they arrived, Rube walked around the church, sweating in his rented tuxedo with dove gray vest, and checked on everything from the red, white and yellow flowers decorating the ends of pews to the organist in the choir loft. The guests began to arrive and Rube was relegated to a small room behind the choir loft so as not to see Kristy before the ceremony. Rube's preacher, Ralph Lee, kept him company as he fidgeted in the limited space. Reverend Lee had been married many years and told Rube that matrimony marked a new beginning. Rube wondered if this beginning would be good or bad. They prayed for a good and fruitful marriage according to God's will.

At five minutes to two, Rube's father and the ushers came to get him. Calvin assured Rube everything was fine.

"How's Uncle Billy?"

"Sober as a judge at Easter morning church service."

Kristy had insisted that Pretty Boy be at the wedding and the caged bird was placed at the back of the sanctuary. Her brother, Dennis, was in charge of the bird. If Pretty Boy started making noise during the ceremony, he was to drop the hood over the cage. Dennis busied himself while waiting for the adults to do their marrying by tormenting the bird. He ran his fingers along the bars of the cage and told Pretty Boy he'd be part of the wedding dinner, if not the entrée, or at least a snack served on Ritz crackers.

While the people were filing in, a young man with blond hair, a mustache and goatee stopped to talk to Dennis. He was curious about the parrot, and asked Dennis if he could pet him.

Dennis, feeling important as "keeper of the bird," and not wanting to disappoint the man, said, "Yes. Just make sure you close the cage door." The man looked a lot like Rube and was certainly a member of his family.

The man reached in, startling Pretty Boy, who promptly pecked him on the finger. He yelped, "Ouch! That hurt!" and carelessly closed the door. Pretty Boy said, "Gawk! Heeere's trouble."

The cue was given and Rube, his father and the ushers filed in. As they waited for the maid of honor and bridesmaids to come down the aisle and take their places, Rube noticed that Uncle Billy's family was seated next to his mother. There was an empty seat where Uncle Billy should have been sitting.

To divert himself from the anxiety that he felt, he looked up and around, taking in the beauty of this very old sanctuary. The ceiling rose on thick wooden beams. It was designed to carry the message of God to the balcony and even to the last row of pews. The stained glass windows on either side, depicting biblical scenes, reflected and improved upon the light of the afternoon sun.

There was a mild disturbance in the back of the church as his old friend, Moochie Dunlop, wedged her body into a pew, putting a strain on the bolts holding it to the floor. Rube became concerned about a small boy sitting in the vacinity, afraid that Moochie wouldn't see him and flatten him like a pancake when she sat down. To his relief, the father reached and snatched the boy out of harms way at the last moment. The three people sitting behind Moochie got up and moved to another location so they would be able to see the wedding.

He noticed Uncle Billy coming down the side aisle with a grin on his face, likely thinking how wonderful, just wonderful the wedding would be.

Kristy's preacher, Kelvin Johnson, and Reverend Lee stood on either side of the pulpit. Everyone's attention shifted to the back of the church when the wedding march began. Kristy's sparkling blue eyes and perfectly tanned skin glowed through the thin, white veil as she clung to her father's arm. Her smile told Rube that this was the happiest day of her life. Their eyes met and he knew how deeply he loved Kristy. Reverend Johnson began the vows.

"Who gives this woman to be wed?"

"Her mother and I," said Mr. Free.

Kristy moved forward as Rube and the rest of the wedding party turned to face the preachers.

Reverend Lee led them in prayer.

"May God bless this young couple as they enter this most holy union. May they always remember and live up to the vows they take today. And, may they live a long and happy life together."

Reverend Johnson stepped in front of the young couple, made some preliminary remarks, and read from the Bible. Then, "Do you, Kristy, take Rube to be your lawfully wedded husband?"

Before she could answer, a wild fluttering of wings came from the back of the church. Pretty Boy had bumped the closed, but unlatched cage door and flew out for his afternoon exercise.

"Come back here you dumb bird!" screamed Dennis.

The ceremony stopped dead in its' tracks as everyone turned to see what had happened.

Pretty Boy was surprised by the amount of space he had, and found that he could fly at full speed without hitting anything. He made three passes around the ceiling of the church, frightened, but feeling the energy and excitement of his large audience.

He landed on the window ledge of the stained glass window depicting Moses' presentation of the Ten Commandments.

"Gawk! I love you!" said Pretty Boy.

His audience laughed and some of them shouted back, "I love you, Pretty Boy."

This encouraged Pretty Boy, and he took off on another flight pattern around the church.

Mrs. Free moaned and bent forward with her face in her hands.

Mr. Free reacted with "What the---," and then made a dash for the rear of the church to find his soon to-be-disowned son, Dennis.

Dennis saw the look in his father's eyes, fled down the side aisle in terror and ducked into the large social hall.

Pretty Boy landed on the railing separating the choir from the dais. "Gawk! Let's make love! Let's make love!" he exclaimed, a polite phrase the bird had learned from being kept in the bedroom.

Preacher Johnson was stunned into an unfamiliar silence. Rube's preacher, having been through a family trauma with Rube before, stepped to his side. "Don't worry, Kelvin. Things will work out fine."

Kristy-with-a-K went into a pout. Her eyes filled with tears. Finally, she said, "Rube, what's happening to our wedding? Can't you do something?"

Rube said, "I'm sorry," putting his arm around her. Desperately, he turned to his father, "Dad, see if you and the guys can catch Pretty Boy."

"Gawk! I love you! Gawk! Let's make love!"

The ushers converged on Pretty Boy. He flew to a standing candelabrum on the altar and knocked it over. Drops of wax dotted the bridesmaid's dresses. The bird settled on the pew in front of Mrs. Free.

"Gawk! Not tonight, Dear. Gawk! I have a headache."

She lunged for the bird, hoping to choke the life out of him before he could say anything else. "Keep your mouth shut! You dumb bird!"

Mr. Free ran back down the center aisle. He caught his wife just as she went over the back of the pew with her legs sticking up in the air. He dragged her back into her seat. "Stay her, Wilma! Don't move!"

"Andy, do something!" She moaned.

Andy Free went running back up the aisle.

Kristy rushed to her mother's side.

Rube joined his father and the ushers trying to catch Pretty Boy. Uncle Billy was missing. The guests began a rhythmic clap. There were broad smiles and open laughter all over the church. Some were shouting, "I love you Pretty Boy," and "Let's make love!" Moochie gave high fives to the people around her and yelled, "Go, big bird, go!"

Preacher Johnson sighed loudly, and asked Preacher Lee, "What can we do?"

"Wait and pray," he soothed.

Pretty Boy landed below another picture window depicting the burning of Sodom and Gomorrah. Rube, the ushers, and six others who had joined the chase, scrambled toward him. Toes were stepped on and hats knocked askew as three of the ushers hurried between the pews.

"Gawk! Let's make love! Gawk! I love you!" said Pretty Boy just before he flew away.

Pretty Boy was used to soiling his cage after exercise. Those below were unaware of the imminent danger and continued to clap. Kristy and her mother cried and held each other.

"This Methodist boy is cursed like he told me," said Reverend Johnson. "I'll never marry a Methodist again, no offense to you Reverend Lee. From now on, I'm going to stick to my own, maybe a Presbyterian now and then."

Pretty Boy flew high in the church and made a nosedive maneuver. As he pulled up, his early feeding let go.

The massive bomb struck Moochie on top of her left ear. One portion splashed down into the ever present bag containing the chocolate pralines, and another portion struck the bald head of the man sitting in front of her.

The man reached up to see what had struck his head. "Ugh!!!" he moaned as he saw his hand.

Moochie was not so concerned about her ear, but the attack on her loved ones, the pralines, was unacceptable.

She raised her fist at Pretty Boy. "You dirty bird! You S.O.B.! If I get my hands on you, I'm gonna pluck your feathery ass!"

She realized where she was and sheepishly sat down. Hands over her mouth, she bent forward to say a quick prayer for forgiveness. The glob caught on her ear fell into her lap. She mumbled another obscenity before regaining control.

Uncle Billy had slipped out for an afternoon jolt of Old Hickory and reeled along the side aisle. He saw the dive bombing attack on Moochie and said, "That's wonderful, just wonderful!" with more awe than irony, and repeated to anyone who looked his way, "This is a wonderful wedding, just wonderful!"

Pretty Boy flew to the front of the church again, and rested on the same choir railing, feeling much better. "Gawk! I have a headache! Gawk! Not tonight."

Rube's mother went over to Mrs. Free and Kristy to see if she could help. Mr. Free had been home and returned with Pretty Boy's special birdseed. He filled the cup in the cage and called, "Here, Pretty Boy. Here, Pretty Boy."

Soon, the guests began chanting, "Here, Pretty Boy. Here, Pretty Boy."

The bird's head perked up as he heard the familiar call. "Gawk! I love you!" said Pretty Boy. Then, he flew to his cage and went inside. Mr. Free slammed the door shut and hustled him outside.

Everyone, except Moochie and the man in front of her, applauded Pretty Boy. One man remarked, "This is the best damn wedding I've ever been to." His wife jerked his coat sleeve.

When the guests realized they were still in church, all became so quiet you could hear a wafer drop.

Brother Lee poked Reverend Johnson who returned from his shocked condition with a start. Lee whispered, "Let's pick up where we left off as though nothing happened."

Moochie got up and headed for the restroom.

The preacher said, "Kristy, Rube and the rest of the wedding party, please come forward and take your places."

The rest of the ceremony went without incident.

Reverend Johnson announced a reception in the social hall immediately following the wedding.

Kristy's makeup was a mess, but it didn't matter to Rube. They kissed, and walked up the aisle, waving and smiling at everyone. Rube thought, the Blankenschipf curse can win only if I let it.

CHAPTER NINE

One of Kristy's cousins, Charles Free, was a news reporter for the Turner Broadcasting System. After Pretty Boy went back in his cage, Charles whispered to his wife and slipped out the side door. He telephoned the station manager, briefly told him the story, and asked that a camera crew be sent out immediately.

Charles then went to Mr. Free, and asked him to not take Pretty Boy home just yet. "Please take him into the social hall so the people will be able to see him."

Before her husband could answer, Mrs. Free interjected, "No! Absolutely not! Haven't I been embarrassed enough already?"

"Please, Aunt Wilma, please. Just let him stay a little while. We'll keep the cover on his cage."

He saw her eyes soften as he continued, "Please, Aunt Wilma. We'll make sure nothing bad happens."

"Well---okay. Just make sure you keep that bird away from me. And, Andy, you make certain that he doesn't say anything else."

Rube and Kristy went to set up the reception line as the ushers led the crowd out and around the church to the social hall.

Mr. Free grabbed the cage, and led his wife inside because they were part of the reception line. He set the cage down on a chair next to him.

The guests were still in a joyous, happy mood as they filed into the hall. Many of them were still laughing and discussing what had happened. They were in a party mood.

As they filed by Kristy, Rube and the parents, there was electricity in the air. Their praise for the wedding was abundant and overflowing.

"What a great wedding!"

"Thank you for letting us be a part of this!"

"May your life together be as much fun as your wedding."

When they got to Mrs. Free, she began to apologize. None of them would accept it, saying there was nothing to be sorry for.

"We've had more fun at this wedding than any we've ever attended," said one of Kristy's aunts.

As the guests approached Mr. Free and noticed the cage, they wanted to see Pretty Boy. "Please. We promise we won't open the cage."

Mr. Free glanced at his wife. She acquiesced to popular demand with a brief smile.

As he lifted the cover off the cage, the camera crew from TBS arrived.

They quickly shouldered their camera and began filming.

The people were shy of the camera at first, but then began to warm to the idea of being on television. Their smiles were a little broader, and their praise a little louder. Many of them insisted on having their picture taken alongside Pretty Boy's cage. There were comments to the bird such as: "I love you, Pretty Boy. Do you have a girlfriend, Pretty Boy? How's your headache? What about tonight, Pretty Boy?"

Of course the camera crew, and reporter, Charlie Free, were delighted with the whole scene. Some of the guests were interviewed as they came through the line.

"What's your relationship with the bride and groom?"

"How did you like the wedding ceremony?"

One man replied, "I think we should have a parrot at every wedding."

Moochie emerged from the restroom with the left side of her head still wet. She made her way to the reception line with "the bag" slung over her left forearm. "Hi,Rube. Thanks for inviting me to your wedding. Honey, it was fun up to a certain point."

"I'm sorry about what happened."

"Oh, that's all right, Honey. I'll get over it."

"Miss Moochie, I want you to meet my wife, Kristy."

"Hi, Kristy. Lord 'a' mercy, the pace of life sure picks up when your husband's around, don't it?"

"Yes, I guess you're right, Miss Moochie. I'm pleased to meet you."

When Moochie got to Pretty Boy, he said, "Gawk! Let's make love!"

She bent over and whispered to the bird, "Thanks for the proposition you dirty bird! I wouldn't make love to you if you were the last featherbrain on earth!"

As she turned her face to the camera, she smiled sweetly.

Later, when interviewed by Reporter Free, she told him that Pretty Boy ought to wear a diaper when he goes out for his exercise.

"I enjoyed the bird's antics up until his unprovoked assault on me and my belongings. Now, I would like to strangle him."

Dennis finally came out from hiding. Once he saw his father talking and smiling in the reception line, he figured his life was out of danger. His dad wouldn't hurt him in front of all the guests.

"Please describe exactly how Pretty Boy got loose at the wedding," said the reporter to Dennis.

"It wasn't my fault. I think a member of Rube's family left the cage door unlatched. When Pretty Boy bumped against the door, it came open, and he just flew out. I tried my best to stop him."

They tried to interview Mrs. Free. The only thing she would say was, "From now on, Pretty Boy's new residence will be the living room, not our bedroom."

When they talked to Reverend Johnson, he told them he was glad he had the presence of mind to keep things under control, and complete the ceremony.

"However, I will ask the committee in charge of the use of church facilities to add a new restriction. No birds will be allowed in the sanctuary."

By the time they got around to Uncle Billy, he had made one too many trips to the car. He talked to just about everyone at the reception, telling them how wonderful everything was. "Moochie, you did a wonderful job of cleaning up. Mrs. Free, it was wonderful how you recovered after going over the back of the pew."

"Mr. Winters, what is your relationship to the bride and groom?"

"Well, Rube is my nephew, but he's like a son to me and Lucille. He grew up with our children."

"What do you think of Pretty Boy, and his antics in church today?"

"Things sometimes happen to birds, just like they do to human beings. Pretty Boy was just doin' things that come natchral. 'Course, I'm sorry 'bout him dive bombin' Miss Moochie. Did I ever tell you the story about how I got my nickname, 'Canary?"

Charlie, sensing they did not want to go there, moved on to interview the newlyweds.

"Kristy, what was your reaction to the disruption of your wedding?"

"I was mortified. I wanted to crawl under a pew. I wanted our wedding to be perfect, but, that was not to be. I'm the one who insisted that Pretty Boy be at our wedding. Now, I'm not sure that was a good idea."

"Rube?"

Rube glanced at Kristy, then decided not to mention the curse. "I was surprised like everyone else, but thought Pretty Boy would be caught quickly. When he wasn't and continued to say embarrassing things, I got worried. Seeing Kristy and her mother so upset was the worst part for me. Kristy is a beautiful bride and I wanted this to be a happy day for both of us. Actually, since we came to the reception, I think we both feel better because our guests seem very happy."

Finally, it was Pretty Boy's turn to be interviewed.

They moved the camera up close, and Reporter Free said, "Hi, Pretty Boy. Could you please give us your bird's-eye view of today's events?" He stuck the microphone into the cage.

"Gawk! I love you," as beak struck foam rubber on the mic.

"Are you sorry for what you did?"

"Gawk! Let's make love!"

"Were you happy to get back in your cage?"

"Gawk! I'm coming! I'm coming!"

At that point, Mrs. Free, standing nearby, lunged toward the cage, knocking people out of the way. She slapped the camera away, grabbed the microphone with her left hand, and gave the reporter an elbow to the throat.

"You dirty bird! I'm going to take you home and wash your mouth out with soap! As for you, Charles, this interview is over!"

"Cough! Cough! Choke! But, Aunt Wilma, I didn't know what he was gonna say!"

"Andy, get over here and get blabbermouth out of here."

In the meantime, the cameraman recovered, and continued to film the scene.

Pretty Boy was given a quick trip home, and the table which held his cage was moved from the bedroom to the living room. Mr. and Mrs. Free returned to the party, not wanting to miss their daughter's departure.

While Kristy was talking to a group of friends, Rube pulled Uncle Billy aside.

"Uncle Billy, I want you to know how much I appreciate you all coming to my wedding. It was special having you here."

"We're happy to be here my boy. I wouldn't have missed it for anything! It's the best wedding I've been to since I married your Aunt Lucille. Where are you going on your honeymoon?"

"To Cancun for a week. Then, we'll come back and fix up our apartment before school starts. Do you have any advice for me as I start my new life?"

"Well, Son, yes I do. Don't worry about the curse. It's just something we have to live with right now. I've been studying the Bible for a long time. Someday I'll find the answer to the Blankenschipf curse. When I do, I'll let you know. In the meantime, you could join in the search by reading your Bible.

There's so much in the Good Book, it would be easy to overlook something."

Rube put his arm around Uncle Billy. "Okay, I'll do that, but not while I'm on my honeymoon."

"I don't blame you, Son. Just know that someday we'll lick this thing." They hugged, and Rube moved over to speak to Aunt Lucille.

Kristy went to change into her traveling clothes, and Moochie waddled to where Rube was standing.

"Lordy, Rube, this has been some kind of wedding. I've enjoyed it in spite of the unprovoked assault. But, I'm glad they took that dirty bird on home."

She reached into her bag, bringing out a box of her treasured pralines. "I didn't bring you a wedding present, but I want you to have these to take on your trip. And, tell Kristy she can have some too, because they won't put any weight on you."

Moochie's sad eyes told Rube that it just about broke her heart to give up the delicious morsels of candy. This was a great sacrifice on her part. He thought, it's not what you give, but how much you miss it that really counts.

He took the box, saying, "Moochie, are you sure you want to give me this?"

"Yes...Yes. I want you to have it," as a tear formed in the corner of her eye.

"Well, I can't tell you how much I appreciate it. Of all the gifts we've received, this is my favorite." He grinned and patted Moochie on the shoulder.

Kristy returned, and the crowd moved outside to send them off to the airport in a hail of rice.

They arrived at the airport and boarded their flight to Cancun without incident. It had been an exhausting day so far. They both fell asleep with the new Mrs. Winters' head resting on his shoulder.

That evening the wedding was on the news. Other networks immediately picked up the story, and by eleven o'clock all were running the story with clips from the interviews, especially the one of Pretty Boy.

Mrs. Free went to bed early with a bad headache. Mr. Free caught the report on CBS, and soon began getting calls from family and friends, wanting to know what he thought about Pretty Boy being on T.V. Actually they wanted to know if he and Wilma were embarrassed. He was glad Wilma was asleep.

The next morning the story was on all the early morning shows, and soon calls flowed in to arrange interviews with Pretty Boy and other members of the family.

That afternoon Pretty Boy's picture and the story were in all the major newspapers, as well as most of the smaller ones. There were headlines such as: "Pretty Boy Disrupts Wedding," "Bird Bombs Wedding," and "Dirty Bird Reveals Secrets."

Mr. and Mrs. Free loved *The Tonight Show*, sitting up in bed many nights to watch it.

Up to this point, Mrs. Free had vetoed any attempt to interview Pretty Boy. Even when Johnny Carson's producer called, she said no. He asked her to hold the phone for just a moment.

"Mrs. Free, this is Johnny Carson."

Her legs wobbled and she almost dropped the phone. Hand over the mouthpiece, she motioned to Mr. Free and whispered, "It's Johnny Carson, in person! I can't believe it!"

"Yes, Mr. Carson. It's nice to talk to you. We watch your show all the time."

"Mrs. Free, I know this has been a little embarrassing for you, but this is a great human interest story. Mrs. Free---."

"Please call me Wilma."

"Fine. Wilma, I want to ask you to do a personal favor for me. We will fly you, Mr. Free and Pretty Boy to New York. My staff will give you the names of three of the nicest hotels in the city to choose from. All of your meals and any other expenses will be paid by the network. Please say that you will come and be on my show."

Wilma was breathless. "Hold on just a minute, Mr. Carson."

She held the end of the phone. "Andy, he wants us to come and be on *The Tonight Show*, all expenses paid. Maybe we could see a Broadway show while we're there."

"Sounds like fun. Let's do it."

"Mr. Carson, we would love to be on your show."

"That's great, Wilma. Now, hold on just a minute and one of the producers will tell you how all of this works. Goodbye, and I look forward to seeing you in New York."

"Goodbye, Johnny."

Mrs. Free had a complete make over and a brand new outfit for the show. The celebrity of it all far overrode the embarrassment of what Pretty Boy might say.

Before they went on the show, they met Ed McMahan back stage. He was as nice as he appeared on T.V.

When they brought Pretty Boy on, the audience went wild with applause and cheers. "Hoorah for Pretty Boy!" "Go Pretty Boy!"

Pretty Boy did not disappoint. Like a born entertainer, his ears perked up when he heard the audience. Before they left for New York, they tried to teach him to say, "Hereeee's Johnnnyyyy!"

As soon as they emerged from the curtain, he began saying it, "Gawk! Hereeee's Johnnyyyy! Gawk! Hereeee's Johnnnyyyy!"

Ed McMahan bent over with laughter, and Johnny smiled broadly, looking sideways at the audience. Introductions were made, and Johnny said, "Hi, Pretty Boy, it's nice to meet you."

"Gawk! I love you."

"Gawk! Let's make love."

Johnny turned his head with a knowing grin. "Right here on the stage?"

The audience roared with laughter.

"Can I hold him?" asked Johnny.

"Sure," said Mr. Free. "But, we'd better put this leash on his leg to make sure he doesn't fly out into the audience" Mr. Free reached into the cage, attached the strap, and brought him out just as someone in the audience shouted, "We love you, Pretty Boy!"

He put him on Johnny's coat sleeve so he wouldn't scratch his arm. Johnny cringed at first, but then began stroking Pretty Boy's feathers. They liked each other immediately, both being in show business.

"Do you like me, Pretty Boy?"

"Gawk! I'm coming! I'm coming!"

Wilma cringed and covered her ears. Mr. Free patted her hand.

The audience went wild again as Johnny gave them his look. Applause went on for a good three minutes.

Pretty Boy was so excited, he fluttered off Johnny's sleeve and onto the table, relieving himself on the papers next to Johnny's familiar coffee cup.

Johnny gave a disgusted look, then ran behind the curtain. He peeked out with a big smile on his face, "Tell me when it's safe to come out."

Mr. Free grabbed Pretty Boy and returned him to his cage.

Tears ran down Ed McMahan's face and he was unable to speak.

The whole room was rocking with laughter and cheers. Johnny came from behind the curtain, waving his hand in front of his nose. Assistants had already cleaned up the mess.

Johnny thanked the Frees for coming, "And, you too, you dirty bird! If I'm ever crazy enough to get married again, you're invited to my wedding."

The people were still laughing and cheering as they left the stage. "Go, Pretty Boy, Go!"

Station *KRLO* in Dallas picked up the story. Somehow they found out that some people from Dallas had been at the wedding. They called Uncle Billy who agreed to an interview.

After he got through telling the reporter and his audience how wonderful everything was, the man asked him if he had seen Pretty Boy on *The Tonight Show*.

"Yes, I did. And, I think he ought to replace Ed McMahan as Johnny's sidekick."

"Maybe so, but what about his unsanitary habits?"

"Well, I'm sure they could fit him with pants. In fact, they could afford to make him a whole outfit, including a straw hat just like mine."

That evening, Ben Bennett called Billy from Chicago to congratulate him on his T.V. appearance. "Perhaps you and Pretty Boy could form a twosome, and call yourselves 'The Dirty Bird Duet.' After all, a 'Canary' and a parrot are birds of a feather. You could sing down at the 'Longhorn." They both laughed long and hard.

"Yes, and maybe I could get Pretty Boy to poop on the mean ole policemen!"

"Yeah. That's a great idea. Well, hang in there old pal. I'll see you the next time I'm in Dallas."

The NBC affiliate in Atlanta arranged an interview with Moochie whom they had seen on *TBS*.

When the crew arrived at Moochie's home in Conyers, they found her waiting for them at the front door. She had a new hairdo with little ringlets all over her head. Her makeup was thicker than usual and her cheeks were especially rosy. The medium high heels that she wore were under great strain, and this kept the members of the crew anxious until she finally sat down in the *Lazyboy* loveseat. They marveled at the strength of modern day plastic when combined with wood.

Sitting on the table next to her chair was a large box of chocolate pralines. There were several *Twinkie* wrappers in the wastebasket under the table.

The crew set up the lights and camera, and were ready to do the interview.

"Ms. Dunlop, how long have you known the newlyweds?"

"Why, My Lord, I've known Rube Winters since he was just a boy. We used to travel a lot together. He's a good friend of mine. Kristy and her family have been neighbors of mine forever."

"What do you think of Pretty Boy now that he has become a celebrity?"

"Well, he's a nice enough bird, I guess. But, Lord, Honey, he sure needs to be potty trained. Besides that, I think they must be feeding him way too much, based on my experience with him. It's a wonder he's not as big as a turkey."

"Did you see Pretty Boy on Johnny Carson's show?"

"I sure did, Honey. I was happy to see that he does not discriminate. He poops on the rich and famous as well as the rest of us."

Rube and Kristy returned from their honeymoon to find that they were now a famous couple in the Conyers area, and that Pretty Boy was a genuine celebrity.

In fact, the next week, Mr. Free was contacted by a Hollywood studio, asking if they could send a representative to talk to him about a possible role for Pretty Boy in a coming "Dirty Harry" movie.

Inside Information

I know you're probably asking yourself, if this narrator is so unhappy with the author and editor, why doesn't he write his own book? Well, I might just do that, now that I know all the tricks of the trade. If I do, you can be sure I'll let the reader in on everything, maybe even some things he doesn't want to read. As for right now, I'm having too much fun as a rogue narrator. It gives me a rush being inside someone else's brain. Besides that, I have a part-time job of narrating for a political speech writer. If you think authors are bad, you ought to try that job for a while.

Herschel sends his fondest regards. I told him I'd help him find a new job when this one ends, which it's likely to do. He's good at sweeping and mopping floors.

Have you ever seen anything like Pretty Boy? Why, he's the damndest bird, in fact the only bird, I've ever narrated about. And, that Moochie is a sight. I love to talk about her. She's my kind of people.

Caresse's mother, Rose, sent Rube's mother a picture of Ruben. She said he looks a lot like Rube at that age.

Clever how the author sneaked in the glimpse of the stranger who left Pretty Boy's cage door ajar. Surely he doesn't think you all would miss that little clue.

Narrator

CHAPTER TEN

Kristy and Rube moved into their new apartment, located near Life College in Marietta, and it was only a short drive for Kristy to Kennesaw State College. They enjoyed decorating their first home. Kristy's parents sent them a bedroom suite, and Rube brought several things from home: his stereo, a recliner and an old dining room set.

The Frees paid for Kristy's tuition and books. Rube's mom and dad agreed to pay half of his tuition. Rube's half was still a lot of money, and he would have to buy books. The rent was five hundred dollars per month.

They both worked part time jobs. Rube became an assistant cameraman for TBS in Atlanta. Kristy's cousin, Charlie, pulled strings to get him the job. As a part-timer, he worked a lot of nights and week-ends.

Kristy got a job as a bartender at the Oak Grove Country Club just outside of Kennesaw. She had no experience, but was trained on the job.

They had two weeks before classes began, and they treated it as a continuation of their honeymoon. They worked in the evenings, but spent the rest of their time together, much of it in bed. They made two trips during that time. One was to the Atlanta Zoo. Neither had ever been, even though they lived near by.

The other trip was to Stone Mountain where they spent the day. They went for a boat ride, then climbed to the top of the mountain. Kristy spread a blanket on a mossy area at the top. They lay there holding hands under God's sheltering cerulean blue sky. There would come a time when Rube would look back and remember how very special this day was. In a way, it was the high water mark of their marriage. They were closer to God, and closer to each other at that time than they ever had been or would be. They lay for a long time, saying nothing. Then, Rube rolled onto his side next to her, saying, "Kristy, I love you with all my heart."

"I love you too, Rube."

After a few minutes, she said, "Rube, does that mean that you love me more than Moochie loves her pralines?" She repressed a smile, but it danced in her eyes.

Rube smiled, "Now, Babe, that would be stretching it a lot, but, yes, I guess I do."

He reached across Kristy and pulled her close. They kissed in a soft, tender way, sealing their love for each other.

They went home every weekend they could, either to Conyers or Winder. When they went to Kristy's home, they laid around the pool and relaxed or studied. Of course, they got to see Pretty Boy on those trips, and they noticed that his vocabulary had been severely restricted by the move from the bedroom. His requests for interviews had decreased since his peak on *The Tonight Show*. He was still in contention for the movie with Clint Eastwood, but they hadn't heard anything for a while.

During this time Rube often thought about the curse, but never discussed it with anyone. It would be too hard to explain, embarrassing, and most people would think he was crazy. He never knew in what ways the curse might manifest itself. It was a source of constant worry. Because of that, he hated Imogene Blankenschipf.

When they went to Winder, Rube wondered about Amy. What was she doing? Where was she? How were things at home? Had she married yet? When he was with his friends, he discreetly asked about her. None of them had heard anything new. As far as they knew, she was still in nursing school.

Cal was working with his dad who was a builder. Will was still at the University of Georgia, and Claude was a junior at North Georgia College. When he saw Will they talked and laughed about the ski trip.

After classes began, Rube and Kristy's lives became a blur of school and work.

Having been an athlete, Rube was very conscious of his physical condition. He had not been able to workout on a regular basis, and was concerned about that. Wally, a friend of his at college, told him about a special they were running at a local health club, so he went to look. He was impressed, and took Kristy to help him decide if they should join. She was all for it.

"Rube, I love it! Maybe I could get back in shape too," she said.

The club had a large workout room with machines and free weights, male and female dressing rooms, a large sauna room, lockers, racquetball courts and a pool.

The membership fee was so reasonable, they joined immediately.

Rube worked out during the day if there was a long break in classes, after class, or in the evening if he didn't have to work.

Two weeks after joining, Rube and Wally went to the club. Rube followed his regular routine as suggested by one of the staff. He changed into his workout clothes and went to the weight room, doing the recommended repetitions. Then, on to the sauna room where he sat fifteen to twenty minutes. After a quick shower, he slipped his bathing suit on and swam ten laps. Then, he returned to the locker room for another shower. He kept his suit on so he could wash the chlorine out. Wally finished his workout ahead of Rube and was standing at his locker.

The sauna room was quite large with three tiers of cedar benches rising from the tile floor. A glass front looked out on a wide hallway with lockers on each side. The showers were at the other end of the hallway.

Rube jumped into the shower and soaped all over, including his swim suit. With eyes closed to keep the soap out, he raised one leg to take the suit off. His foot caught in the lining, and he fell against the pressure latched door. His soapy body flew onto the wet tile floor of the hallway, sliding almost to the sauna room. As Rube went sliding by, Wally yelled,

"Safe!" and slid his hands across each other in the manner of a baseball umpire.

The ten men in the sauna room were startled at first, then broke out in wild applause, shouting, "Go, man, go! Yeah! Way to go, Rube!"

Rube, red faced, jumped up from the floor without thinking about whether he was injured or not. He quickly put his left foot back into the bathing suit, raised a fist in triumph, and took a deep bow.

The group in the sauna went into a frenzy with applause, cheers and taunts. Someone shouted, "Take it off! Take it all off!"

Rube turned around, quickly dropped his suit from behind, mooning his tormentors, and made his slippery way back into the shower. He stayed a long time, washing the soap off, hoping the humiliation would go along with it.

By now, he was getting used to this kind of thing and just tried to relax and enjoy it as Uncle Billy had suggested.

School went well for Rube because he was interested in health and the human body, and he had a genuine desire to help people. The first term was difficult until he got used to the medical terminology. Then, each quarter seemed to get easier as his understanding of how the body worked, increased.

Most of the professors were very approachable, and made every effort to help the students become competent chiropractic physicians. There was one in particular that Rube liked a great deal. Doctor Herbert Wilkins had streaks of gray in hair which he combed straight back. His kind, healing eyes gazed out over a thin nose which required frequent attention. He had taught at the Canadian Chiropractic College for many years, and was well known for his knowledge, as well as his dedication to the profession. He taught technique classes, and was also director of the Clinic. He often ended his demonstrations or explanations with the statement: "If you do that, things will work out quite nicely."

It became a common saying around campus, and was used in just about every conversation. Such as, "Wally, you don't know what you're talking about so shut up. If you do that, things will work out quite nicely," or, "Katie, if you will go out with me tonight, things will work out quite nicely."

Even some of the other professors picked up the phrase, and began using it to relate to the students. "All right, Students, if you study your notes so that you know them backward and forward, things will work out quite nicely on the test tomorrow."

Rube even found himself using the term at home and work. "Kristy, if you will put the book down and come over here, things will work out quite nicely," or "Jim, if you move that set of lights, and let me get my camera over there, things will work out quite nicely."

It became a craze overnight, and reminded Rube of Uncle Billy's phrase, "That's wonderful, just wonderful." In fact, Dr. Wilkins reminded Rube of Uncle Billy in some ways. He was so helpful and kind that everyone around him felt good and wanted to work hard for him.

Dr. Wilkins "sniffed" his long, thin nose often as he lectured. There was no apparent reason why he sniffed, but he used it to good effect, as many people use "Uh." It was his pause to think of what he would say next. "Now, would be doctors (sniff), if you will look on page sixty-seven (sniff), you will see a picture of the genito-urinary system (sniff). Note that the renal arteries branch off from the aorta (sniff), and the kidneys are located just beneath the twelfth ribs (sniff)." He had a strong jaw which jutted forward as he spoke. There was always a tolerant smile on his thin lips as he guided his novice underlings. Each student had the feeling that Dr. Wilkins liked him or her personally.

Charlie Connerly, a member of Rube's class, was blind. He had a Seeing Eye Dog, Blue Streak, Blue for short. Blue was very calm and obedient, as are all of the dogs chosen for that kind of duty. He lay at Charlie's feet, quietly, even during the most boring of lectures. At times, he put one paw over both eyes, and laid there for a minute before bringing it back down. Occasionally, he shook his head back and forth, rolled his eyes, laid his ears back or perked them forward. Some of the students in class became obsessed with these actions, and began to assign meaning to them. Rube swore, and others agreed, that Blue knew exactly what was being said. Wally claimed that if they could find some way to test him, he would most likely be the valedictorian.

Before long the students were being distracted by Blue's reactions. Word soon reached the faculty. Every now and then, a professor would glance over at Blue to see what his reaction was, especially if the teacher was inexperienced.

One day in class, Dr. Wilkins said, "Would be doctors, if you will kindly look at me, instead of Blue, when I'm showing you this technique, things will work out quite nicely."

Wally Thomas and Andy McKay said they were working on a code for Blue, so they could take him with them when they took the National Board Exams.

Another thing about Blue that some of the students noticed, was his gait. When he walked down the hall beside Charlie, his front paws were two or three inches to the left of his hind paws. It was like watching a misaligned old truck driving down the highway. One day, Rube pointed this out to Dr. Wilkins. Dr. Wilkins said, "Hmmm. I think you're right."

Apparently, Dr. Wilkins had spent some time thinking about the dog's problem, because the next day in class, he cleared off the desk, and said, "Would be doctor Charlie, bring Blue up here."

He palpated the dog's lower spine, and pointed out how one of the spinous processes was rotated to the right. He laid Blue down on his side, and adjusted that vertebra. "There, that ought to work out quite nicely."

He then lifted Blue off the desk, and set him down. "Charlie, walk him up and down the aisle."

Charlie did so, and sure enough, his gait was completely normal. The class applauded. Wally leaned over to Rube, and said, "I wonder if Blue will be able to talk now."

Rube had no idea that Dr. Wilkins, his favorite professor, would play such an important part in his life.

There were other incidents in Rube's college career which reminded him that the curse still lurked in his life.

During fourth quarter, Rube's class was taking a course on emergency medical procedures. The class was taught by Doctor Fred Harmon who had been an emergency medical technician before attending chiropractic college.

He used a resuscitation manikin, sometimes called Resusciannie, to demonstrate the procedures, and to allow students the opportunity to practice prior to the final examination.

The final was given in the clinic, and Dr. Harmon asked two other doctors to help him administer the test, including Dr. Wilkins.

While they were standing in line waiting to have their "affair" with Resusiannie, Wally offered Rube a piece of bubble gum, to calm his nerves. He took the gum, and was still chewing when he was called in to take the test.

Dr. Harmon said, "Rube, here is the situation: a lady is driving her car along the highway. She suddenly feels chest pains, pulls off the side of the road, opens her car door and falls out onto the pavement. You are driving behind her and see what happened. What would you do? You have five minutes, starting now!"

Rube, very nervous, said, "First, I would move her, but only if she was in imminent danger of being run over."

"All right, now show us what you would do."

Rube put his fingers on the carotid artery, and leaned his ear close to her mouth to see if she was breathing. Not hearing or feeling signs of life, he immediately moved to her side, giving five thrusts to the sternum with his hands locked together. He quickly moved to the side of her head, and put his hand under her neck causing her head to tilt backward. He opened her mouth to check for any obstruction. Next, he put his mouth over hers and blew his bubble gum deep into her throat. "Oophs!" he said, reaching his finger in to try to retrieve it.

"What is it? What happened?" said Dr. Harmon.

"I'm sorry, Sir. I blew my bubble gum into her mouth."

"Oh, no! Let me see if I can get it out."

No one could reach the gum, nor could they find tweezers long enough. Finally, Dr. Harmon said, "We'll have to take her apart."

They began the process as Rube stood and watched, feeling like a dummy himself. He bit his lip and thought, damn all the Blankenschipfs who ever lived. Dr. Wilkins came over, put his arm around Rube and said, "Don't worry, Son, go back and stand in line while we fix Resusciannie. Just be glad we don't use real people." He grinned. And, as he walked Rube to the door, he whispered, "It'll be okay, forget it. Remember, God has a sense of humor, too."

Things did work out, but it was very embarrassing. Wally asked, "What happened Rube, did she die while you were working on her?"

After the details got out about that fiasco, it took a week for the quips and jokes to die down.

"Rube, what else do you carry in your doctor bag besides bubble gum?"

"Yes, the patient survived her heart attack, but she choked to death from the bubble gum."

"Dr. Winters, would you please demonstrate for us your technique of blowing bubble gum down a patient's throat?"

The kidding was not malicious, and Rube knew he just had to ride it out.

One day while sitting in the cafeteria, Rube was asked by an underclassman if he would be student doctor for him and his wife. Rube, needing clinic visits for the quarter, quickly agreed. He arranged the time to do the physical and X-ray examinations that afternoon, and gave them an appointment for the next day.

All treatment had to be given under the direct supervision of a licensed clinic doctor, although he did not have to be in the treatment room.

The clinic doctor on duty the next day happened to be Dr. Larry Gooch. Rube really liked him and he was very popular with the rest of the students. His dark brown hair was parted on the right, swooped down across his forehead, then draped over his left ear. It was his left hand's job to make sure none of the strands escaped from behind the ear. His face was always serious, but his voice and manner said otherwise. He taught a diagnosis class, as well as technique classes, and was very competent. He had one flaw, if you wish to call it that. His speech was such that you would swear he had just stepped down off a tractor after spending all day in North Georgia, plowing the red, clay dirt. Peppered among myelencephalitis and kyphoscoliosis were such phrases as "Is here, at are, rat cheer, over yonder and cowpractor." When he used Dr. Wilkins saying, it came out, "Ever thang will work out <u>quite</u> nicely," with emphasis on the i's.

It was a marvel to all the students, especially ones from northern states, that he could have gone through high school English classes, four years at the University of Georgia and four years at Palmer Chiropractic College, and still talk that way. The students knew that speech patterns were learned skills, and could be altered by practice and/or regular contact with people who spoke differently. The conclusion was that Dr. Gooch was different. Somehow, his speech pattern had been written into his genetic code and could not be changed, or maybe he just liked it.

Prior to the appointment with student Bill Lockman and his wife, Ann, Rube asked Dr. Gooch to look at their X-rays, and give whatever advice he felt appropriate. After looking at Ann's X-rays he said, "Rube, Ah thank she's got a slight rotatory scoliosis with a high right shoulder. Her occiput is high on the left, and C2 is rotated to tha right. I thank you need to have her lay on the table in a supine position. Then, place the second phalangeal joint of yore left hand on tha transverse process of C2 rat cheer, like 'is here. Then, ah'd turn her up on her side, and Ah'd use at are drop piece to adjust her atlas."

"Okay, Dr. Gooch, I think I know what you mean."

"As fer as Bill is concerned, 'is here X-ray shows 'at L5 is rotated left, and so's his right ilium. Ah'd have him prone on tha table. Then, Ah'd use 'at are drop piece on 'is ilium. Ah'd git 'im up on his left side, and Ah'd adjust that thar L5 back in place."

"Well, thank you Dr. Gooch. I appreciate your help."

"Okay, Rube, if Ah can he'p when they come, jes' give me a holler."

When Bill and Ann came in, Rube went out to greet them, led them to the adjusting room, and gave his report of findings.

Ann wanted Bill to be treated first, since this was her first experience with chiropractic. Bill was adjusted without incident, and sat down to watch.

Ann, a pretty girl with long blond hair, climbed on the table face down, so Rube could palpate her spine. He loosened her spine, then asked her to turn onto her back. She did so, and after finding the same vertebra rotated as on the X-ray, he adjusted it. There was a slight "pop," and he asked if it hurt. She said, "No! It felt good!"

Then, he asked her to turn on her side as he cranked the handle to raise the headpiece. Unfortunately, her long locks had fallen into the gears, and as they turned, her hair caught, causing the mechanism to lock up.

Ann tried to raise her head, but could not without pain. "Ouch! It hurts! I can't raise my head!" Her eyes shifted from surprise to panic.

Oh no, Rube thought. Not again. I can't believe this is happening.

Bill jumped up, "Are you all right, Honey? Here, let me help," as he tried to pull her head up.

"No! Don't pull. It hurts!" screeched Ann. "Oh, Bill, get me out of here," she cried.

Rube was desperately trying to get her hair untangled as Dr. Gooch came into the room after hearing the commotion.

"What's goin' on in here student Rube? Sounds like somebody got their fanger caught in tha door."

"No Sir, it's just that Ann's hair is caught in the table, and I'm trying to get it loose."

Bill said, "Honey, it'll be all right. I'll just find some scissors, cut your hair, and get you loose."

"No! No! Don't cut my hair," she screamed and covered her face with her hands.

"Okay, Honey, I won't cut it. But, what else can we do?"

Rube piped in with, "I've got some WD 40 out in my car. Do you think it would help if I got it, and sprayed the gears?"

"No! Don't spray that stuff on my hair! It would ruin it!" said Ann as Bill stroked her forehead, trying to calm her down.

"Y'all wait rat cheer, and Ah'll go see if Ah can find tha janitor, and get him to take this here table apart," said Dr. Gooch. He hustled out of the room.

The open ceilings of the cubicles in the clinic did not allow secrets, and by now word was out that something was going on in room nine with one of Rube's patients.

Soon, the ladies who worked the front desk came to see if they could help. Just as Dr. Gooch returned, one of them asked, "Do you want me to call the E.M.T.'s?"

"No, Emily, Ah don't rekin tha medical folks have any spacial knowledge about gettin' hair unstuck. Besides, it'd be down right embarrassin'! I left word fer tha custodian ta come over here as soon as possible."

Ann was still crying, and Bill was holding her hand. "It'll be all right. Don't worry, we'll get you out."

Rube rested one hand on the spring held headpiece, put his other hand over his eyes, and bent his head down, desperately trying to think of what else he might do. As his weight shifted forward, the spring let go causing the headpiece to drop.

Suddenly, Ann felt less pulling, and realized that she could move her head.

Rube dropped to his knees, and fished her hair out of the gears. Thank you Lord, he thought.

"I'm free, Bill, I'm free!" Ann cried. Her husband hugged her, wiping tears from her eyes.

"Ann and Bill, I'm really sorry about this. I'm sorry your first adjustment turned out so badly. If you want another student doctor, I understand," said Rube.

Ann said, "No, no. It's not your fault. It's just one of those things. When I come back, I'll have my hair tied up so it won't get in the way."

After they left, Dr. Gooch could tell that Rube was really discouraged. He went over and put his arm around him. "Rube, did Ah ever tell you 'bout tha time my mama got her hair caught in tha ranger when she'us washin' tha clothes?"

"No, Sir."

"Well, it'us tha dangdest thang. It'us one a them thar automatic rangers, and her hair got caught as she'us puttin' a sheet through. It dragged her head right up ag'inst them thar rollars, an' she comminced to holler fer someone to shut the rangers off.

"Well sir, Paw run over thar, and shut it off jest before it pulled tha roots out. He later told her that maybe he should 'a' let her head run on through tha ranger. That it might 'a' improved her personality.

"Rube, you have to understand that it's tha bad thangs that happen to us in life, that causes us ta grow. If those thangs didn't happen, we wouldn't learn some of tha most important lessons. So, always look for tha lesson, learn it and move on. It can only hurt you, if you dwell on negative thangs that happen. Do you see what I'm sayin'?"

"Yes, Sir. I do. Thank you, Dr. Gooch."

Rube went home and wrote down what Dr. Gooch said. He promised himself from then on, if bad things happened, that's how he would handle it.

The next day, when Rube walked into the cafeteria, he was not surprised by the comments from his fellow students.

Wally said, "What happened, Winters? Did you blow your bubble gum down another patient's throat?"

"Tell us about your new hair yanking technique. Does it work as well as the toggle?" kidded Andy.

"You all just don't appreciate true scientific research," said Rube. "I was looking for a new way to help my patients relax, feel more comfortable."

Rube enjoyed college life. It was fun, and he learned a lot about health and healing, even something about people. But, the greatest lesson he learned was how little he knew. Even so, he was certain that one day he would know enough about healing to help many people. And, he was determined to defeat the Blankenschipf curse, no matter how long it took.

CHAPTER ELEVEN

Kristy graduated from Kennesaw after two years, and got a job teaching special education at the Conyers Middle School. The fact that she had a full time job, relieved their financial stress, and made life easier. Their time together was limited because when Rube was not working, he was studying. Still, they settled into their lives together, and were happy in love. They made the moments they had together, special. Often, as Rube studied, Kristy sat next to him and wrote lesson plans for the next day. And, there was their closeness in bed which gave them a chance to express their deep love for each other. They dreamed of the day when Rube would be in practice, and they would be able to have children.

Rube's last two years of college went by quickly. He worked hard in his courses, and became more and more confident in his ability to help people live a healthy and more comfortable life.

Before Rube graduated, he went to see Dr. Glasson, his chiropractor in Athens. His parents told him Dr. Glasson needed help in his office, and was thinking of retiring. Dr. Glasson informed Rube that the only thing standing in the way of his retirement was finding a doctor that would take good care of his patients. "Rube, I think you might be that person. I hope you will consider coming to Athens, and working with me for a year. I can teach you all that I've learned over the years, and you can get to know the patients. If things work out as I think they will, you like the patients and they like you, then you can buy the practice."

Rube was so excited about the offer he could hardly wait to get home and share the news with Kristy. He had always wanted to live in Athens, there were a lot of things to do, and yet, it was not nearly as congested as the Atlanta area. When he told Kristy, she was delighted. It wasn't far to drive to her school, at least until she could find another job in or near Athens. Also, this would be within driving distance of both sets of parents.

"Besides," she said, "it's an established practice, and will be much easier than starting a new practice."

It was fun to think about the possibilities of their new life in Athens as Rube finished chiropractic college that spring. He had already taken and passed the Georgia Board Examination and part one of the National Board Examination. He was confident that if he studied hard he could pass the remaining exam when the time came.

Kristy finished her teaching year two weeks before, and Rube graduated on June 15, 1988. They celebrated by splurging on dinner at The Abbey on Peachtree Street in Atlanta.

When they got home they sat at their small dining room table, over coffee, and talked of having their first child, and how they would raise it.

Rube had flipped the radio on, as usual, when they first came in. When Anne Murray's "May I have this Dance," began, he looked at Kristy, smiled, and said, "May I?"

"How can I refuse my handsome guy?" she said as they rose.

She flowed into his arms on the small kitchen floor, and their bodies drifted to the rhythm of the music. She rested her head on his shoulder, and he pulled her close. When the song ended, her back was to the counter. He pressed harder, and kissed her on the neck.

"I have an idea, Mrs. Winters. Why don't we start that family tonight?"

"Are you sure you don't want to think about it a while longer?" she said teasingly.

"No. My mind's made up. I think we should start immediately." He grinned.

It was then a race to see who could get undressed the fastest, leaving clothes strewn from the kitchen to the bedroom.

Their love that night was an expression of joy as well as passion. Their wish for a child seemed to push their sensuous desires to new heights. Rube fell asleep with Kristy's head on his left shoulder, embraced by the smell of her body and remnants of White Diamonds.

By the end of summer, Rube had settled in with Dr. Glasson and was doing most of the X-ray and physical examinations. He was learning the office procedures and enjoyed getting to know the patients.

Kristy loved her summer vacation, and found out six weeks ago that she was pregnant. She wanted a girl, Rube wanted a boy, but they agreed to be happy with either.

In the middle of August, Kristy went to spend the day with her mother in Conyers. Mrs. Free was almost as excited about the baby as she and Rube. Kristy left early Wednesday morning so they could shop in the morning, and spend the rest of the day by the pool.

They embraced and kissed. Then Rube stood by the back door and watched as Kristy got into her little red Toyota. He waved and said, "Call me before you leave Conyers. And, drive carefully, Okay?"

"Don't worry. I will. See you tonight," as she slammed the car door.

Rube had an uneasy feeling as he turned to go in and get ready for work.

At about six o'clock that evening she called Rube to tell him she wanted to wait for her father to get home and have dinner with them.

Rube said, "That'll be fine, I'll stop and pick something up on the way home. I love you. Call when you start home."

"Will do, Honey. See you later."

It was eight forty five when she called to say she would be leaving in a few minutes to come home. She waved good-by to Mom and Dad, drove across town, and turned left on Highway 138 which would take her to Highway 78 and on to Athens.

She did not put her seatbelt on, thinking that it might harm the baby if there was an accident. Because of that, she would drive safely and not so fast. Just as Kristy was merging onto Highway 78, there was a light blue, nineteen-seventy-nine Dodge pickup pulling away from a small bar in Monroe, Georgia. The large, gruff looking man had just had a nightcap which put his already high blood alcohol content into orbit. He was the type who got mean when he got drunk, and the bartender was glad to see him go. He felt sorry for whomever might be home waiting for him.

He had made this trip in this same condition many times before, and had no doubt that he could do it again.

A red Toyota went past as he turned onto Highway 78. He picked up speed, and soon overtook the Toyota which was only going about fifty five, the speed limit. He asked, "Why in hell is this guy goin' so slow?" He yanked the wheel to the left causing the old truck to shudder as the wheels re-tracked with each other. He kicked the gas pedal to the floor, picked up speed until he thought he was past the car, then, twisted the wheel to the right. His right rear fender grazed the left front fender of Kristy's Toyota.

Surprised, she jerked the wheel to the right trying to avoid more impact. The car spun around on the shoulder of the road. It rolled one time before starting down the deep embankment. It turned over two more times before coming to rest against a large boulder next to a barbed wire fence.

Kristy had screamed, then desperately tried to protect herself as the car twisted and rolled, throwing her against the left door and window, then, the right side, the ceiling, the dash and windshield. She lost consciousness half way down the embankment, and was left at the mercy of the forces involved. When the car came to rest, her body was crumpled into a ball in the right, front floorboard. The motor died and everything was quiet and still.

The big man in the pickup drove on as though nothing had happened. "These damned people who can't drive ought to stay off the road," he snarled.

A few minutes later a man and his wife came by. She saw the torn up dirt on the side of the road, the tracks leading down, and finally the crumpled car.

"Frank, there's a car down there!"

He slammed on the brakes and pulled to the side.

"Sharon, I'm gonna have to go down there and see if I can help. You take the car, go back to the station we just passed, and call 911."

He slid more than climbed to the bottom of the ravine. The right door was wedged against the rock, and the other door was so badly damaged that he couldn't open it. He yelled, "Can anyone hear me in there?"

No response.

The left side window was partially broken. He peered in, and finally saw Kristy's crumpled body lying in the corner. "Hey! Can you hear me?"

Not expecting an answer, he looked around for something he could use to break the rest of the window out. He found a rock the size of his head. He drew it back to smash the window, then stopped. Thinking the rock might go through and hurt the person more, he moved to the back, side window and smashed the glass. Then, he heard a moan.

"Ohhh. My baby..."

Oh no! he thought, There's a baby in there.

His eyes searched the car, desperately trying to find the baby.

"Please Lord," he prayed, "Protect them both. Please don't let them die!"

Just then he heard sirens, and scrambled back up the bank to make sure they found them. Sharon, his wife, drove up just in front of the State Patrol car. The Good Samaritan saw the flashing lights of the ambulance a half mile down the road.

He led the two patrolmen down to the car, yelling over his shoulder, "Show them where we are, Sharon."

It took the EMTs and policemen an hour to take apart much of the left side of the Toyota so they could lift Kristy out as carefully as possible.

To Sharon, watching from above, it looked like they were lifting a rag doll onto the stretcher. When the EMTs hauled her to the top of the embankment and she saw her blood soaked body, she turned away. Her husband, trailing behind, reached her side. They embraced, then fell to their knees in tears of sorrow for this young mother. The junior patrolman came over to console them as tears rolled down his cheeks.

They arrived at the Athens Regional Hospital thirty minutes later with Kristy desperately clinging to life. They found no sign of a baby, but Kristy kept mumbling, "Baby...baby." Finally they decided that she must be pregnant. They told the emergency room doctor of their suspicion as they rushed her into an examination room.

The senior patrolman stepped to the phone on the emergency room counter. This was the part of his job he hated, but knew that it must be done. He picked up the phone, and dialed the number found in Kristy's wallet.

"Hello, Mr. Winters?"

"Yes."

"Mr. Winters, this is Patrolman Curtis of the Georgia State Patrol. There has been an accident."

Rube's breath caught in his throat, and his chest seemed to sink in as he bent forward holding his stomach. "Yes," he mumbled.

"Mr. Winters, your wife, Kristy, has been in an accident, and is in the Athens Regional Hospital on Prince Avenue. Do you know where it's located?"

"Yes, Officer. Is she hurt badly?" he heard himself say as he tried to comprehend what was happening.

"I'm sorry, Sir, I really don't know what her condition is. We just brought her into the emergency room. Please come right away."

"Okay. I'm on my way."

"Lord, please don't let anything happen to Kristy," he said as he grabbed the car keys, and ran out the door.

The five minute trip was a blur as he tried to get there quickly, thinking of Kristy at the same time. My God, he thought, why is this happening to us? Is this that damned curse raising its' ugly head again? Damn it! Damn it! Damn it! Then he thought of the baby. "No Lord! Surely you're not going to take the baby from us," he screamed as he pulled into the first spot he saw.

He ran from the parking lot into the emergency room, and up to the counter. He puffed, "My wife was just brought in. How is she? Can I see her?"

"Are you Mr. Winters?"

"Yes."

"Mr. Winters, they are treating her for shock, and she is having X-rays done right now. I'll tell the doctors you're here, and they will talk to you just as soon as they can."

"Okay," he said, seeing no other choice.

"Mr. Winters, if you don't mind, would you please give us some information about your wife, and about your insurance?"

"All right. But, please, let them know that I'm here," he urged.

She motioned for someone to see that it was done.

After about fifteen minutes which seemed like an hour, Dr. Slocum came out, introduced himself and led Rube into a small room off the adjoining hallway.

"Dr. Slocum, I'm a doctor of chiropractic, and understand about the body. So, please feel free to tell what you have found out so far about my wife's condition. And, please call me Rube."

"Okay, thanks for telling me. That will make my job easier. First of all, there are multiple contusions of her head, body, arms and legs. She was not wearing a seat belt, and was thrown all over the car. We suspect that she has several broken ribs---we're waiting for the X-rays to verify that. There may be internal injuries in her chest and abdomen. We don't know that for sure. We strongly suspect an internal head injury with possible swelling and/or bleeding. Her blood pressure and heartbeat are now stable, so we're going to send her right away for an MRI of her skull, chest and abdomen."

"Is she conscious? Can I see her?" Rube's eyes pleaded as he reached for the door knob.

"No, she has not regained consciousness yet, and we don't know just when or if that will happen. Dr. Winters--- Rube, is your wife pregnant?"

"Yes. Is the baby all right?" He closed his eyes and turned his head, not wanting to hear what the doctor might say.

"We thought maybe she was. We don't know for certain about the baby yet. We called Dr. Oliver, an obstetrician/gynecologist to examine her and give us his opinion about the baby."

"That's her doctor, the one she went to for her pregnancy," Rube offered.

"Good. That will make it easier."

"Please tell me, Dr. Slocum, is Kristy going to make it?"

"We just don't know yet, Rube. We'll do all that we can," as his eyes teared for an instant. Rube could tell that he was trying to maintain control as all doctors are expected to do.

"When can I see her?" stammered Rube, wiping his cheeks with his sleeve.

"When all the tests are done we'll put her in intensive care. One of the nurses will notify you as soon as that happens."

Rube went back to the waiting room and sat for a long time with his face hidden in his hands. He could taste the salt of his tears as he asked, why Kristy and our baby, Lord? They don't deserve this. Why not let it be me? Please save them, Lord, and I'll do whatever you direct me to do. Suddenly, he sat up straight, realizing that he had to call Kristy's parents, and his own parents. How could he tell them? What would he say?

He walked over, picked up the phone and began dialing. He turned toward the nurses' station so he would know if they came to tell him about Kristy.

"Mr. Free, this is Rube-----------
--------."

Rube could hear Mr. Free's voice crack as he tried to control his emotions with Mrs. Free sobbing in the background, "All right, Rube. We're on our way."

Then, "Hello, Mom," his voice shaking.

"Hello,Rube----What'swrong?"

"Mom----I'm at the Athens Regional Hospital. Kristy and the baby-------------------."

"Hold on, Son. We'll be with you soon." She slammed the phone down, caught her breath and went to tell Calvin.

Rube glanced at the nursing station, then went back to the waiting area. He paced back and forth, not being able to sit. He watched the clock on the wall-------------thirty minutes------then forty before the nurse came to tell him that his wife was in intensive care on the third floor.

He clenched his fists, waiting for the elevator to rise. Identifying himself to a nurse, he was quickly taken down the hall to a room that was teeming with machines that seemed to be alive. The nurse directed him to Amy's bed.

A nurse with her back to Rube was holding Kristy' wrist while looking at her watch and softly chanting, "Come on girl, you can make it, come on girl---." She looked vaguely familiar to Rube. As he approached, the nurse turned around. It was Amy, his high school friend!

Amy was not surprised to see Rube because she had read Kristy's chart and knew who she was. Rube, on the other hand, was stunned by the whole scene. His wife was barely recognizable. Her scraped and bruised body was lying there with a tube protruding from her nose, an intravenous drip attached to one arm, and there were monitoring devices attached to her head and body.

Amy stepped aside. "Rube, I'm so sorry! I'm on duty now. I hope that's okay. I'll take good care of her. I promise."

Rube stepped up and took Kristy by the hand, as tears rolled down his cheeks. "Sure it's okay, Amy. I know that you'll do all you can."

"Dr. Slocum will be in as soon as he has looked at the CT scans, MRIs and the X-rays. He's doing that now," said Amy as she left.

"Thank you."

Rube leaned over Kristy as best he could and whispered, "Honey, I love you. I'm sorry this happened. Please get better. Please!" He kissed her on the cheek, then stood there for a long time, looking at her unmoving face with only the rise and fall of her chest telling him that she was still alive.

Amy came back, "Rube, your mother and father are here."

"All right," said Rube, "Give me a few more minutes. Then I'll go out so they can come in and see Kristy."

When he walked into the waiting room on the third floor, his mother began to cry and fell into his arms. His father embraced them both.

"Is she going to be all right, Son?"

"I still don't know, Mom. Dr. Slocum is supposed to let us know as soon as he has the results of all the tests."

They sat and Rube told them the events of the day. All he knew was that the car had gone off the road, down an embankment and into a large rock.

Shortly, the Frees rushed into the room. "What happened, Rube?"

He explained again, briefly.

"Can we see her?" asked Mr. Free.

"Sure," said Rube. "We can take turns, and stay for short periods of time. I think that'll be okay with the nurses."

"You all go first," interjected Rube's dad.

They were all back in the waiting room when Doctor Slocum came to explain his findings.

"The X-rays show four fractured ribs, and it's a wonder that her lung was not punctured on that side. There are multiple contusions as you have seen."

Kristy's mother sobbed quietly as Mr. Free held her hand.

"The external bleeding has been stopped, and we're treating the wounds to prevent infection."

"Good," said Rube's dad.

"There is a hairline fracture just below the left shoulder. The ligaments and tendons have been torn in the left knee which probably hit the dashboard or was caught by the steering wheel. There is a fracture of the frontal bone in her skull, probably from hitting the windshield. This resulted in a serious internal head injury which we are very concerned about. The CT scan and MRI show some swelling and bleeding in the brain. Both can be life threatening."

"No! No! Please, no!" screamed Mrs. Free. She was embraced by Mr. Free, and continued to sob.

Dr. Slocum paused. "I'm sorry," he said. After a few seconds, he continued. "It will be very dangerous if the swelling and bleeding continue. We're doing all we can to slow that process down. All we can do at this point is wait and see what happens. We should be able to tell more by tomorrow morning.

"What about the baby?" asked Rube.

"Dr. Oliver has examined Kristy. He said that as far as he can tell at this time, the fetus is okay. There is no heartbeat at this stage, so we can't be sure. But, there is no bleeding in that area which makes him hopeful that the baby is still viable. It's too early for the baby to survive on its' own. Dr. Oliver will continue to monitor its condition as we proceed."

"Is there anything else we can do, Dr. Slocum?" asked Rube.

"All you can do right now is be with her, Rube. If there is any change in her condition, we'll let you know immediately. I'll be back in touch with you late tomorrow morning after more tests are done."

Rube spent the rest of the night standing or sitting next to Kristy with his hand resting on her arm. He watched her eyes and mouth closely, looking for movement. Now and then he kissed or touched her forehead. Never before had he been so afraid. As he sat listening to the bleeps of the monitoring machines, watching the drip, drip, drip of the tube leading into Kristy's arm, he thought how good their lives had been. Even though the struggle for both of them to get through college had been difficult at times, knowing they had each other made life not only bearable, but a joy. Jerry Reed's old song, *She Understands Me*, kept popping into his mind. His father was a big fan of Reed's, playing his records all the time as Rube was growing up. A line in that song, "We've seen the rain, and the sunshine, together..," repeatedly rippled through his mind. He hadn't thought of that song in over twenty years. As he sat, half asleep and half awake, he wondered what else might be stored in his subconscious memory. Was everything that he had ever seen or heard lying there, waiting to be brought to the surface at some point?

His parents and the Frees offered to come in and sit, but Rube declined.

Amy came in with coffee for Rube, and checked Kristy's vital signs. "Everything is fine right now, Rube. I'll be going off duty at six o'clock. Please don't tell my supervisor, but, here's my phone number. If there is any change, would you please give me a call. If there is anything I can do, or if you have any questions, please let me know, no matter what time it is. Okay?"

"Okay. Thanks, Amy."

At eleven o'clock that morning, Dr. Slocum came to report on the latest test results. "The swelling has slowed, and the bleeding has stopped as far as we can tell. That is a good sign. I don't want to get your hopes too high, because she still has a long way to go, and we don't know the effects of the damage that has been done. We won't be able to assess that until she regains consciousness."

"You think she will regain consciousness, though?" Rube asked.

"I think so, but we can't be sure. Her ribs, of course, will be very painful, and will take considerable time to heal. The cuts and abrasions will heal fairly quickly. As far as we can tell at this time, there is no serious damage to the internal organs. We suspect that there may be some bruising in the liver, and possibly the spleen. Those should heal with time. The left arm will have to be in a sling, and the left knee may need some support when she gets to the point where she can walk.

As far as the baby is concerned, we are still very hopeful. There doesn't seem to be any damage to the fetus. Dr. Oliver will continue to monitor that situation."

"When do you think she will regain consciousness?" asked Mr. Free.

"We are hopeful that it will be soon, but we really have no way to tell. It could be within hours, or it could be two weeks or even longer."

Amy was back on duty at one p.m. When she came in to check on Kristy, Rube was surprised. "Amy, I didn't expect you back until tonight. They don't give you much time off, do they?"

"Oh, I'm just filling in for one of my friends," said Amy without adding, at my own request. She worried about Kristy and her other patients. Secretly, she was concerned about Rube.

Rube wanted to be there when Kristy woke up, so he refused to go home. His parents and the Frees took turns going home for some rest, and then returning. Rube sat in the chair next to Kristy, waiting and watching for some sign that she was going to be all right. He would doze off for a while, then wake up when Amy or another nurse came in. After three days, he finally gave in and went home for a while so he could take a real shower, and see if there was anything that needed to be done there. He had already called Dr. Glasson and explained the situation. He knew there would be no problem about his job.

When he got home, there was a message on the answering machine. He pushed the message button, and heard Patrolman Curtis' voice, "Mr. Winters, this is Patrolman Curtis, State Patrol. I wanted to touch base with you about the accident, and tell you what might have happened. Please give me a call at 706-542-8660."

Rube picked up the phone and dialed the number.

"Georgia State Patrol. Sylvia speaking. How may I help you?"

"This is Rube Winters. May I speak to Patrolman Curtis?"

"Patrolman Curtis here, Mr. Winters. How's your wife doing?"

"We still don't know for sure, but the doctors are hopeful that she's going to be all right."

"Mr. Winters, we think the accident was caused by a hit and run driver. As far as we can tell, someone driving a light blue vehicle pulled in too soon while passing your wife's red Toyota, and struck her left, front fender, pushing her off the road, causing her to lose control of the car. There was a light blue paint mark on that fender. Apparently, that person kept on going. We're still trying to locate the vehicle, but so far have had no luck."

"Okay, Officer Curtis. Thanks for the information. I hope you'll keep looking for the person who caused this, so that he can't hurt others the way he has my wife."

"Don't worry, Mr. Winters. We will. I'll let you know if anything new turns up."

He had been so concerned about Kristy, this was the first time he had thought about who might have caused the accident. He wondered what kind of cold, callous person could leave the scene of an accident where another person's life was in danger. It was frightening to think that there might be people out there without morals, who had no love for their fellow man, and cared only for themselves. He pushed that thought aside, knowing that he must spend his mental energy to get Kristy and the baby well. It was beginning to sink in now that it was going to be a long haul. He wondered if their lives would ever be the same.

He finally fell into an exhausted, fitful sleep that night with thoughts of Kristy, the baby, the hit and run driver, and Amy running through his mind. There were so many conflicting thoughts and emotions. Would Kristy survive? Would she be the same? Would the baby survive? Was it a boy or girl? He already felt love for the child, and promised himself that he would be a good father.

He found himself trying to fathom what kind of person the other driver was. Were they male of female? A teenager? Did they have a wife and children of their own? What were they thinking? Were they remorseful? Were they afraid? Finally, to shut his mind up, he said, "Lord, I turn that person over to you for your mercy or vengeance."

His thoughts turned to Amy. How lucky they were that she had been there to take care of Kristy. She was a loving, caring person, and Rube felt secure, knowing that she would do all that she could to help them. For the first time, he realized that her beauty had only been enhanced by the few years since he had seen her. Her hair was longer, and her dark brown eyes still demanded your attention. He refused to allow his thoughts about her to go beyond that point.

At five a.m. on the sixth day, Rube was standing by Kristy's bedside, looking down at her peaceful face, silently praying. Suddenly, her eyes popped open, then closed.

"Kristy! I'm here Baby. Open your eyes. I love you. Please open your eyes!"

Her eyes slowly opened, blinked several times, and stayed open longer.

"Come on Baby, keep your eyes open. It's Rube. I love you. Please come back to me," he said as he reached and pushed the signal for a nurse to come.

"Rube, what happened?" said Kristy as her eyes slowly closed again.

"Kristy, it's me, Rube. You were in an accident, but, you're going to be okay. Do you hear me, Babe?"

Amy came into the room as Kristy opened her eyes again.

"Where am I? What happened??"

"Baby, you're in the hospital. You were in an accident, but you're going to be all right."

Amy had tears in her eyes as she checked the monitoring devices and I.V. "Rube, do you want me to call your parents and the Frees?"

Rube thought for a minute. "No, let's not wake them quite this early. I'll call them in an hour or so."

"Rube, what are you doing here? Where's my baby?" said Kristy.

"He's right here, Baby," as he laid his hand on her abdomen.

"Is he all right?"

"The doctors think the baby's going to be fine. Don't you worry ."

Rube answered Kristy's other questions as best he could, and tried to reassure her that everything was going to be fine. Her eyes slowly closed. Rube called Amy back in to ask her if she had gone back into a coma. Amy lifted both of Kristy's eyelids and said, "No, I think she just fell asleep. She's tired, and has been under sedation for a long time. I think she's going to be fine. I'll have Jean notify Dr. Slocum right away," as she pushed the intercom button.

"Will you watch her, Amy, while I go down and call her parents and Mom and Dad?"

"Sure, I'll be right here with her."

CHAPTER TWELVE

The next year, from the time Kristy left Athens Regional in late August until the following August, was a living hell for Rube Winters. He thought often of the baby inside his wife, and wondered how it was being affected by the thoughts of fear, suspicion, hate, worry and jealousy being expressed by Kristy.

Of course, Kristy was the one who had been injured, and it was no picnic for her either. Rube realized that, and was determined to help her through this. He remained hopeful that the old Kristy would return soon.

While Kristy was still in the hospital, Dr. Slocum sat down with Rube, and informed him that sometimes, after an injury such as this, the victim has a change of personality. He noticed her curtness and argumentativeness when he discussed her condition with her, and suspected that this may be the case with Kristy, although he couldn't be sure since he had not known her before the accident.

Rube said, "There has been a change. I have seen the same traits you mention, and she is suspicious of everything I say or do. Even her parents have remarked that something is wrong. Maybe she'll get better with time. I hope so."

"Maybe. But, I suggest that we call in a psychiatrist for an evaluation. Is that all right with you?"

"Yes. I'm not certain that Kristy will co-operate. But, I will try to explain it to her and her parents."

The psychiatrist, Dr. Worley, interviewed Rube, the Frees, and finally Kristy. His conclusion was that there was a change in her personality. At this stage he did not know if this was temporary or permanent. Nor, did he know the exact form these changes would take. He said there were signs of hysteria at this point, since she was overly excitable, unstable and over reactive. He also thought that she might be narcissistic or paranoid to some degree because she was afraid she was being abandoned, and that Rube would not be able to take care of her. "All we can do is wait and see exactly what form or forms this takes, then treat it with psychotherapy which may include medication." Rube shuttered at the thought of their tiny child being subjected to mind altering drugs.

"Is there a chance that this can go away?" asked Rube.

"Yes. But, the longer it remains, the less likely it is to go away."

Rube showed Dr Worley's report to his parents and to the Frees. They both offered to help in any way they could.

Rube stayed home with her the first week, kept the house clean and prepared all the meals, going out only for short times to get groceries. He waited on her, hand and foot, getting her a magazine, fluffing her pillows, fixing her coffee or tea, et cetera. Whatever he did was never right or never enough. "This coffee's not hot enough or sweet enough. Why do you have the television turned up so loud? This glass has a spot on it." If he didn't check on her for a while, "Where have you been? You don't care about me, do you?" If he checked on her more often, "Quit bugging me. Can't you see I'm trying to rest?"

When he went out to shop for groceries, he always faced a barrage of questions when he returned. "Where were you? It shouldn't take that long to go shopping. Did you get what I told you to get?"

"Yes, Baby."

"Did you get the half and half?"

"Yes."

"What are we having for dinner?"

"Steak."

"Well, make sure mine is well done. You know I don't like raw meat."

"Yes, Dear. No problem. I will do it."

Rube was beginning to feel like a mushroom; in the dark and covered with fertilizer.

When the week was up, he looked forward to going back to work. He loved his patients, and enjoyed helping them. Most of them were thankful, and returned his love. Also, Dr. Glasson had a good staff that he enjoyed being around. They tried to help him in every way they could. They were sympathetic to his plight, and always asked about Kristy.

Kristy wanted to know why he had to go back to work. Rube explained that he had to work in order to pay their bills. "Well, what about me? You don't care what happens to me, do you?"

"Yes, Kristy, I care a lot about you, but I have to work. You'll be all right. Your Mom and Dad have helped me hire a person to come in during the day to help you with the house. Dr. Slocum says you need to get up more, walk, and do some of the housework. He says it would be good for you."

"Dr. Slocum doesn't know how much I hurt."

"I know, Honey, but you need the exercise. Mrs. Shelly Houseman, the lady we hired, is very nice. She'll take good care of you. I'll call you as often as I can."

"You don't care about me. You just want to get back to your precious patients."

"Not true, Sweety. I love you. See you tonight."

Rube noticed, but said nothing, that Kristy was letting herself go. She was a fanatic about being clean, but rarely combed her hair and never put on makeup. At the same time she sprayed herself and the entire house with White Diamonds perfume. Rube had liked it before, but now found it stifling and repulsive. Her once beautiful figure was gradually disappearing.

The weeks turned into months, and things remained the same. After three months, Mrs. Houseman met Rube in the driveway. "Dr. Winters, I'm sorry, but I just can't take it anymore. Your wife is just too demanding, and there is never a thank you or please. I've never been treated this way before. So, I'm just going to have to quit. I'm Sorry."

"Okay, Shelly. I'm sorry too, but I do understand."

He went inside to face the usual barrage of questions and demands. "Why didn't you call me this morning? Where did you eat lunch? Who did you have lunch with?"

"Some of the staff."

"Who?"

"Ginny and Ellen."

"So, you had lunch with Ginny again. Are you in love with her? Are you having an affair, Rube? Why are you doing this to me?"

This stunned Rube temporarily. She had never taken this tact before. It frightened him. How long had this been building up in her mind? "I'm sorry, Kristy. I didn't know that you were concerned about that. I won't have lunch with them anymore. I promise you that nothing is going on. Nothing. Okay?"

Later Rube wondered if he had been completely honest. He had dreams about Amy Buchanan and Cousin Caresse Lafayette at times. Okay, many times.

They had not had sex since the accident. Rube was sleeping in the guest room so as not to disturb her. If he sat on the bed next to her, tried to put his arm around her, or even hold her hand, he was rejected. It was always, "No, Rube. I don't feel good. I have too much pain. It might hurt the baby."

There was never any reference to him or his feelings, how he felt about things, what he would like to eat, whether he was tired, or how things had gone at the office. If he ever mentioned anything about himself, he was called selfish.

One day at the office, he had some free time, and called Dr. Worley, the psychiatrist. He explained the situation, and asked the doctor if there was anything that could be done.

"Dr. Winters, we can prescribe a mild sedative for her. I'm reluctant to give her the stronger drugs because of the pregnancy, unless it's absolutely necessary. I would need to see her in my office before I could give a prescription."

"Okay. I agree we don't want to take chances with the baby. I'll call you if we decide to come in. Thanks."

Kristy was sleeping well and Rube couldn't see the need for a sedative.

To be fair, he decided to mention it to Kristy. She accused him of trying to dope her up so she wouldn't know what he was doing.

She didn't know, but he was glad to drop the subject.

That evening he tucked Kristy in as usual, and kissed her on the forehead. That's all she would allow. "Is there anything else I can get you, Honey?"

"No," she said, turning on her side.

As he lay in bed, he realized that it would be up to him. There was no help, and very little hope. He had managed to find another helper to come in during the day, but didn't know how long she would last. He found the only advantage to sleeping alone was that you could cry when you needed to. He prayed for the patience and strength that he would need in the days ahead.

Two weeks later he came home to find that the latest helper had been fired. From that time on, after a few weeks, they were either fired or quit. Finally, there was no one else available.

"Kristy, I can't find anyone to come in and work. It looks like we'll just have to do it ourselves."

"If you cared about me, you would find someone."

The next day, on his way to the office, he had a thought, but pushed it out of his mind. All day long, the same idea kept popping into his brain. He thought, there's no way that could work.

Two months ago, his old friend, Moochie Dunlop, had come into his office suffering from what she called a "brain twisting" headache.

"Honey, it's one of them kind that grabs hold and won't let you go." Grinning, she said, "You don't reckin it's a residual of that dive bombin' attack on my pretty self, do you?" Rube had done the examination, all the time trying to decide which of his adjusting tables would be wide enough and strong enough, and whether the X-rays would penetrate sufficiently to give a clear picture of her spine. He treated her twice and the headaches went away. The last time he saw her she said, "Lord-a-mercy, Dr. Rube, you sure do good work, and I'd like to keep comin', but livin' on disability benefits like I do, I just can't afford it."

Finally, just before he left to go home, he picked up the phone and dialed the number in Conyers.

"Hellooo."

"Hello. Is this Moochie?"

"Yes, Honey. Who's askin'?"

"This is Rube Winters. Remember me? I'm the one who untwisted your brain."

"I sure do, Honey. How's that old dirty bird doin'?"

"He's fine, as dirty as ever."

"Lord, I hope not! My ear will never be the same!"

"Moochie, have you heard that Kristy was in a bad accident?"

"Yes, I heard that. How's she doin'?"

"That's what I want to talk to you about. I'd like to do that in person, if possible. Is there someplace I could meet you?"

"Well, Honey, I always have breakfast at the Huddle House over on the strip, just off I 20. Why don't you meet me there in the mornin'?"

Rube thought for a minute. "Sure, that will be fine. Tomorrow is Thursday, so I don't have to be at work until one o'clock."

"Okay. I'll meet you there at eight o'clock."

"Fine. I'll be there. By the way, are you working anywhere right now?"

"Lord-a-mercy, no! I haven't worked in two years. My ankles just won't take it anymore. I finally got hooked up on disability."

That gave Rube hope.

When he got home, he had to wash the dishes, straighten the house, and start a load of clothes. After he fixed dinner, he sat down beside Kristy, being careful not to sit too close.

"Kristy, I have to get up early in the morning and meet someone in Conyers."

"What's her name?"

"Kristy, this is someone I want to talk to about becoming our helper."

"Oh, really? What's her name?"

"I would rather not mention her name before I find out if there's any interest on her part."

"Oh. I see. You want to meet a woman and not tell me her name---."

"Wait a minute, Honey. It's nothing like that. Okay, it's Moochie Dunlop. Surely you're not jealous of Moochie. Besides, I have no idea if she's even interested in a job like this."

"Rube, you have completely lost your mind! Moochie is a crazy woman. I couldn't put up with her all day. Besides, she would eat us into bankruptcy."

"I know that Moochie has her faults, but, I can't think of another soul that wants a job like this. It's our last hope. Also, I've learned to like Moochie. Basically, she's a good person. Please don't get mad if I just go and talk to her."

"Do what you want. But, just remember that I told you so."

The next morning Rube found the Huddle House and pulled into the parking lot at precisely seven fifty-seven. He noticed a nineteen eighty-seven Pontiac Grand Prix sitting in the handicapped parking spot, and listing to the left as though it needed new shocks. He parked, went inside, and immediately spotted Moochie sitting in the outside chair of a table next to a built-in bench. The chair was different than every other chair in the restaurant, and had obviously been imported to handle a special job. Moochie smiled broadly when she saw him, and rose to her feet as the chair gave an audible sigh of relief.

"Rube, Honey, how's my old airplane buddy?"

"I'm fine, it's good to see you again. You're lookin' good. Have you lost some weight?"

"No! No! I've finally got that all figured out. For years, I would lose five pounds and then gain ten pounds back. That went on for years until recently when I decided that I was creating the very problem that I wanted to get rid of. I got pencil and paper out and put it all down in black and white. If my numbers are correct, it's clear that I was going about it the wrong way. Now, I concentrate on not losing the five pounds to begin with. That way, I figure that in ten years, I'll be way ahead of the game. See what I mean?"

"It seems to add up," said Rube.

"Sit down, and she'll be over in a minute to take our order."

"Thank you. I'm really sorry to bother you like this, but I'm at the end of my rope."

"What can I get for you folks?" asked the waitress.

Rube said, "Go ahead, Moochie. I'm buying."

"Why thank you, Honey. All right, I'll have four eggs over light, with bacon, a side of hash browns, a large orange juice, plenty of jelly, extra butter, and a large cup of hot java. Oh, and bring us a plate of biscuits."

"You, Sir?"

"I'll have two scrambled eggs, a small bowl of fruit, and a small cup of coffee."

"Lord-a-mercy, Honey! You're goin' to waste away eating like that."

"I'm not very hungry. I guess I'm too worried about our situation."

He then explained everything that had happened: the accident, the fact that Kristy was pregnant, and the present situation.

Moochie listened intently with only an occasional "Lordy!" or "Mercy!"

When he got through, she said, "Boy! You are in a mess! What could I possibly do to help?"

"I know this may sound crazy, but, I want you to go to work for us. It's a long drive from Conyers to Athens, so I was thinking you might consider living with us for a while. We have an extra bedroom. The job pays well, and would include your room and board. There would be no cost to you. We'll pay you in cash if you like. I must tell you that this whole thing would depend on whether Kristy accepts it, and whether you all get along."

Their food arrived and Moochie opened four biscuits, and slathered them with butter and grape jelly. She chugged half the orange juice and said, "Lordy! I just don't know about all this."

Rube said, "I hope you'll at least come and talk to us----see the house," as he sipped his coffee.

As she dumped five creams and five packets of sugar into her cup, she thought. The disability check is not nearly enough. It barely makes the payment on my house, and keeps food on the table. The month always lasts longer than the money. I always have an anxiety attack, and then go into depression when I realize there is no money to buy chocolate covered pralines. It must be the same feeling a cocaine addict has when there is nothing to snort, she thought. The idea of having her room and board paid for, plus having the extra money to buy pralines was too much to resist. Besides, she liked Rube and Kristy.

"Well, I might be interested, Honey. When can I meet with you and Kristy?" she said, waving a fork full of eggs.

"How would tomorrow evening at seven o'clock be?"

"Fine."

"Great! Here are the directions I've written down. It tells you how to get to our house. If you get lost, just give me a call, and I'll come and meet you."

"Okay, Honey! I'll look forward to it," she said as she got up, taking the last biscuit with her, and followed Rube to the cash register. Rube, feeling empathy for the chair, patted it gently as he came around the table.

He followed Moochie to the Grand Prix, and held the door as she got in. "Thanks again, Moochie. We'll see you tomorrow night."

Rube spent the rest of the morning, and that evening convincing Kristy to at least talk to Moochie. He told her it was their last hope of finding someone to come in and do some of the work. Otherwise, she would have to start doing some of the work herself.

She reluctantly gave in and agreed to the meeting.

At five minutes past seven on Friday evening, Moochie called. "Lord-a-mercy, Honey! I must be lost. I'm over here at 441 and Hog Mountain Road."

"Okay. Sit tight. I'll be there in ten minutes." When they got back to the house and went into the living room, Kristy was sitting there with a sullen look on her face.

"Kristy, I'm sure you remember Moochie from our wedding."

"Sure. Hi, Moochie."

"Have a seat," said Rube. "Can I get you something to drink?"

"No thanks. I'm fine," she said as she tried once, unsuccessfully, to cross her legs, settling for a demure ankle cross.

Kristy said, "Well, I don't know why Rube invited you here. I don't need any help. I'm doing just fine."

"Why, Honey, it don't sound like you're doin' fine to me. It sounds to me like you're in a heap of trouble, and Ole Moochie is here to help out."

As the conversation progressed, Rube could sense that Kristy was responding, at least to some degree, to Moochie's straightforwardness. She had a way of cutting through the crap, and getting down to the real truth. Kristy's sarcasm and curtness was like pissing on a piece of North Georgia granite to Moochie. It didn't appear to penetrate her psyche at all. She just went on telling it like it was, and at the same time offering to help. Rube was surprised, and impressed with the inner strength that he saw coming from Moochie during this conversation.

Towards the end of the interview, Moochie mentioned one stipulation if she did take the job.

"Oh? And what's that," said Kristy.

"That you never allow that dirty bird, Pretty Boy, or whatever his name is, in this house as long as I'm here. Being bombed by a dirty bird will not be one of my duties," she smiled.

"I think we could agree to that," said Rube, as Kristy sat there grinning in spite of herself.

All parties agreed that the alliance should be on a trial basis. Either party could end the relationship at any time. That weekend Rube borrowed his Dad's pickup truck and helped Moochie move into the third bedroom.

They had used the insurance money from the accident to buy a nineteen eighty-six Chevy Nova. It could be used by Moochie and/or Kristy to do the grocery shopping, et cetera. Rube was hopeful the shocks would be strong enough.

After the first week, Kristy tried to fire Moochie.

"You never listen to what I have to say. You don't care about me, only yourself. You're fat and you're ugly, and I want you to pack up your stuff, and get the hell out of this house!" said Kristy, holding her own protruding stomach.

"Well now, ain't you the nice one. And, you talk about me not caring, after the way you treat me and your husband. You ought to be ashamed of yourself, Girl. It don't bother me none though. Hell, I'm used to it. Nobody's ever liked me---my entire life. People don't usually like fat and ugly people. Lord! Even my parents didn't like me! I've been shunned all my life. So, go on, Girl. Sulk around all you want to, but I ain't goin' nowhere."

Kristy wheeled around, went into her bedroom, and slammed the door.

Moochie heard her crying. She fixed a pot of tea, and took a cup and a praline to Kristy.

"Here, Honey. This will make you feel better."

Kristy stood up, grabbed Moochie around the neck, and just stood there sobbing, "I'm sorry, I'm sorry, I'm sorry."

"It's all right, Honey. You ain't hurt me none. Now, sit down here and have your tea."

Rube could tell there was a slow, but definite change taking place in the household. Moochie had Kristy up and helping do some of the housework. They took a walk around the block every afternoon. Rube was delighted one day when he came home, and Moochie told him they had been grocery shopping that afternoon. Kristy, sitting at the table with a cup of coffee, smiled.

"Honey, you wouldn't believe it! Why, those dummies had stacked up a big display of cokes in front of one of the aisles. Well, me and Kristy come sashaying up one aisle, and went to make our turn to go down the next one when one of my sidecars (as she patted her hip) collided with that display. Lord-a-mercy! You should'a' seen them cans go flyin'. Ain't that right, Kristy? There must 'a' been hundreds of them. They began to roll all over the place. One old lady stepped on one, started to fall, and caught herself with one arm in her cart, clean up to her armpit. One man, tryin' to get out of the way, jammed his cart into the rear of the person in front of him, and that set off a chain reaction. It reminded me of a rear end collision on I 85 in mid morning traffic. Ain't that right, Kristy? Why, Lordy, Rube, it was the worst mess you've ever seen. Well, sir. This female Assistant Manager came prissin' over there where we were standin'."

"What seems to be the problem here?" she said.

I said, "What seems to be the problem is that one of your dummies around here stacked up a whole pile of coke cans right smack in the way."

She said, "Well, Madam, couldn't you go around them?"

I said, "Hell, Madam, that's like askin' if an eighteen wheeler could make a U-turn on one of them streets in downtown Athens. Ain't that what I said, Kristy?"

Kristy nodded, and grinned.

"Well, Sir, we went on doing our shopping like nothin' had happened. Didn't we Kristy? While all them people began pickin' up coke cans. It was the damndest thing you've ever seen."

Their grocery bill went from fifty dollars a week to one hundred and fifty. Rube didn't mind at all. He was happy to pay it. A tremendous pressure had been lifted off his shoulders.

Still, things were strained between him and Kristy. Moochie knew this, and, of course, she knew from the beginning that Rube was sleeping in the guest bedroom. One day she had a talk with Kristy.

"Kristy, I been meanin' to talk to you about somethin'. You ain't been sleepin' with your husband. Why?"

"That's none of your business, Moochie."

"Well, Honey, I don't like livin' in an unhappy house. So, I'm makin' it my business.

"Now, it seems to me like I've heard that certain unalienable rights is written into our constitution. And, there's also somethin' in there about life, liberty and the pursuit of happiness. So, I figure it must be written somewhere in there about a man's right to sleep with his wife. Now ain't that right? Why, Lord-a-mercy, Honey, I think you may be in violation of the Constitution of the United States of America!"

That evening, after dinner, when Kristy went into her room to get ready for bed, Moochie said quietly to Rube, "Honey, I think you ought to sleep in your own bed tonight."

"But, Moochie, I don't think she will---."

"It'll be all right. Just go on in there and go to bed like you normally would. Okay?"

"All right, I'll give it a try."

Kristy was in bed, reading, when he went in to take his shower.

When he came out, he casually went over and turned the covers back on his side of the bed, and sat down. There was no objection. He stood two pillows up on the headboard, slipped under the covers, and sat up. He reached and grabbed the book, *Midnight in the Garden of Good and Evil* by John Berendt, which he had been reading prior to the accident.

After a while, Kristy put down her book, turned the light off and lay on her back.

He continued to read, but was becoming very nervous, scared and excited at the same time. After a few minutes which seemed much longer, he laid his book on the table, turned the lamp off, and lay on his back.

Finally, he got up enough courage to reach over and lay his hand on top of hers. No reaction.

"Kristy, I love you."

No reaction.

He rolled onto his left side, and put his right hand on her abdomen, "Kristy, we haven't even talked about what we're going to name our baby."

No reaction.

Rube put his hand across her, raised up and kissed her on the lips. "I love you, Kristy."

She allowed the kiss, but responded only mildly.

He laid his leg across her thigh.

She said, "Be very careful."

The next morning at breakfast, before Kristy got up, Moochie asked, "How did it go?"

Rube gave her the thumbs up sign, and said, "It was a good start, thanks to you."

Moochie smiled broadly, and patted his hand.

Later in the day Rube was sitting in his office when a thought crossed his mind. Had they ever caught the person who ran Kristy off the road?

He picked up the telephone and dialed Patrolman Curtis' number at the station.

"Yes. How can I help you?"

"Patrolman Curtis, this is Rube Winters. You may remember me from a few months back. My wife was run off the road by a hit-and-run driver."

"Yes. I remember. How's she doing?"

"Well, she's recovered from her physical injuries and I'm thankful for that. I'm also thankful that you and the others were there to help that night."

"Wasn't your wife pregnant? I never did know for sure," said Officer Curtis.

"Yes she was, and the baby is fine. Thanks for asking," replied Rube. "I was just wondering if you ever caught that person."

"No. I'm very sorry, Mr. Winters. Normally, we would have found that vehicle by now. It must be someone who lives in an isolated area, or that does not drive the vehicle much."

"Okay. I was just curious."

"Don't worry, Mr. Winters, we'll keep looking until we find them."

"All right. Thanks. Please call me if there's any progress."

Rube doubted they would ever know the truth.

Things went along fairly smoothly until February. The baby was due in the middle of March, and Kristy had put on more weight. Her abdomen looked like she had swallowed a small watermelon. Kristy's personality took a nose dive as the birthdate neared. She was cranky most of the time now, and she never had a kind word for Rube.

On an evening in late February, after they had gone into their bedroom and prepared for bed, Kristy said bluntly, "Rube, I want a divorce."

Rube went from stunned to devastated in a matter of seconds. He dropped his head, grabbed his stomach, and sat down on the side of the bed. He was trying desperately to digest and comprehend what his wife had just said. How could this be? He thought over and over.

"Did you hear what I said?"

"Yes---yes, I heard."

"Well?"

"Kristy, why? What have I done?"

"I don't think you love me, and I know I don't love you."

"What do you mean? When did you come to that conclusion? Why?"

"I just don't love you anymore, if I ever did. Do you understand? Maybe the accident made me realize that. I just don't know."

"Kristy, Honey, you're just upset. You've been through a lot with the accident and pregnancy. But, we can get through this," he pleaded as he got up and walked toward her.

She turned her back and crossed her arms, "What is it that you don't understand? I've thought about it and made up my mind. It's over."

"But---," Rube choked, "what about our baby?"

"I'm the one who's suffering through this pregnancy---not you. I'm the one who will have this baby, and we don't need you," she growled, grabbing her robe as she went into the bathroom and slammed the door.

Rube stood there for a minute until the anger inside overwhelmed him. He pounded her side of the bed with his fist, picked up her pillow and flung it at the bathroom door. Then, he went into the closet, grabbed his arms full of clothes and headed for the guest bedroom. He fell on top of the bed. His head was swirling. It was as though his brain had been scrambled. He went back over each word she had said, and let it sink in. He cried. Prayed. Then, cried again. At one point he thought, it's not her fault. It's the paranoia from the accident or depression from the pregnancy. He finally decided he didn't know what to think. "I want a divorce. I don't love you anymore," kept playing over and over in his mind until early morning when he finally fell asleep. He dreamed of the Blankenschipf curse and damned every Blankenschipf who ever lived.

CHAPTER THIRTEEN

The next day his patients did not receive his full attention. His mind kept wandering back to those words, "I want a divorce." When he arrived home at six-fifteen, he didn't know what to expect.

Moochie met him at the door with a long face. She had been crying. "She's in the bedroom, Honey, and she won't come out. Says she wants to talk to you right away. I haven't been able to talk any sense into her."

Rube walked into the bedroom and closed the door.

Kristy had been waiting all day to say, "When can you be out?"

Once again Rube was surprised. It hadn't even entered his mind that he might have to leave their house. How naive of him.

"Kristy, please listen. I don't want to leave you. I love you. Don't you remember what a wonderful life we had before the accident? I'll take you to any doctor you choose. Let's just try to get some help for our situation. Okay?"

Rube could only see her back as she gazed out the window and said, "No. I want you out as soon as possible."

"What about our baby? I don't want to leave you when you're going to have our baby. Please, let's just calm down and talk this out. All right?"

"There's nothing to talk about. I don't love you, and I want you out of here. What do I have to do to get that through your skull? Just leave!"

Rube felt as though he had been punched in the chest. He bent forward, then straightened up, calling upon his anger to get him through this. He grabbed his suitcase from the bottom of the closet, threw his clothes from the dresser into it, and stomped to the guest bedroom for his hanging clothes. Moochie was there waiting for him.

"Rube, Honey, what happened?"

"She wants me to leave. I don't understand it. I haven't understood her since the accident. I don't know anything else to do, but leave," said Rube as he ripped clothes from the hangers.

Moochie shook her head, "I know the pregnancy and everything's been hard on her, Rube, but, Lord-a-mercy, there's something wrong with that girl---in the head. You know what I mean?"

"I know, but the only thing I can do right now is move out."

"Then, I'll leave too. I'll start packing."

"No! No! Moochie. Please don't do that. She needs you so badly, and I need you to stay here with her and the baby. I don't know what would happen if you weren't here to watch out for them. Please stay for my sake."

"Okay, Honey, don't worry. I'll stay for you and the baby. Here, let me help you pack those shirts."

When finished, he picked up his suitcase, set it down, and turned to face Moochie. He was unable to speak, but grabbed her, and held on for a long moment. She hugged him back, and kissed him on the cheek.

"I'm sorry, Honey, I thought we could do it, but it didn't work out," said Moochie.

"It's not your fault. You did all you could. I'll be all right. I'll call you tomorrow."

He was already out of the driveway and onto the main road before he realized that he had no idea where he was going. He pulled to the side of the road. He didn't want to go home and upset his parents. Their health had not been good over the past year. Besides, he didn't want to face questions for which he had no answers. Why does she want a divorce? Is there another man? What did you do? What about the baby? He just started driving, and after about an hour of wandering around the streets of Athens, he ended up at the office.

He put his suitcase in a closet, went in and laid down on one of the adjusting tables. He lay there quietly, trying to sort out his cluttered brain. He couldn't really blame Kristy because he knew her mind had been altered by the accident. He wondered if the person who hit her knew the devastating effects of what he had done. Was this caused by the curse, or not?

He thought, what have I done wrong? Maybe it's my fault. He knew that he hadn't been perfect, but he tried to please her in every way he could. Nothing was ever good enough. He wondered why things like this happen to people who have done nothing wrong.

Their lives and that of their unborn child had been changed in an instant by a single irresponsible act of another. It was not fair. How could God let something like that happen?

Then, he remembered something Uncle Billy said to him years ago, when he was depressed about not making the sixth grade baseball team after trying so hard. He said, "Son, My motto has always been, when you're down and can't get up, get up anyway!"

He went on to explain, "Don't get caught up in the devil's trap of trying to figure everything out. Sometimes, there are no answers, least ways, not for us normal, everyday human beings. You just get up and go on, and I have never seen it fail. Never. Things always work out. Maybe not the way you planned or wanted, but, it will work out for the best."

They were sitting at Aunt Lucille's dinner table as Uncle Billy fingered the spoon sticking out of his ice tea. "Remember one thing, Son, you are not the one in charge. I finally figured that out, after all the things that have happened in my life. Now, I just sit back, relax, and enjoy life. Let the one in charge worry about the rest.

"I know that you've wondered why I always say, 'That's wonderful, just wonderful.' Well, Son, it's because I know that whatever has happened to them is for the best, at least in the long run."

Rube sat up on the table, and decided that he would not allow this to get the best of him. "I will do whatever I have to do, and do the best I can. Hopefully, that will be enough to get us all through this."

The next day, he found a small apartment only a few blocks from the office, on Prince Avenue. Then, he went and bought a few sticks of furniture to fill it.

He also called Moochie to see how things were.

"Moochie? How are things going?"

"Lord-a-mercy, Rube. I worried about you all night, wondering where you were."

"I'm fine. I decided to spend the night at the office, you know the phone number here. I found an apartment today. I'll let you know as soon as I get a new number. How's Kristy, and the baby?"

"Well, they're doin' fine as far as I can tell. She's in taking a nap right now."

"Moochie, I want you to do me a favor. If there is any problem, if you or Kristy need help, in any way, call me right away. I don't care what time it is. Okay?"

"Sure, Honey. I'll do it. By the way, the baby will be coming before too long, what do you all plan to name it?"

"I don't know. I was never able to get Kristy to discuss names. For a girl I like Melissa or Julie, and for a boy, Ben, Wade or Sam."

Moochie said, "Well----if the subject comes up, I'll see that those names are pitched into the pot."

The thought of not being part of choosing a name for their child deepened his pensive mood.

Rube said, "Thanks. I appreciate all that you've done for us. I've never told you this, and I should have. You're a beautiful person, and I love you."

There was a long silence on the other end of the line. Finally, Moochie sniffled, "I'm sorry, Honey, you caught me completely by surprise. No one's ever said those words to me. I don't know what to say."

Rube said, "You don't have to say anything. I'm just telling you how I feel in my heart. You're my best friend, and I wanted you to know. I'll talk to you soon," and hung up.

Within two weeks Rube was served with the divorce papers from Kristy's lawyer, the cause being incompatibility. He tried to call her, but Moochie couldn't get her to come to the phone. Finally, he just went to the house and knocked on the door. Moochie answered. She said, "I've been talking to her, Sweetie, but I can't get through. There's no way to reason with her," as she led him into the living room.

Kristy came out. "What do you want?" she said.

"Kristy, I'm sorry if I've done anything to hurt you. If I have, please forgive me. I just want to talk to you for a minute about your decision to file for a divorce."

"What about it?" said his wife.

"I want you to please reconsider. I know the accident has been a terrible strain on you. It wasn't your fault. I'm very sorry that it happened. Our child will be born very soon. For his sake, please, let's try to make it work. I want to be part of his life, and your life. Let's see if we can sort things out."

"No! Absolutely not! I have nothing to say to you. Talk to my lawyer." She went in, closed and locked the bedroom door.

Rube stood there for a minute with his mouth ajar. He had never experienced such coldhearted hostility before. She gave no causes, no reasons, no charges which he could even attempt to refute. What could he say or do? There were no leads to follow, and only one conclusion to reach. This marriage was over.

But, what about my child? he thought. He always thought of it as being a boy. He didn't know why. Maybe it was a man thing, a secret hope. How would he be raised? Where would he live? Would he be able to see him often?

Would Kristy re-marry? Would his stepfather treat his son well? Then, he realized that he was not in charge, turned and walked out the door.

Three weeks later he got a call from Moochie. It was ten-thirty in the evening. He had just finished eating popcorn, and was watching a Clint Eastwood movie. Clint was getting a haircut when three of the meanest looking characters Hollywood could find, walked in, muttered a few words, and drew down on Clint. They were unaware that he already had his Colt 45 drawn, lying in his lap. He shot all three of them dead before they could clear leather.

"Rube, Moochie. Kristy is in labor. The pains are ten minutes apart. I've already called Dr. Oliver. He said to call him back when the pains were five minutes apart, or if her water broke. I've already got her bag packed, just in case."

"Okay. Just sit tight and follow Dr. Oliver's directions. I'm going to come over, but I'll just park out on the street and wait. I don't want to upset her. If anything happens---if you need me to help, blink the side porch light. This may be false labor. Anyway, I'll wait around for about two hours. If nothing happens, I'll go back to the apartment, and give you a call. Okay?"

Rube sat in the car and watched the light. Thoughts ran through his mind, mostly about Pretty Boy's antics at their wedding, and the wonderful life they had spent together while in college. It had been more than an hour now, and he had become mesmerized by the light. He was fantasizing about the baby, trying to picture its face. Would it favor him or Kristy? The first blink of the light didn't register. When it blinked again, he shot up in his seat, opened the door, and ran up the driveway. When he reached the side door, he heard an agonizing scream, and Moochie saying, "It's all right, Honey. Just relax, things are going to be fine."

Rube pushed the door open, and saw Kristy lying in the middle of the kitchen floor. There was a puddle of watery fluid around her. Panties lay at her side.

"What happened?"

"Her pains got to five minutes. I called Dr. Oliver. He said bring her on in, and that he would meet us there. I got her up, but this is as far as we got. Her water broke, and she sank to the floor."

"It's all right, Honey. Rube's here now, and everything's gonna to be just fine," said Moochie.

Kristy opened her eyes and screamed, "You son-of-a-bitch! You're the one who got me into this mess!"

Rube grabbed a pillow from the couch, and put it under Kristy's head.

"How far apart are her pains, now?"

"About a minute."

"Okay. I want you to get on the phone and call the hospital. Ask to speak to the maternity ward. Get Dr. Oliver on the phone if he has arrived. Tell them it's an emergency. I don't think the baby is going to wait. Whether he's there or not, tell them to send an ambulance right now."

Rube bent over Kristy, "Hold on, Baby. Everything's going to be all right. Take deep breaths and try to relax."

"You try to relax, you bastard! Don't you understand? I can't stand this pain! I need a shot or a pill! Do something!" she yelled as another pain struck. Clinching her teeth, she jerked her head to the side.

By this time, Moochie had Dr. Oliver on the phone. She handed it to Rube.

"Dr. Oliver---Rube. I don't think she's going to be able to make it to the hospital. Her water has broken, and her pains are less that a minute apart. What should we do?"

"Rube, don't worry. Everything is going to be all right. You're going to have to deliver this baby. But, I'll be right here with you. Just do what I tell you to do. Okay? There's an ambulance on the way."

"Okay. Moochie, get a clean sheet from the closet."

"Now, Rube, look at the opening and see how far she's dilated."

"I would say about two inches."

"Okay. Now. Can you see the baby's head?"

"Yes. I can just see the top."

"Now. Have Ms. Dunlop get Kristy to breathe deeply, and push. You watch to see if the dilation continues."

Kristy screamed every time a pain struck.

Moochie kneeled beside her, "Kristy, I know this is hard for you, but you're goin' to have to help us so we can get this thing over. Okay? Now, try to relax as much as you can. Each time I say push, I want you to bear down as much as possible. Okay, push!"

Kristy realized this was her only way out of the pain, and began to cooperate. Each scream was followed by a push.

Moochie said, "That's it, Girl. Push hard."

"Damn it. I'm pushing as hard as I can. Why don't you push for a while, fat ass." She screamed.

Moochie said, "I'll let that pass for now, but when you get through this, I'm goin' to pinch your nose off."

Kristy came close to a grin before another wave hit.

Sweat beads were rolling off Moochie and Rube, as well as Kristy.

"The head's coming out! Keep pushing Kristy! Get me some towels and wash cloths," said Rube, his hands trembling.

"Remain calm, Rube," said Dr. Oliver, "We're doing fine so far. Now, hold the baby's head, reach in slightly and see if you can turn the shoulders to make things easier."

"Okay. That's done. The baby has blood and mucous all over his face. Should I wipe it off?"

"Yes, just take a warm wash cloth, and gently clean his face. Now, we've got to get through this next phase. Have Kristy continue to push. You keep supporting the baby's head."

"Okay," Rube said through the bloody phone. His hands and both knees were soaked.

"Moochie, wet me a wash cloth with warm water. Kristy, keep pushing. You're doing fine!"

"Fine, my ass! I can't do this anymore!"

"Yes you can. Just hang in there, Baby."

Moochie handed him the cloth, then began wiping the floor with a towel.

Holding the baby's head with one hand and the phone with the other, "Dr. Oliver, the shoulders are coming out!"

"Okay. Now, lay the phone down for a minute. Keep supporting the baby's head, reach in and see if you can just gently pull on the baby's shoulders. That should make things easier for Kristy. Okay. Go ahead."

As Rube pulled on the shoulders, the baby slid out.

"Kristy, it's here! It's a boy!" he said as he cradled the tiny little body in both hands.

"Moochie, hold the phone up to my ear. Dr. Oliver, the baby is here. What do I do now?" Then, panic crept into his voice as he said, "He's not breathing!"

Soothingly, Dr. Oliver said, "That's okay, just remain calm. Now, wrap a clean towel around the baby's body. Turn him over, clear any mucous from around his nose and mouth. Use your finger to clear his mouth, being careful not to hurt him."

Moochie handed him a clean washcloth.

"Okay. That's done," said Rube.

"Now. Holding him face down, slap him on his backside."

Rube did that and the baby sputtered, giving a loud cry. Rube yelled into the phone, "He's breathing!" as they heard the ambulance pull into the driveway.

The emergency medical technicians rushed in, laid the baby on Kristy's chest, and loaded them on the stretcher.

Dr. Oliver asked to speak to one of the technicians.

"Dr. Oliver, this is Courtney. We've got them ready to transport."

"Okay. I'll be waiting for you when you get here."

Rube took the phone back. "What about the cord, Dr. Oliver?"

"Don't worry about that. We'll take care of it when she gets here. Congratulations! You and Ms. Dunlop did a fine job. I'll talk to you here at the hospital after we get Kristy taken care of."

After they had carried Kristy and the baby out, Rube and Moochie turned and looked at each other. They both smiled, then fell into each others arms and began to cry. Only now did they realize how scared they had been.

They cleaned things up, grabbed the suitcase from Moochie's car, and headed for the hospital.

A short time after they arrived, Dr. Oliver came to the waiting room.

"You two are to be commended. I couldn't have done it better myself. We got the cord cut and tied. They're both cleaned up, and in fine shape. The baby weighed in at six pounds, ten ounces. Kristy is worn out, of course. I just gave her a light sedative. You may go in and see her for a few minutes if you like."

As they entered the room, Kristy smiled weakly at Moochie. Rube took her hand, and placed his other hand on her head. "You really did a good job, Kristy. I'm proud of you."

She said, "Thanks," then rolled to her other side and closed her eyes.

Moochie sat in a low chair next to her bed, while Rube looked out the window. He was deeply hurt. He was secretly hoping that when the baby came, things would be different. That was not to be.

Moochie hoisted herself from the chair. "She's asleep now. Let's go out in the waiting room."

They sat in the large neo-natal care unit, surrounded by the glass windows overlooking the little cribs, changing tables and incubators. Rube could see his son a few rows back. He and Moochie took turns going back to see him up close, although they were not allowed to hold him.

Rube stood there, staring at his son, sometimes for a whole hour. He wanted to pick the baby up, and hold him to his chest. He realized that this time alone with him was precious. He didn't want to miss a moment of it, because in the morning things would be different. There would be other people to visit him, and he would be taken in to see his mother. He wondered how it was possible to be jealous of someone so new and tiny.

Early the next morning, he called Dr. Glasson, told him the good news, and asked him to take care of his patients. Then, he drove Moochie home so she could straighten the place, freshen up and drive her own car back to the hospital. Rube urged her to sleep for at least a couple of hours.

"Okay, Honey, maybe I will. I'm awful tired. I'm not used to staying up all night. Nor am I used to being on a fast. You know, anything over two hours is a fast for me." She looked at

Rube and smiled, "Do you realize I haven't had a praline since yesterday afternoon?"

There was an almost audible sigh of relief by his Toyota Camry when Moochie stepped out, and it had a lot more pep as he drove back to the apartment.

He spent a lot of time at the hospital over the next two days looking at his son, and talking to his and Kristy's parents. He made one more attempt to talk to Kristy, but there were only short sentences by him, followed by long periods of silence.

He found out from his father that she had named the baby, Samuel Neely. He was happy about that, but wondered where she got the name Neely. He finally decided that it must be a family name.

Kristy refused to let Rube take them home. She said she and Moochie could handle things just fine.

Rube was relieved that Moochie was going to be there to help Kristy with the baby. He was sure that Mrs. Free would also spend some time with her daughter.

He called Moochie daily to check on Samuel. He went to visit him two or three times a week. During those visits he got only brief glimpses of Kristy, and never talked to her. His lawyer called to let him know that the uncontested divorce was final on the twenty eighth of April. Rube's hands began to shake, and his voice cracked as he said, "Okay, Brett. Thanks for letting me know." He dropped the phone on the cradle, laid his head on the desk and cried. It was finally over and Rube now knew the true meaning of a broken heart.

CHAPTER FOURTEEN

Wendall Buchanan had wished a thousand times that he could tell his daughter, Amy, about his life. Maybe, just maybe, she would understand and not hate him for what he had done to her mother. He hated himself. Why wouldn't she hate him. How could he tell her about other things he had done, such as running that woman off the road. He was drunk, but how many things can you blame on whiskey? Someone had to pick the bottle up. His blackouts were often followed by graphic, scary dreams. If he drank enough, maybe they would go way.

The Bridges at Toko-Ri was playing on television when he extended the recliner. His chin dropped and his head fell to the right. He was eight years old again, back in the same old dream. His body shuddered as he began to recall every detail of that day.

The young boy lay bleeding and sniveling on the ground; shirt and pants torn to shreds; cuts and scratches over most of his body. Many times during the ordeal he had thought it better to just curl up and die. All of this came on his eighth birthday, and his mama told him she would cook a blackberry pie, his favorite, if he would help his father and older sister, Kathleen, pick berries. She wanted enough for two pies, and enough to put up ten jars for the winter months.

A large field not far from the house had been timbered off. A few scrub oaks and sycamores remained, but it was covered with brush, briars of all kinds, and plenty of blackberry bushes. Only half of the berries were dark enough to pick, but his daddy wanted to get a head start on the other families who would soon converge on them.

Arthur was a stocky man of thirty eight with dark brown hair combed straight back. There was no break between his facial and chest hair, so he had to shave to a point below his collar. Without a shirt, he reminded the boy of the picture of a bear he had seen in school. When mad the veins in his neck stood out like ropes. He was a strict disciplinarian, and if you broke one of his rules, you paid the price. The boy learned that very early in life, and had the scars to prove it. He had even been questioned at school about some of the wounds he suffered. His teacher, Mrs. Ashford, was especially concerned about the deep cut on the back of his hand about three months ago. He told her he was slicing a piece of ham, and the knife slipped. Actually, he had taken his daddy's good pocket knife without asking, and used it to cut a forked limb off a tree to make a slingshot.

The big bear was furious when he caught him with the knife. He said, "Boy! I've told you before, you don't take something that belongs to somebody else. That's called stealing!" He hit him with the back of his hand. "Do you hear me now?!"

"Looks like I'm gonna have to teach you a lesson the hard way! Come over here, and lay your hand on this table. Get over here!"

The boy was scared and crying, but knew he had to do what his daddy said. He slowly walked over and put his hand up on the table.

When his daddy grabbed his hand, he said, "Now, you know what they do to thieves in them A-rab countries? They cut their hands off! You want me to do that to you, Boy?"

"No Daddy! Please don't do that," he wailed.

"I'm goin' to teach you a lesson you won't forget," and with that, he dragged the knife across the boy's hand.

The scared little boy screamed and ran into the kitchen. His mama washed it off, poured some rubbing alcohol over the wound, and tied a kitchen towel around it. She held him tightly, soothing him quietly, not wanting to be heard in the next room.

The boy knew that his mama loved him, but she was scared and shaking almost as much as he was. She had suffered her share of beatings as well, and always tried to appease his father. The streaks of gray in her black hair, and the deep wrinkles across her brow belied her age. Heavy makeup could not hide the torment in her eyes. It was her job to keep the tenuous peace at any cost, even if it meant allowing these things to happen to her children. She told him once that she was glad she didn't have another child after him.

His sister had not been spared from the cruel abuse. She had turned twelve a few months back. After that, for some unknown reason, her beatings had suddenly stopped. Now she appeared to be his father's favorite. He even put his arm around her, and kissed her from time to time. Still, she was too scared to come to her brother's assistance, even though she wanted to.

His daddy's rule was that you didn't eat any berries until you had taken them back to the house and washed them. There might be chemicals on them from the surrounding farms, and besides, it slowed your picking down.

It was four-thirty and he hadn't eaten since lunchtime, not even a snack after school. He was hungry, and dinner was a long time off. When his father looked the other way, he popped three berries into his mouth. Unfortunately, his father saw him chewing.

"Did you eat a blackberry, Boy?"

"No, Sir!"

"Come here! Open your mouth. What's that blue stuff I see?"

"I'm sorry, Daddy! I was hungry, and I thought just a few berries wouldn't hurt."

"All right. The worst part is you lied to me! You see this blackberry patch here? It's only about thirty feet wide. I want you to crawl through that patch on your hands and knees, all the way to the other side. You hear me?"

"Yes Sir." He knew it would do no good to argue or plead with his father. He never gave in. Never.

"Now, Boy. If you don't make it all the way through, and I have to drag you outta there, it means no supper for you, and you go straight to bed when we get home."

He said, "Okay, Daddy. I'll try-----."

He got down on my hands and knees as Kathleen and his daddy resumed picking berries. He stuck his head through an opening between two bushes, and tried to wiggle his shoulders through, but there was not enough room and the sharp briars caught his shirt. When he laid his hand on the ground, he screamed with pain, as several of last years thorns stuck in his hand. The old, dried up thorns were much sharper, and hurt more than fresh ones. They cut like a razor. He wanted to keep his hat on to protect his head and eyes, but knew if he was going to make it, he would have to put his hands on the ground. He took it off and put it under one hand at a time as he moved through the thicket. Still, the needle-like thorns shot into the palm of his hand every now and then, causing him to scream out. When the pain became unbearable, he stopped, prayed and cried for a while, then, moved ahead.

At one point he got caught by the briers between bushes, and couldn't move either way without excruciating pain. The pickers were tearing through his clothes and into his skin. He thought, I'm going to die here. There is no way I will ever get out of here. Even if Daddy wanted to help, he couldn't get me out. He wanted to die. He finally just gave up, and let himself go, hoping the end would come soon. The relaxation that comes just before death, caused his body to sag, and finally drop to the ground.

After a while, he realized that he was not dead. Lying flat on his stomach, he was able to move his right arm. He reached forward and grabbed the base of the bush where there were no pickers, and pulled as hard as he could. Inch by inch he was able to free himself, and move on.

Then, just ahead he saw movement and two small eyes stared at him from a diamond shaped head as a forked tongue flicked in his direction. He was paralyzed by fear. He closed his eyes, dropped his head and waited for the fangs to dig into his head. He waited for awhile, afraid to move, but became hopeful the longer he didn't feel the bite. Finally, he opened his eyes. Hearing a flutter of movement to his left, he cut his eyes in time to see a flipped up tail working its way through the underbrush.

He was bleeding profusely now from the scrape and puncture wounds, and could feel himself getting weaker. He could hear Kathleen faintly, pleading with his daddy to help him.

He said, "Shut up, Girl, and get back to work. This'll make a man out of him."

"But, Daddy. He's only eight."

"That don't matter. It's time he learned a lesson."

He crawled a couple of feet, rested, then again.

When he was only a few feet from the end, he began to hope that he could make it. His will to survive, and the inner strength that could only come from God kept pushing him forward. He got through the last clump of briars, and passed out.

A few minutes later his peace was shattered by the terrible pains which racked his body from head to foot.

"Get up Boy, and get back to work!"

He rose to his hands and knees, and finally staggered to his feet.

"Go get your bucket, and start where you left off."

He could taste the combination of blood, sweat and tears that had run into his mouth as he lay on the ground. He wiped his mouth with his shirt sleeve. Glancing up at the perfectly clear, beautiful blue sky, he wished with all his heart that he could just float away to that peaceful place.

He staggered back to where he had dropped his pail. He picked it up and began picking berries. He was light headed, but knew that he must keep going if he wanted to eat. After ten minutes, he dropped the bucket, staggered back two steps, looked up at the spinning sky, and fell back into the red, clay sod.

The next thing he remembered was his mother's quiet voice, "Here, Son, I brought you some soup and cornbread."

He opened his eyes, and looked up at his old and beaten mother who had only lived thirty six years. He began to cry again, this time for her.

"Mama, I was just hungry. I wanted something to eat."

"I know, Son. It's all right now. Here, let me raise you up so you can eat your soup."

After he had eaten, she said, "Wendall, I'm goin' to have to get your clothes off so I can treat your wounds."

"Is it gonna hurt, Mama?"

"Yes, Son, it will sting some, but it has to be done, otherwise you'll hurt even more."

When she took his shirt and pants off, she could see that he was swollen and red over most of his body. She took a cloth, splashed some alcohol on it and began dabbing at all the scratch and puncture wounds. Each time, he winced with pain, and drew in a breath, knowing that he couldn't scream and wake his father.

"I'm sorry, Son, but it looks like you've got a dose of chiggers, too."

She finally finished, and pulled the covers up over him.

"You're a good boy, Wendall. I'm so sorry that you have to go through this."

"It's okay, Mama. Don't you worry none. I'll be all right."

He quickly fell asleep as the eventual cooling affect of the alcohol overcame the pain long enough for his tired body to relax.

Wendall shifted his weight in the chair and turned his head to the left. Soon he was back into a deep sleep.

At eleven-thirty one night when the boy was sixteen, he was startled awake by his mother's scream, and a loud crash. He sat straight up in bed.

He heard from the other bedroom, "You damn bitch! Why didn't you fix me somthin' for dinner? Get your ass into that kitchen and fix me somethin', you hear?!"

"Arthur! Please don't hit me no more. I thought you'd eat somethin' at the bar."

He had heard this kind of thing before, but now his rage jumped above a threshold of hatred and shame that could no longer be contained by his fear of his father. He took his hands from over his ears, grabbed his hair and pulled it as hard as he could, and let out a primordial scream from deep in his soul.

As he went through the living room, he grabbed a metal lamp, pulling the cord from the wall. When he entered the bedroom, his father was sitting on top of his mother, pounding her in the face with his fist.

No longer in control, the teenager flew across the room, raising the lamp at the same time. He swung his weapon with both hands, expressing all of his hatred with one stroke. The metal clanked as it struck the hard bone of his daddy's skull, opening a gaping wound. The bear said, "What the---?" as the force of the blow sent him rolling into the wall. The young man was standing over him in an instant, swinging his club time and again. He heard his father's arms break as he tried to defend himself.

He would have killed him for sure if his mother hadn't grabbed him around the waist and pulled him away, pleading, "Wendall, please, Son. Please don't hit him no more!" He turned and threw the lamp at the mirror, smashing it to pieces.

"Mama, get your things together, we're leavin'!" he said.

"But, what about your father, Wendall? He's hurt bad. We've got to help him!"

"To hell with him! He don't care about us. All he does is hurt us. I hate him! I never want to see him again! Let's go!"

"No, Wendall. I can't go. Don't you see that I love him. I can't leave him like this. Besides, where would we go?"

"I don't know, Mama. But, I'm goin'. I can't stay here no more!"

He never saw his father again until he was stone cold dead, lying in a mortuary as though he was the most serene and peaceful man on the planet.

His mother met him at the door, leading him to the casket, as she cried softly. "He was a good man, Wendall. He loved you very much."

He couldn't think of anything to say that wouldn't hurt his mother. He thought, he never gave any indication that he cared about me. If there had even been a clue, it would have made the beatings easier to take.

As he sat next to his mother at the funeral, his sense of smell was almost as confused as his brain by the sickeningly sweet smell of the mixture of flowers. He was startled by the feelings of love for his father that awakened in him as the preacher read from the Bible. He thought to himself, this can't be. How can you love someone that you hate so much?

Wendall was startled awake by the bombing of the bridges on television. He reached for the half empty Budweiser with his left hand and took a swallow.

The love/hate relationship was never clarified in Wendall's brain, and it carried over into his own family. He never understood how to go about giving and receiving love from Thelma and Amy.

His mother loved his father even though he beat her. Wendall figured that must be the way to gain a woman's love and respect. He would never forget the first time he hit Thelma. It happened during a fit of rage over something small. He felt great remorse. Later, she came to him on her knees and told him how sorry she was. After that, it became easier for him to use force. She seemed to respect him more after that, and it gave him a sense of power over his own life, at least within his own four walls. Life outside his home was another story. When he lost his job, or someone talked back to him on the outside, there was nothing he could do about it without ending up in jail. Home was the only place where he felt safe, secure, and in control, the only place he could really let his feelings out. Still, most of the time, he was sad, depressed and full of self loathing because he had become a reincarnation of his father.

Wendall wished he could tell Amy how much he loved her. Now she had grown up and moved away. He feared his chance was gone forever. There was just him and Thelma. He didn't know why, but it seemed impossible for him to tell either one of them what was really on his heart. Maybe it was the shame.

143

The only real accomplishment of his miserable life, and the thing that he was most proud of, was that he had never raised his hand to his daughter, Amy. She had been a well behaved child from the very beginning, full of unconditional love for him. Even so, there had been times when he wanted to slap her or even beat her, but he had resisted. He never understood exactly why. Maybe he didn't want his daughter to have the same feelings he'd had toward his father. Sometimes he would turn and storm out the back door, and go for a walk alongside the cotton field. At other times he would simply take it out on his wife.

Amy never knew all the facts about her father's early life, only bits and pieces that she had picked up from her mother and the few times she had been with her grandmother.

After Amy moved to Athens to work and go to school, Wendall became even more despondent. He tried to overcome his deep depression by spending more time drinking in sleazy bars. Many times when he got home, if he was not too drunk, he would slap Thelma around, just to remind her that he was still boss. In his lucid moments at home, he sat in his chair and watched championship wrestling, boxing or some other program containing violence. It was the only thing on television that he could identify with anymore.

One evening in late May, he was sitting in his chair, sleeping with his head bent forward and to the side, spittle seeping out of the corner of his mouth.

Thelma came in and tapped him lightly on the hand, "Wendall, it's time for bed."

No reply.

She bent over closer to his ear, "Wendall, Honey, it's time to go to bed."

The last thing Thelma heard was, "Damn you!!!," as the back of his hand caught the right side of her face, spinning her around and throwing her off balance. She stumbled backwards, clawing at the air, unable to regain control. Her scream was cut short when the back of her head struck the slate hearth, breaking her neck. Her head lolled to the side, and there was one last spasm as her soul prepared to flee.

Wendall rose from his chair, "Thelma !!!! "Thelma!! I didn't mean it!" as he rushed to her side, lifting her head, only to see it flop forward onto her chest.

He screamed, "Thelma, it was an accident! I didn't mean to hurt you! Please, Thelma, talk to me! Please! Please! Please!" He leaned across her lifeless body and pounded his fist against the floor, then raised up.

"Thelma, please don't die, Honey! I love you. I've always loved you! Please don't go. You're the only one I've got!" He tore at his clothes and pounded his head with both hands.

Tears flowed down his cheeks, much as they had forty years ago as he lay bleeding from the vicious blackberry bushes, and his equally vicious father.

"No! No! No!"

Wendall knew it was over for him. "There is no way I could face Amy! No way! And, there is no way that I will go to prison," he screamed.

He rose, walked into the bedroom, and took the single barrel, twelve gauge shotgun out of the closet. He walked back into the living room, and sat down in his chair.

"I love you Thelma. I love you Amy. I'm sorry."

He leaned forward, placed the barrel in his mouth, and pulled the trigger, splattering blood and brains on his favorite chair and the adjacent wall.

Wendall's television continued to promote the entertainment value of violence to an audience who could not hear, and was no longer amused by man's cruelty to man.

The phone rang helplessly on its cradle. It was Amy calling to check on the only two people she had ever loved as family. Puzzled, she hung up the phone, and decided to drive out and check on them tomorrow. Little did she know that the circle of violence had been broken, and that the burden of shame was hers to bear.

CHAPTER FIFTEEN

Rube was busy with the practice, especially since Dr. Glasson retired on the first of May. It was now his practice, and there was increased pressure because all the responsibilities were his. Even so, his happiest times were at the office. The work gave his life meaning.

His personal life was empty and without purpose. There was no one to share his thoughts and feelings. He spent his evenings reading or watching the tube. At times he met Cal or Will for a beer. But, they had lives of their own. Rube felt like an intruder. He continued to see Samuel once or twice a week, and talked to Moochie almost every day. The baby was growing, and according to Moochie waking up only once during the night for feeding. Moochie said he favored Rube more and more each day. He felt proud, and yet, sad at the same time, since he wouldn't be part of his son's day to day life. During the day, when he thought of Sam, he tried to imagine what he might be doing at that time. He pretended to look into his eyes, then hold him close. It wasn't like being there, but, at least it was a connection. He cherished those moments. When Kristy was teaching, if he could arrange time out of the office, he would call and drive the short distance to see Sam and Moochie.

It was a Thursday afternoon at six-fifteen when Rube received the call. His last patient had just left.

Sara said, "Dr. Winters, there's someone on the phone for you. I couldn't make out her name, but she said it's urgent."

Rube went to his office and lifted the phone, "Hello."

There was sobbing on the other end of the line.

"Hello----Hello," said Rube.

Finally, after a long pause, "Rube? Is that you, Rube? It's awful---I don't know what to do."

"Yes, this is Rube. Who is this?"

"I'm so sorry to bother you, but I didn't know who else to call. I'm sorry---." Then, her voice broke into a sob.

Finally, Rube recognized the low, sensual voice, "Amy! Is that you?"

"Yes. I need your help. Tell me what to do---," she said, on the edge of hysteria.

"Amy, calm down. Where are you, and what happened? Were you in an accident? Are you hurt?"

"They're dead. My mama and daddy are both dead!"

"Okay. I want you to tell me exactly where you are."

"I'm at a convenience store up here on Highway 78. It's the Golden Pantry, I think. It's on the corner of Johnson Road and 78, on the left side. Please hurry!"

"I will. Now, hang on." He held the phone away for a moment, trying to think of what to do. Then, he said, "When we hang up, I want you to pick up the phone again and dial 911. Can you do that?"

"Yes---I think so---."

"All right, you've got to be strong. Tell them about your parents, and make sure you give them the address. Got it?"

"Yeah---address."

"I'll be right there. Don't move. Stay where you are. I'm on my way." He threw his clinic jacket off, and grabbed his keys. As he went by the front desk, "Sara, you'll have to close. There's an emergency. I have to leave right now. I'll call you later."

Knowing her father, Rube wondered if he finally went too far and killed Mrs. Buchanan. But, what could have happened to the old man? When he arrived at the store, Amy was slumped over the wheel of her Honda Accord, next to the pay phone. When he pulled up behind her, she jumped out and ran into his arms, holding on and sobbing.

He guided her to the passenger side and helped her in. "Now, please tell me what happened."

"They're both dead. I don't know what happened to Mama, but Daddy was shot. It was terrible, terrible!"

Rube handed her his handkerchief and held her hand, "Okay, take your time and start at the beginning. You did call the police, right?"

"Yes," she stammered, then took a deep breath and continued, "I talked to Mama yesterday at lunch time. Things were fine. Then, I called last night and got no answer. I knew that Daddy might be at the bar, and I thought Mama might be out for a walk. I got worried today when I called, and there was still no answer. After work, I came out to check on them. That's when I found them. I just slammed the door and ran to my car. Then, I called you."

"All right, don't worry. The first thing we've got to do is meet the policemen at your house, and tell them what happened."

"I can't go back in there, Rube. I just can't!"

"That's okay. You can stay in the car."

She was sitting on the other side of the seat, shivering.

He turned the car around and put it into drive. He reached across, took her hand, and pulled her over next to him. He put his arm around her and rubbed her shoulder as they drove back to the house.

Rube asked, "Amy, was there any sign of a break-in?"

Her voice shaking, she said, "Not that I could tell, and I doubt if Wild Thang, Daddy's dog, would let anyone get close to the house." Rube knew Wild Thang personally, and did not doubt her word.

The deputies had not arrived yet. Rube didn't want to block the driveway, so he parked out in front on the edge of the road next to the infamous embankment where he and Amy had experienced the treachery of the slippery red clay. It brought fleeting memories of that dreadful night a few years back. What had seemed so dreadful then, paled in comparison to the present situation.

"Do you want to wait here or go up and sit on the porch?"

"I'd better go with you so the Rotweiler doesn't chew your leg off. Then, I guess I could sit on the porch."

"Okay. If you need to, you can always come back to the car."

They got out and met in front of the car. Rube put his arm around her in a protective way as they walked up the driveway. When they passed the old, light blue, Dodge pickup, Rube noticed a large dent in the now rusty right, rear fender. Red paint had been ground into the patches of blue. That set off an alarm in Rube's head. His mind went back to what the state patrolman told him about the vehicle that struck Kristy's car. He rubbed his hand over the rusty dent, and thought, my God! Could this be the truck that ran Kristy off the road?

"Amy, what bar did your dad go to when he wanted to drink?"

"Well, he had several, but his favorite was the one over in Monroe. Why do you ask?"

"No reason. I was just curious," as he tucked it into the back of his mind, knowing he would have to deal with that later.

As they approached the porch, Rube saw Wild Thang and heard a low growl that sent chills up his spine. He quickly shifted to Amy's right side.

Rube, trying not to show his fear, said, "Better tie him up to protect the policemen."

Amy said, "Yeah, you're right." Then, walked over, grabbed the snap end of the chain attached to the porch and clipped it to Thang's collar.

Rube relaxed and walked Amy to the swing, "Will you be all right?"

She nodded, "I think so."

"I'm going in just to look around. Okay?"

He opened the front door and stepped inside. His nostrils were immediately assaulted by the pungent smell of death. The television was still blasting away with Dan Rather reporting on one African tribe taking revenge on another by killing hundreds of women and children. Wendall's chair had been knocked flat on its back and splattered with blood. Wendall was lying just above the chair, his face missing. The wall next to the chair had small and large blotches of blood and other matter. There was still a faint smell of powder from the shotgun which lay out in front of the chair.

Rube, feeling nauseated, bent forward, put his face in his hands and thought of blue sky for a minute to settle things down. He then turned and walked toward the fireplace. Amy's mother was lying in front of the hearth, her swollen face and neck turned to the side. There was a red bruise on the right side of her face. Hearing the wail of a siren, he turned and walked outside. The dark brown sheriff's patrol car rolled in behind the pickup and fell silent. Two officers got out, hands cautiously resting on their weapons. They saw Amy and Rube standing on the porch. Sensing no danger, they walked toward the house.

When Wild Thang cleared his throat, the youngest officer drew his thirty eight and hunkered down.

The other deputy said, "Damn it, Owens, stash it." Through his teeth, "If I have to tell you again about pulling your weapon unnecessarily, I'm goin' to take it away."

Owens struggled to regain control as they joined Amy and Rube on the porch.

"I'm Deputy Bill Stephens and this is Deputy Owens," said the senior officer who appeared to be in his forties. He had dark brown, short hair, and looked as though he had outgrown his uniform. His neck hung over the strained collar, the belt was under considerable stress, and his pant legs were about an inch too short. But, he was obviously the one in charge.

Deputy Owens blushed and shifted from one foot to the other. He was in his twenties with sandy blond hair that stood up in all directions. There had been a futile attempt to part it on the left side. He had sharp features and thin lips which were turned down to match the grim look on his face. He deferred to Officer Stephens by standing behind and to his right side.

"I'm Rube Winters, a friend of Miss Amy Buchanan whose parents are inside." They shook hands.

"Miss Buchanan, please tell us what happened."

Amy explained everything that had occurred. Then, asked, "Can I go home now?"

"I'm sorry, Miss Buchanan, but we'll need you to come to the Sheriff's office and give a formal statement. We're going to go inside now and look around. Then, we'll probably call the coroner, and a team to examine the scene to determine just what happened."

The shadows from the trees were longer now as the sun began its slow descent. They walked over and sat down on the swing with Amy still clinging to his arm, leaning her head against his shoulder, crying softly. Rube enjoyed her closeness, but couldn't allow himself to think about it now. The sweet smell of honeysuckle hung in the air.

"I guess I should have stayed here to look after them," Amy said.

"You have to pursue your own life, you can't live your life for your parents. This is not your fault." He thought about how much she had already sacrificed during her high school years because of her father. "You couldn't be with them every second."

"Yes, I guess you're right. I've dreaded something like this for a long time."

"I'm finding out that things like this happen in our lives whether we want them or not. My Uncle Billy says we have to accept the fact that we're not in charge, do the best we can and move on," said Rube.

"Maybe so, but still, I wonder why. I wish I could have prevented this." She sighed and dropped her head.

The officers came outside with Deputy Owens looking pale, his eyes twitching.

Deputy Stephens said, "Owens, put tape around the house. Then put tape across the driveway when I leave.

"Miss Buchanan, we'll get the coroner out here right away. Did either of you touch anything in the house?"

"No. I ran to my mother, bent over her, then got up and ran out of the house."

Rube said, "The only thing I touched was the doorknob."

Amy and Rube followed Deputy Stephens down the driveway. He called over his shoulder, "Owens, you can put the tape up now. Wait for the coroner, and try not to shoot the dog." He muttered something about the quality of people they had to hire nowadays.

Rube and Amy followed the patrol car back to the sheriff's office. Rube said, "Amy, you know they're going to ask you a lot of questions. They may even ask if you want a lawyer."

She said, "Oh---well, I don't care about that. They can check my story out if they want to."

Rube gave a brief statement, then waited for Amy as she was questioned by Deputy Stephens and the investigating officer.

It was apparent that Amy had been crying when she emerged from the session with the officers. Her face was streaked, and her body seemed to sag with the weight of having relived the events of the last few hours. Rube rushed over to support her.

"I'll be okay," she said.

"Miss Buchanan, we'll let you know what we think happened as soon as we get the preliminary report from the coroner. Please notify the funeral home that you mentioned to us, so they will be ready to receive the bodies when they have been released."

They drove back to the Golden Pantry to get Amy's car. "I'll follow you back to your apartment since I don't know exactly where you live. Are you sure you're okay to drive?" asked Rube.

"Yes, I think so. I'm so sorry to get you involved in this. It's just that I had no one else to call. Daddy's mother died two years ago. I've never met his sister, and know only that she lives somewhere in North Carolina. Mama's parents are both dead, and what family she has, lives in Virginia."

"Don't worry about that. I don't mind helping out in any way I can. I'll be right behind you."

As they drove back to Athens, Rube thought about the strong possibility that Mr. Buchanan was the one who ran Kristy off the road near Monroe on that fateful night. An event which had changed his life, and the life of Kristy and his son, forever. He had often wondered what kind of person could do something like that. Now he knew. And, there seemed to be an empty space in his heart where he had nurtured his hatred for that person. How can I hate someone who is dead, and has no face, he thought. The only thing that he knew for sure was he could not tell Amy about his suspicion, at least not yet. At some point, he would have to call Patrolman Curtis with the State Patrol, and tell him about the truck. Maybe Curtis could check it out quietly to see whether Wendall's truck was the one that caused the accident. Without a license plate number, it would be very difficult to prove. In his heart he knew that Wendall was guilty, but bringing that out would not help anyone, and could only hurt Amy.

Rube parked on the street, and met Amy at the front door of the apartment. He could hear barking inside as she opened the front door. They were assaulted by a wagging, yapping, slobbering bundle of energy who appeared to be overjoyed by their presence.

"Okay, Didhe, just calm down. It's only us. Rube, this is Didhe."

"Diddy? D i d d y?"

"No. D i d h e. His full name is Didhebiteya. He's a mutt that my daddy gave me."

"Where did you come up with such a name?"

"I didn't. That was my daddy's idea. He said, that way you can call your dog, and check on his victims at the same time."

"Oh. I see---." Rube was amazed to learn that Mr. Buchanan had any trace of humor about him. "Sounds like a good idea to me."

Didhe was just a big, brown dog with floppy ears who could not wag his tail without wagging his whole body. Rube had no idea how many breeds might have been represented, but somewhere in his lineage he suspected a coon dog was involved because Didhe sniffed everything in sight. He had already sniffed Rube from head to toe.

Rube sat on the green, plaid couch while Amy sat on the matching chair. They talked briefly about their high school days, and their one and only date.

Rube said, "I'm sorry about what happened that night. I really wanted to date you again, but could not come up with a safe way to do that. I figured your daddy would kill me if he ever got his hands on me." Rube could tell that Amy was weary from the grueling day that she had been through, and he wondered if he should even mention his situation. Then, he decided that he wanted to get it out in the open. Besides, maybe it would get her mind off her own problems. "Did you know that Kristy and I are divorced?"

"I heard that from Will. I also know about the birth of your son through my hospital friends."

"She was never the same after the accident. I kept hoping she would get better, but it never happened. I tried to hold things together for Sam, mainly, but it was impossible. I still love Kristy, the way she was before."

"I'm sorry. I know you've been through a lot. I had no one else to call. I---." Amy began to cry.

"No. Please don't cry. I'm glad you called. You were a great help to me and Kristy when she was injured." Rube reached over and patted Amy's hand. He then leaned back on the couch and rubbed his brow.

"There's something else I need to tell you, and I don't know quite how to explain it. My life has been cursed according to Uncle Billy." He held up his hand. "Please don't laugh. I know this sounds crazy, but since I was very young, weird things keep happening to me and those around me. I don't want to bring more grief into your life. That's why I'm telling you about it now. After you're through this, I'll walk out of your life so you won't be affected."

Amy closed her eyes and put her hand over her forehead. Then, she looked up, "Thanks for telling me, but I don't believe in curses. That's absurd. I could say that I was cursed too. My situation made it impossible for me to have a social life. I knew that if I was ever to have a life of my own, I would have to leave home. My mother was the only thing that kept me there. I was concerned about her. Don't get me wrong, I loved my father, but I knew that he was abusing my mother. I just didn't know how badly. But, I wasn't cursed. I was born into that situation. Besides, things happen to all people."

"Yeah, I guess you're right," said Rube, not wanting to discuss the details. "Did your father ever hurt you in any way?"

"No, no. He got angry, but he never harmed me. Maybe if he had, I would have called the police, or somehow gotten help for him and my mother. But, who do you turn to for help in a situation like that? If he were arrested, he would be out in a few days. Then, things might get worse. Besides, we couldn't have survived without his income. I just didn't know what to do."

"I understand," said Rube. "There are a lot of people who face that same dilemma every day. In some areas there are shelters for battered women, but not nearly enough. Have you eaten anything?"

"No. I haven't thought about that."

"Would you like to go out to eat?"

"Not really. I might have something here. I could fix us a sandwich. Would that be all right?"

"Sure. That would be fine. But, do you feel like doing it?"

"Yes. I would rather be busy. That way, I can forget about the sadness in my heart."

"May I use your phone?" said Rube. "I want to let Sara, my office manager, know what happened."

"Help yourself. I'll get us something to eat."

Rube ate while Amy picked at her food, taking a few bites. Then, she blurted out, "Rube, what do you think happened to Mama and Daddy?"

He thought for a minute, "Was that your daddy's shotgun?"

She nodded, "Yes."

Rube said, "Are you sure you want to talk about this?"

"Yes. I need to know."

"It looks like your daddy shot himself. From the look of your mother's face, I would say he hit her. Maybe that killed her or maybe she hit her head when she fell."

After dinner, Rube said, "Amy, it's getting late, and I know you're very tired. I should go on home and let you get some sleep."

Suddenly, she began to shake, and covered her face with both hands. After a brief period, she regained control and raised her head. "I'm sorry. It's just that I hadn't thought about being alone. I don't know if I can go to sleep." Her cheeks were wet with tears.

He moved to her end of the couch, sat next to her, and put his arm around her. "Don't worry, Amy. I won't leave as long as you need me here. Are you going to work tomorrow?"

"I hadn't thought of that either. Do you think I should? I can't imagine sitting here, by myself, all day."

"I agree. I think it might be better to go on to work. At least your mind would be occupied by something else. I'll have to go into the office and see the patients who are already scheduled."

"I guess I'll do that. If things get too bad, I'll just come home," said Amy. "The police have my work number in case they need to get in touch with me."

"Okay. I'll meet you here after work, and take you out to dinner."

"That sounds fine. I'm so lucky to have a friend like you. Thanks for everything."

They sat and talked for a long time. Amy told him about her father's difficult life. She related the little she knew about what had happened to him in the blackberry patch. In turn Rube told her what had happened to him after they brought Kristy and the baby home from the hospital.

Amy said, "I'm so sorry about your wife and son. I know it has been a terrible ordeal for you. I wish there was some way I could help."

"Apparently there is nothing that can be done for Kristy. I tried to make it work, Amy, but it finally became clear to me that our marriage was over. Our divorce is now final. I wish it had never happened, but wishing doesn't make it so. Now, I'm trying to figure out how to become a part of my son's life. I'm lucky that I have Moochie, a good friend of mine, there to take care of them. She keeps me up to date on what's happening."

Finally, Amy fell asleep on Rube's shoulder. After he was certain that she was sound asleep, he gently laid her head on the couch as he raised her legs. He then found a pillow and blanket in the bedroom, came back and made her comfortable. He was struck by her natural beauty as she lay fast asleep, exhausted after the dreadful events of the day. Her skin was slightly tanned, and perfectly smooth, even without makeup. Her lips were full and slightly open, and her breath came in soft waves. Her silky brown hair fell above her right eye, and then swept back, just below the right ear. Suddenly, Rube's heart began to beat faster and he felt an overwhelming desire to kiss her. But, he just couldn't do that. Not now. Not under these circumstances.

The chair was a recliner, and he was able to sleep fitfully, using a pillow from the couch. He dreamed of the boy in the blackberry patch, and the circle of violence.

The next day was hectic. After making sure Amy was all right, he rushed home, took a shower and hurried to the office. He hardly sat down during the morning, but caught himself thinking about Amy as he worked on the patients. After lunch he called Moochie to check on Sam. He knew that Moochie would answer because Kristy had resumed her teaching job in Conyers about two weeks ago.

"Hi Moochie, how's our boy doing?"

"Why, Lord-a-mercy, Honey, he's doin' just fine. He's sleepin' right now. He took his bottle and fell asleep in my arms."

"Is he playing basketball yet?"

"Not yet, Honey. But, I'll tell you one thing. He's a strong boy. He can pull himself up to a standing position in my lap."

"I wish I could see him. I miss him every day. How's Kristy doing?"

"She's doin' just fine---about the same, really. I don't know how she does at school, if they notice the difference. Here at home we have an understanding. She knows that I don't take any of her crap. I tell her like it is, and that's it. If she don't like it, tough titty. I guess I ought to tell you that she is seeing another man. They went out to dinner on Wednesday night. He coaches and teaches at her school. I can already tell that I don't like him. He's too slick. You know what I mean? Outwardly, he acts very nice and considerate of me, Kristy and the baby. But, I can tell that he doesn't mean it. See? He's only out for one thing, and I think you know what that is."

Rube didn't know what to say. He had known this might happen, but had not allowed himself to think about it. How stupid of him. Of course, other men would be interested. She was a very attractive woman. He realized that he no longer had a legal claim on Kristy, and no right to be jealous. Still, as illogical as it might be, it hurt him deeply that she would go out with another man. Then, he thought of his feelings for Amy and felt guilty.

He stammered, "Oh, I'm sorry to hear that."

"Don't worry, Honey, I'll watch out for his sorry ass."

"Okay. I love you and Sam. Give him a big hug and kiss for me." He had wanted to tell her about the situation with Amy, but just couldn't.

The afternoon was not as busy as the morning, and he wondered if the day would ever end. He did not give his patients the attention they deserved. His mind wandered from Amy and her situation to Kristy and his son. His thoughts and emotions were a jumbled mess. He hated Wendall for what he had done. But, at the same time he was sorry for the life that Wendall had lived, and Mrs. Buchanan's misery and suffering. He was sad that Amy was all alone now, with no family to look after her. At the same time, he was happy to be back in her life after all these years. She had always been in the back of his mind, a dream that had never been experienced. Could it happen now? He was angry that Kristy was going out with someone else. How could she do this to him? How could she do this to their son? What if she got married again? How could he bear to see another man raising his child? He could understand why a parent would take their own child and run away. Finally, he admitted to himself that he was jealous of Kristy, not the person she was now, but the one he had fallen in love with, married, and conceived their child with. Tears welled up in his eyes as he thought of that Kristy. Was she dead forever? What if she returned? He hoped so for Sam's sake. But, then, could their old relationship be reclaimed? How would that affect his deepening love for Amy? It was all so confusing. His mind was exhausted by the end of the day.

He called Amy when he got home to his apartment.

"Hi, Amy. How was your day?"

"Hey. It went okay. Work helped occupy my mind, but I still thought about it all day. I got home about four o'clock and called the Sheriff's Office. I talked to Officer Stephens. He said, they may never know for sure what happened, but it looks like Daddy hit Mama causing her to fall against the fireplace. The fall broke her neck. Then, Daddy, likely upset by what he had done, committed suicide with the shotgun. They do not suspect foul play, and he thinks the bodies will be released tomorrow, and sent to the funeral home in Winder. I'll have to make some arrangements and decisions. I hope I'm up to it."

"Don't worry. I'm gonna help you with all that. I'll be right over. We'll go get something to eat, and talk about what needs to be done. Okay?"

"Okay. Thanks. I'll see you in a few minutes."

When he got there, he knocked on the door, and heard a "Come in," from somewhere in the apartment. He opened the door and was greeted by Didhe, who jumped up, licked him on the face and all over his arms before he could get him to settle down, and stop wagging his brown, shaggy body. He found Amy lying across the bed, with mascara running down her face.

He sat down on the bed and put his hand on her shoulder. "What's wrong?"

"I called information and got Aunt Ruth's number in North Carolina. I just finished talking to her. She's bedridden with arthritis and diabetes, and can't come to the funeral. She has no contact with Mama's relatives in Virginia."

He patted her shoulder. "It'll be all right. We'll just have our own funeral if we have to. Things will work out just fine. Wait and see."

She rolled onto her side, tears in her eyes, but with a faint smile on her face. "Rube, do you know that you're the best, and only friend that I've ever had? I was always afraid to have good friends because I knew I could never take them home with me. So, I just made superficial friends that I needed to work with. I've been a loner, really, although, I don't want to be that way."

"Well, from now on you can forget about being a loner." He leaned over and kissed her forehead.

CHAPTER SIXTEEN

Since Amy and her parents had never attended a church in the area, Rube suggested Ralph Lee, his preacher at the First Methodist Church who had presided over his infamous, head caught in the spindles of life, performance, as well as his bird splattered wedding to Kristy (neither of which he mentioned to Amy). Rube called and made the arrangements. He briefly told him what had happened and gave him background information about the Buchanans.

"Who is Amy?" asked the preacher.

"A friend of mine from high school. She called me for help when this happened."

"How's your wife? Kristy, was that her name?"

"Yes, Kristy. She's fine, I guess. Reverend Lee, I'm divorced. There was an accident, and Kristy has not been the same. I'll tell you more about it when I see you."

"Okay, Rube. Where will the service be?"

"At the Smith Funeral Home in Winder."

"Is there anything else I need to know about the funeral? Pretty Boy won't be there, will he?" Rube heard a chuckle.

"Oh. No. I haven't seen him in a long time." Rube smiled, "Our relationship was never the same after the wedding."

"Okay," Preacher Lee chuckled, "I just wanted to make sure. I'll be there unless I hear from you."

"Thanks. We'll see you on Monday."

The visitation on Sunday night was a lonely affair. Her father's casket was closed. Amy bought her mother a beautiful dress with a high collar to cover the swollen neck. Rube suspected it was the only descent dress she had ever worn. The bruise on her jaw was covered with heavy makeup.

Her mother had no friends. They always lived in isolated areas with few, if any, neighbors. She had never worked outside their home.

Amy and Rube sat there by themselves, holding hands. At eight-thirty, when they were getting ready to leave, an older man walked into the lobby of the funeral home, looking confused. There was a slight stagger as he walked over and looked at the blank sign-in book. He decided that he couldn't or wouldn't sign in, and came on through the large door where they were sitting. When he saw them, he tried to lift his shoulders, but the weight of the well-worn sports coat seemed to drag them back down. He stopped momentarily as though he was going to turn around and walk out. Before he could do that, Rube was across the room with his hand out, closely followed by Amy. The man declined to shake, showing Rube his gnarled hands. They introduced themselves.

"I'm jest an ole friend of Wendall's, an' wanted to say my goodbyes." The corners of his mouth looked as though they were permanently turned down, and there was a small streak of tobacco juice in one of the creases that followed the line of his mouth. The lower part of his face was much lighter than the top part, and it was obvious that this was the first time he had shaved in a long time. His sad eyes continually looked down toward the floor, and it appeared to be unbearable for him to look up for more than a second.

Amy took his hand and held it. "Thank you so much for coming. He would be so proud that you came. I'm sorry, I didn't catch your name."

"William Arrington the Third, Ma'am. But, ever' body calls me Bud. You must be Wendall's daughter. He always talked about you. Said you'us the pride and joy of his life. Tha only good thing that he ever did. He'us mighty proud of you, Ma'am."

"Thank you for remembering that, Mr. Bud. I loved my daddy very much. I'm sorry the casket has to be closed, but I guess you know what happened."

"Yes 'am. I understand."

Rube said, "Come on over and have a seat, Bud."

As they sat down, Rube could see that Bud's hands were swollen with rheumatoid arthritis. Rube now understood the grimace of pain on his face when he offered his hand.

"How did you get to know Wendall?" asked Rube.

"Well, me and him wuz ole drinkin' buddies. 'At's where I met him, out there at the bar in Monroe. I always had trouble sleepin' at night because of ma hands and all. They hurt like the dickins, 'specially at night. So, I'd go over to the bar and get drunk before I went home to bed. It was either that or take them damn pain killers."

"Did he have other friends at the bar?" asked Amy.

"No 'am, not really. The others thought he'us mean actin'. Me and him was pretty much shunned by the regulars.

"I knew he was hurtin' inside from somethin' that happened earlier in his life. Last fall he stopped comin' for awhile. When he come back, he'us really worried about somethin', wouldn't talk much. We'd just sit and drink together. I guess we both figured some company was better 'n no company at all."

"Did he ever say what was bothering him?" asked Rube.

"No. He wouldn't talk about it. When I'd ask about it, he'd jest say it wasn't nothin', and order another drink. One night he cried, off and on, until I got tired and went home to bed. I reckin we'll never know what was botherin' him."

Rube felt sick to his stomach, but tried not to let on, for Amy's sake.

They left the funeral home, and walked Bud to his old Chevy pickup, loaded with trash and old beer cans.

When they got back to Amy's apartment, she asked Rube to call the preacher and tell him that she had decided to just have the service at the grave site, since she didn't expect many people to be there. As far as she knew, it would be her and Rube. Reverend Lee said that he would call the funeral director and have the bodies delivered to the Rose Hill Cemetery at two o'clock the next day.

How do you measure the value of someone's life? Rube wondered. Is it by the amount of wealth they accumulate? By the position they have achieved? By the strength of their character? By their good deeds, or how many times they attended church? Perhaps it was by how much they had suffered. He knew if it was based on the number of people who attended their funeral, Thelma and Wendall's lives had not been worth much. Still, they had conceived and raised Amy. If you have children who have children, etc., does that mean there is always a chance that your life can be redeemed?

When he got back to his apartment, he called Bud to let him know the new arrangements. He told him how much it would mean to Amy, if he attended. Next, he called his parents and asked them if they could please attend, since it was close to their home. Finally, he called Kristy's home, hoping Moochie would answer.

"Hello." It was Kristy.

"Hello, Kristy. Rube. It's nice to hear your voice. How are you doing?"

"Fine. Did you call to speak to Moochie?"

"Yes. But, I'm glad you answered. It's been a long time since we talked."

"I'll call Moochie to the phone," and Rube heard the phone as it was dropped to the counter.

Rube's relatively good mood was shattered. A slap in the face would have felt better. He wondered why he continued to expect the old Kristy to appear.

"Hey, Rube! How ya doin'?"

"Hi Moochie, I was doing pretty good until I talked to you know who, now I'm not so sure. How are you? And, how's our boy?"

There was a faint "click" on the line that went unnoticed by Rube or Moochie.

"Why I'm doin' fine, Honey. As for that boy, he's a sight to behold. Why, he's crawlin' all over the place. He laughs all the time, and has two teeth comin' in. He's the love of my life, Rube. I don't know what I ever did without him."

"That's wonderful, Moochie. I miss him and you a lot. I wish I could be there with you both as he goes through all these changes. Give him a big kiss for me when you get a chance.

"Moochie, I want to tell you something, and ask you to do me a favor. Are you out of earshot of Kristy?"

"Yes, I think so."

"Do you remember the nurse at Athens Regional when Kristy was there? The one that I told you I had gone to high school with?"

"Yes."

"She found both of her parents dead last week. From what the police say, her father hit her mother who fell and hit her head. Then, he shot himself."

"Well, Lord-a-mercy, sakes alive, that's awful," said Moochie.

"It was a terrible scene. She called me for help. The funeral is tomorrow, and I'm not sure that anyone will be there except Amy and me. I wondered if there is any way you and Sam could attend?"

"Well, Kristy goes to work tomorrow. What time is the funeral?"

"It's at two o'clock in Winder at the Rose Hill Cemetery. What time does Kristy get home?"

"She gets home about four thirty. So, maybe we could make it. We'll try."

"Okay. I appreciate it, Moochie. You're a good friend."

He had already talked to Sara, his office manager, on Friday. She made calls and rescheduled his Monday afternoon appointments.

He hung up the phone and walked into the living room. Amy was sitting on the couch with her shapely legs crossed. She was wearing a white tank top and pale blue shorts. She patted the space next to her as he crossed the room.

He sat down and put his arm around her. She rested her hand on his thigh. Didhe came over and laid down directly in front of Rube. He looked as though he expected something to happen, his head erect and his tail flipping from one side to the other.

"Didhe looks a little anxious, do you think he needs to go out?" said Rube.

"No, he went out a little while ago. He'll be okay," said Amy.

She continued, "It's so sad that my parents had no friends, no one to confide in, or even talk to for that matter. Daddy had Bud to talk to at times, but Mama had no one. She talked to me, of course, but not about things that must have been weighing on her soul. They both tried to protect me from anything that would make me sad. Daddy was able to draw a veiled curtain over the ghosts of his past by absorbing our modern day opiate, television, with his eyes, and drinking himself into a stupor. Mama always watched the programs he liked, in order to keep the peace. She chose to tiptoe around every aspect of their lives so as not to rile the monster inside the man she married. Looking back on it now, I can't understand why I didn't see what was going on and try to do something about it. Actually I did see, but chose to push it into the back of my mind. I guess I was just trying to protect myself."

"I would say that's a pretty normal reaction, especially since there was no real solution, and nothing you could do under the circumstances," said Rube.

"Maybe so, but I guess I'll always wonder if I could have made things better," she said as she snuggled closer.

So far Rube had been able to push his romantic desires aside and concentrate on helping Amy get over the loss of her parents. It was becoming more and more difficult, especially with her so close, and knowing that she had feelings for him as well. He turned slightly as she looked up into his eyes. His right hand reached for her shoulder as their lips met. He pulled her close, rotated his body and slowly placed his right knee across her leg. She moaned softly and rolled her body closer. Their breath became heavier as they kissed again. Suddenly Rube felt another breath and wetness on his arm. He turned his head and saw Didhe, mounted on his leg with a glazed look in his eyes as though Lassie had finally come home.

He rolled to the right and kicked straight out, trying to repulse this unwarranted molestation of his leg.

"Damn! Get out of here, you crazy dog!" he yelled as he got to his feet.

He turned to find Amy convulsed in laughter. He began to chuckle, fell back on the couch, and finally surrendered to the humor of it all. Every time they looked at each other, they started laughing again.

Finally, Rube said, "I still think your dog needs to go outside."

"I have a better idea. Follow me," she said as she took his hand, led him into the bedroom and closed the door.

The next day when they arrived at the cemetery, the caskets had already been unloaded and placed on the framework, secured by the straps which would later be used to lower them into the ground. There was a small mound of dirt between the caskets and larger ones on the outside. As Amy and Rube stood off to the side, the workers carefully draped green blankets to cover the framework, straps and loose dirt in front of the caskets. Several rows of chairs had already been set up under the tent.

Amy, wearing a black jersey, form-fitting, dress, turned away from the scene, burying her face in Rube's chest.

"Are we going to be the only ones here?" she asked quietly.

"It will be okay, even if we are the only ones here. I know Preacher Lee will be here in a few minutes."

As he comforted Amy, he saw an old Chevy pickup turn off the main road and onto the gravel trail leading to the gravesite.

"Amy, isn't that Bud's truck?"

"Yes. It looks like his. Maybe we won't be alone."

As the man got out of the truck, he lifted his shoulders and stood at his full height, but only momentarily, as he quickly realized the burdens that were his to bear. His shoulders gave way to gravity, and his head bent forward as he limped past the markers representing other souls who had already lost the battle of life. Briefly, Rube wondered, what is so precious about life that makes humanity cling to it so tenaciously?

Bud wore the same blue plaid sports coat, and had added a dark brown, clip on tie to go with his black shoes. He dressed up out of respect for his old friend, Wendall, but shaving had been too much to ask because of his arthritic hands. The gray-black stubble was beginning to show through his pale skin.

Amy gave him a quick hug, "Hi, Mr. Bud. Thanks for being here."

"Yes 'am. I got to thinkin' about Wendall, and felt honor bound to show my respect this last time."

"Hello, Bud, glad you could come," said Rube as he carefully shook his arthritic hand.

"Well, I didn't plan to come. I wus just sittin' there thinkin' about Wendall, feelin' sorry for him. Then, I got to feelin' sorry for myself. I won't have nobody to talk to now, when I go to the bar to drown my sorrows. I'll miss him."

Tears formed in Amy's eyes as Rube put his arm around Bud and led him toward the tent.

As they stood and talked, a gray sedan pulled in behind Bud's truck. They watched as Reverend Lee got out and walked toward them.

"Hello, Rube. How are you?"

"Fine, Reverend Lee. It's good to see you again. This is Amy Buchanan, Mr. and Mrs. Buchanan's daughter. And, this is Bud Arrington, a friend of Wendall's."

"I'm pleased to meet you both. Miss Buchanan, may I speak to you privately for a moment about the arrangements?"

As preacher Lee led Amy away, Rube and Bud sat down and continued their conversation.

When Rube's mother and father arrived, he walked out to greet them with a hug. "Thanks for coming, Mom and Dad. It will mean a lot to Amy."

Rube was thrilled when he saw Moochie's Grand Prix turn onto the cemetery trail.

"Hey! It's Moochie and Sam!" he exclaimed as he and his mother and father rushed over to greet them. Rube realized that his parents had only seen Sam a few times since he left the hospital.

He reached for the rear passenger door handle just as Moochie got out of the car, causing the door handle to drop a foot. He missed, but adjusted and quickly opened the door, released the strap on Sam and lifted him out of the car seat. Tears came to his eyes as he hugged his son to his chest.

"Hi, Moochie. Thanks for coming and bringing my big boy."

"No problem, Honey. Ain't he a sweetie?"

Rube's Mom and Dad stood by anxiously waiting their turn to hold the baby.

"Here, Mom and Dad, hold him for a minute. Hasn't he grown a lot?"

"He sure has. We haven't seen him for a long time. He really favors you, Rube, especially when you were a baby," said Mom.

Moochie grabbed Rube in a bear hug. He was thankful that he was taller than she, and still able to breathe once she let up on her initial squeeze. He couldn't help but notice a resident box of chocolate pralines on the front seat.

They made their way to the tent where they met Amy and Bud. Rube's Mom and Dad had known Reverend Lee for years, and Moochie had met him at the wedding. But, Sam was the big star and had to be held by everyone. Rube could tell that Amy was especially taken by the baby. When she saw him, her face lit up like a child seeing Santa Claus for the first time. She didn't want to give him up. Sam had been the only one able to divert her attention from the funeral.

Rube whispered to Reverend Lee that these were the only ones likely to attend.

"Rube, is there anything else I need to know before we start?"

"Not that I can think of. There are no spindles out here for me to get my head caught in, so things should work out just fine."

Preacher Lee burst out laughing. Then, caught himself and turned somber again as the others looked his way.

"Well, I guess we'll start the ceremony. Please take your seats."

Everyone was able to sit on the front row, with Amy and Rube in the middle. Mrs. Winters held the baby, and Moochie sat on two folding chairs (just to be safe) next to Bud. Bud had perked up a bit since he met Moochie, and Rube couldn't help but wonder if a burning ember had sparked to life somewhere under that blue plaid sports coat.

Rube sat next to Amy and gazed across the emerald green landscape while waiting for the ceremony to start. A dark green 1991 Jaguar rolled up behind Moochie's car, and what appeared to be an old man in a slouched hat and trench coat got out. This was curious because it was a warm day. The only thing Rube could make out under the hat was a mustache and goatee. The man leaned on a cane and hobbled down a row of markers as though looking for a specific grave.

Reverend Lee moved to a position in front of and between the caskets so as not to show partiality.

"Ladies and gentlemen, we are gathered here today to honor the lives of Thelma and Wendall Buchanan, Amy's parents, who were tragically taken from us a short time ago.

"Let us pray. Our Heavenly Father, we ask you to accept your children, Thelma and Wendall, into your kingdom. They both led difficult lives and we ask for your understanding and your grace. Please have mercy on their souls.

"Now, please listen as I read of David's confidence in God's grace in the twenty-third Psalm.

'The Lord is my shepherd; I shall not want.
He maketh me to lie down in green pastures:
he leadth me beside the still waters. He
restoreth my soul; he leadth me in the paths
of righteousness for his name's sake.

Yea, though I walk through the valley of the
shadow of death, I will fear no evil: for
thou art with me; thy rod and thy staff they
comfort me. Thou preparest a table before
me in the presence of mine enemies; thou
anointest my head with oil; my cup runneth
over. Surely goodness and mercy shall follow
me all the days of my life; and I will dwell
in the house of the Lord for ever.'

"Amy, I want you to know that God recognizes the good in all people. In spite of the hardships your parents endured, their goodness has been expressed in and through you. They were so proud of you, because you represented the God Spirit within them. You were their souls' connection to their Maker, and they sensed that.

"They are at peace now, and we leave them in the hands of a merciful and loving God.

"I quote to you from Ecclesiastes 3:20, 'All go unto one place: all are of the dust, and all turn to dust again.'"

The Reverend stepped back and turned to the left to recognize the deceased. His left foot landed on the deceptively solid looking green carpet, and quickly disappeared, followed by his right leg. His right hand clutched the rest of the carpet and began dragging it through the opening in front of Thelma's casket.

Rube had not been caught completely by surprise. A red light went off in his head when he saw the preacher turn and lift his left leg. Fleetingly, he thought, I wish I had warned him about the carpet covering the gap. Rube lunged forward from his chair, then dove, head first toward the gap. He was able to grab the back of the reverend's hand, but unable to stop the momentum, and was dragged in on top of the preacher.

"Damn!" mumbled the preacher, then realizing someone was there with him, said, "You didn't hear that, Rube."

"No Sir, I couldn't make out what you said. Are you okay?"

"Physically, I guess I'm all right, but any dignity that I had, has been crushed. Could you please get me out of here before that casket comes crashing down on us?"

"Okay, Preacher, I'll get you out. I'm so sorry about this!"

Amy had her head remorsefully bowed when the incident happened, and when she raised up, the preacher and Rube had disappeared.

"What happened!? What happened!?" she cried.

The rest of them sat in stunned silence momentarily.

The grandmother was holding Sam protectively to her chest.

Mr. Winters ran forward, laid down and peered into the hole to see if he could help.

"Are you all right? Rube, can you hear me? Give me your hand and I'll pull you out."

"We're okay, Dad. Let me get Preacher Lee up to the opening, and you can pull while I push."

Moochie said, "Lord-a-mercy, Honey. I ain't never seen nothin' like it. It's like one of them magic shows. Bud, why don't you see if you can help?"

"Yes 'am, I reckin I can help." He carefully removed his sports coat, and laid it across the back of the chair.

"Lord, Honey. Hurry up! They could be dead by the time you get around to it!"

Mr. Winters grabbed the preacher by one hand, and Bud told the preacher to grab his arm in stead of his hand, while Rube pushed from below. It was a different man who emerged from the hole. The hair which had been so carefully combed to cover the top of his head was now pushed over, making him look like a hippie on one side. His tie was askew, and the red clay had done its best to re-decorate his pants and coat.

Rube was able to climb out with a helping hand from his father and Bud. He was none too pretty himself, with red dust covering his head and face. He took his shoes off and poured the dirt out. For some unknown reason he looked up to check on the man in the trench coat. He was no where in sight and the Jaguar was gone. Rube scratched his head, then turned to Amy.

"I'm really sorry about this. Something bad always happens when I'm around. I should have stayed home so this could be a peaceful event. I'm sorry."

"Rube, it's okay. It wasn't your fault. Sometimes things just happen for no reason. I'm just glad you're both okay."

Sam was the only one who enjoyed the whole thing.

He was cooing, smiling and doing his best to talk. Rube wondered if his son had inherited the family curse.

"Rube, that was the bravest thing I've ever seen, you divin' head first like that to try to save the preacher," said Moochie.

"Well, I just saw it comin' and hoped I could get there in time."

The preacher had brushed himself off, straightened his tie, and raked his hair back into place with his hand. Even some of his dignity had returned.

"Well, ladies and gentlemen, I'm sorry about that interruption.. It just goes to show that even preachers misstep at times. I only wish that Rube had been a mite quicker with his heroic effort to save his old preacher. Anyway, I fully expected something to happen. I just didn't know when it would take place.

"Now, please allow me to close this ceremony with a brief prayer. Dear God, we thank you for your mercy and grace without which we would all be lost sinners. Please help us to express your love, your joy, your wisdom, your healing and your peace. And, give us the courage and patience to live this life to the best of our ability, and a sense of humor to get us over the rough spots. Thank you for being with us even during our foibles and ineptness. During those times, we pray that you will be able to laugh along with us. In Jesus name, we pray. Amen."

Somehow, the events of the funeral melded the small group together. They stood around hugging, smiling and consoling each other. Moochie gave Bud one of her famous hugs. The only problem was that he was not tall enough to keep breathing during the process. As his face disappeared between the massive breasts, Rube became genuinely concerned about

Bud's survival. Not wanting to interfere, he waited for what seemed like an eternity, then slapped Moochie on the shoulder to make sure he got her attention, saying, "Moochie! What about me? Don't I get a hug?"

She suddenly let go of Bud who blinked several times, and began to sink to the ground as he gasped for air. Rube grabbed him by the arm, and slapped him on the back with his other hand. His lungs sprang into action, causing a loud sucking noise as the air rushed in. As the color returned to his face, he said, "Wow! I've never been hugged like that before!"

Rube thought, I hope you never are again, 'cause I don't think you'd survive it. Before he knew it, he was fighting for his own life, as Moochie granted his request.

The group finally said their goodbyes and moved toward their cars, knowing that the funeral director needed to complete his job. There were more goodbyes and waving as the preacher and Bud drove away. Rube noticed earlier that Moochie had given Bud a slip of paper which probably contained her phone number.

Rube's mother cried softly as she handed Sam to him, not knowing when she might see her grandson again. Dad put his arm around her and walked her to their car.

Now it was Rube and Amy's turn to get teary eyed as he placed the baby in Moochie's arms, saying, "Thanks again. Maybe someday we can all be together, permanently."

"I hope so, Honey. But, in the meantime, don't you worry none, Ole Moochie's gonna take good care of this precious baby."

On the way home Rube and Amy sat quietly. Amy, thinking about her parents, and wondering where her relationship with Rube would go. He was the only thing she had left now, and she had loved him since high school. Could they make a life together?

Rube thought, since my son was born, every time I see him, I go from very happy to extremely sad when I have to leave. That's not right, but how can I ever make him a major part of my life? His mind shifted to the virtual certainty that

Wendall was the one who ran Kristy off the road, causing her mental condition and Rube's separation from his son. Would that eventually affect his relationship with Amy? He knew that he would have to call Patrolman Curtis and tell him of his suspicion so they could stop looking for the guilty party. Should he tell Amy, Kristy's parents or his parents, for that matter?

On Tuesday, he did what he knew he must do, even though he dreaded opening the whole matter up again. When the state patrolman came on the line, Rube said, "Patrolman Curtis, this is Rube Winters. My wife is the one who was run off the road a few months back. Remember, you suspected that it was a light blue vehicle?"

"Yes. I remember that case. We still haven't found the vehicle involved."

"Well, I think I know who did it, and I wanted to let you know so you can close the case."

"Okay, who do you think did it?"

"It was a man by the name of Wendall Buchanan. He was the father of a friend of mine from high school. Last week the friend called me, telling me that both of her parents were dead. You may have read about it in the newspaper. Mr. Buchanan apparently struck his wife, causing her death, then he shot himself. My friend called and asked me to help her through this. When we went to her parents' home, I saw the truck, a light blue 1979 Dodge pickup. It had a dent on the right, rear fender. Also, I found out that Mr. Buchanan frequented a bar in Monroe, and he might have been there on the evening of the accident."

"Dr. Winters, your evidence is circumstantial. Are you sure you want us to close this case?"

"Yes, I'm almost positive he did it. A man that I have since met, told me that he and Wendall drank together at a bar in Monroe. He told me that Wendall was very worried about something during that time, but he never told him what was on his mind."

"You may be right, but in order to close this case, I would need to interview his friend in Monroe, and perhaps his daughter."

"Patrolman Curtis, I was hoping to avoid that, since she has lost both of her parents, and is very upset right now. She wasn't living with them at the time. I don't believe that his friend knows anymore than I've told you. If you want me to, I'll come to your office and give a statement. The truck is still sitting at their home on Johnson Road in Barrow County."

"Okay, Dr Winters, you come to the Post and give a statement. In the meantime, I'll go have a look at the truck to see if the paint on the truck is a possible match with our sample from your wife's car. Still, you know that all of this will be part of the public record, and others will have the right to know. That is, if anyone ever asks."

"Yes. I understand. I just don't want innocent people to be hurt unnecessarily."

Inside Information

I don't mind telling you I cried while narrating the chapter about Amy's father, Wendall. Even worse was the affect it had on Thelma. The poor woman never did anything wrong, but she suffered and died because of what Wendall's father did. It's strange that life has ripples just like a pond. But, pond ripples end at the shore. The ripples of life may reverberate through generations.

Did you catch the author's, not so subtle, introduction of the stranger at the cemetery? I knew you would. It's so obvious. What you may not know is that Kristy called the guy the day before and hired him to keep an eye on Rube. The guy couldn't believe it. He was going to be paid to tail the man he was already tailing. Kristy didn't know it, but his father had given him the lifetime assignment of seeing that the family curse was carried out.

I have no idea why Kristy wants a private investigator to spy on Rube. See, I don't have a clue until it's clear in the author's mind.

The author is being very coy. He wants you to figure everything out. If he knew I was telling you this, he would cut out my tongue and throw it into his piranha aquarium.

Narrator

CHAPTER SEVENTEEN

The morning after the funeral Rube got a call from Moochie. "You're not goin' to believe this, Honey. That ex of yours has gone completely off her rocker. Last night she chewed my 'larger than life' ass, as she called it, out for going to the funeral. I said, why Lord-a-mercy, what's wrong with goin' to a funeral. She said, 'You thought I didn't know you were there, didn't you? You were sneaking around behind my back. But, I know what both of you are doing. I have my sources.' I said, well screw your sources. I will attend any funeral I want to. That's what I told her."

"Hmmm. I wonder if she's been listening to our conversations. We'd better be careful from now on," said Rube.

"You know what else she said? Said her and Coach Siefert were goin' to South Carolina this week-end and get married. Said you'll have to stay here and keep Sam. Just like that. No please or thank you. Can you believe it? 'Course I don't mind doin' it because I love my little Sam. But, can you imagine that? Those two have never gotten along, fight all the time. I've warned her about him many times."

"I'm sorry to hear that. Sounds like there's going to be problems down the road. I wonder why she's doing this," said Rube.

"I'll tell you why, Honey. She's a woman, and some women don't want another woman to have her man, even if she hates his guts and has kicked him out on the street. It's purely spite. That's all it is. Besides, she's crazy as hell."

"I'm sorry this is happening, Mooch. All we can do is hang in there. Do the best we can, and see what happens. I'll see you and Sam this week-end."

The next week Siefert moved in. Moochie kept her distance. She was hurt several times, but never said anything, when he referred to her as "Fatso" behind her back. She knew that he had been abusive to Kristy, and she worried about four year old Sam. Kristy always made sure Moochie was there when she went out, so he wouldn't be alone with Siefert.

One night Kristy had to go to a meeting at school. Moochie was in her bedroom folding clothes. She finished and entered the hallway leading to the living room. Sam dragged his truck with one wheel missing across the coffee table, leaving a scratch. Siefert screamed, "You little Bastard! What do you think your doin'?" He then slapped Sam across the room with an open hand.

Moochie's three hundred pounds had never moved so quickly, sore ankles and all. Within an instant she had Siefert by the shirt with both hands, lifting his two hundred pounds off the couch, carrying him with his feet dangling across the room, slamming him into the wall, leaving a hole that shadowed his body. His eyes were the size of ping pong balls as she grabbed him by the hair with her left hand, and reached around between his legs and grabbed his testicles with her right hand. She then drove his screaming face into the short shag carpet. Siefert lost his breath temporarily as Moochie looked up to see Sam with tears on his cheeks, but with a twinkle in his eye as a crooked grin played across his face.

Coach Butch caught his breath and screamed like a hyena caught in the jaws of a mother tiger. "Please, Moochie, please, please, please!"

Moochie let up slightly, "Now, listen to me, Coach. I don't want you to ever lay your wicked hands on Sam, or Kristy ever again. Do you hear me, Coach?" Her grip tightened.

He screamed, "Yes, yes. I hear you! I won't hurt them!"

"Ever?"

"Never! I promise with all my heart."

"Listen carefully, Coach. If you ever do, and I hear about it, I'll find you wherever you are, and I'll finish pulling your sorry testicles out by the roots. You do hear me, don't you, Coach?"

"Yes! Yes! Please Moochie. I promise!"

"Now, Coach, while we're havin' this little conversation, what's my name?"

"Moochie."

"Miss Moochie to you."

"Yes. Miss Moochie."

She tightened her grip. "Is my name Fatso?"

"No! No! No! Miss Moochie. Miss Moochie."

"Okay, now I'm gonna let you go, and I want you to go to your room like a good little boy. Understand?"

"Yes, Miss Moochie. Thank you! Thank you!"

She let go and Siefert crawled past Sam into the bedroom. A few minutes later, while cuddling Sam, she heard the bath water running.

When Kristy got home she knew what had happened, but asked anyway, "Moochie, what happened to the wall?"

"Well, Honey, your hubbie and I had a nice little heart to heart." That's all that was ever said.

The following week a "Cease and Desist" order was delivered to Rube's office. He was not to come within a hundred yards of Kristy's house or see Sam. He went to the back room, laid his head on the desk and wept. Kristy knew how to hurt him the most.

CHAPTER EIGHTEEN

Brett Garner, Rube's attorney assured him that his right to see Sam would be restored. It was a matter of time and the expense of fighting it out in court. The main charge was that Rube had taken Sam without Kristy's permission.

Rube wondered if there was a connection between the stranger at the cemetery and Kristy or was it just part of the curse. He concluded that Kristy had heard the conversation between him and Moochie, and that the "dust to dust" adventure of Preacher Lee followed the pattern of the curse. He didn't discuss it with Amy because she didn't believe in curses and didn't want to hear it. In fact, no one believed him when he told of his penchant for disaster. Well, maybe Preacher Lee was beginning to believe. Even so, he couldn't admit it openly. Preachers are supposed to be mentally stable. What would the church members say if he began to talk about curses?

Rube and Amy saw each other regularly, and spent the night together most of the time at his or her apartment. They talked briefly about marriage, but made no definite plans. Amy didn't want to push Rube into it, knowing what he had been through with Kristy, and his concern for his son. Rube, knew that he loved Amy very much, but at some level he still felt married to Kristy. He knew that didn't make sense, and he was too shy to discuss it with Amy. He believed that with time, his feelings for Kristy would dissipate, and that he and Amy would be married.

Each year Rube was required to take twelve hours of chiropractic education in order to be eligible to renew his license. His state organization offered a seminar at the Hyatt Regency Hotel on River Street in Savannah, and Rube signed up to attend. He asked Amy to go, but she was scheduled to work at the hospital that weekend.

It was a long drive from Athens to Savannah, and he didn't want to make it alone, so he called Wally Thomas, his old friend from Life College. He was now practicing in Washington, Georgia. Wally was a big man with a cherubic face, and a shock of thick brown hair curled down, covering most of his forehead. A mischievous grin was plastered on his face most of the time. Life amused him, and not even the smallest nuance of character or action escaped his notice. It was as though life was a special television program, created just for him. If there was humor in any situation, Wally would find it, and magnify it as necessary to make others appreciate it.

Rube hadn't seen Wally for a long time, and he was certain they would have a lot to talk about on the trip to the coast. Rube found his house amongst the old houses on Main Street, and pulled into the narrow driveway, got out and walked to the front door, dodging pine cones that had fallen on the path. The clapboard house had been white at one time.

Wally told him he had bought an older home and was planning to renovate it as he had the time and money. Millie, Wally's wife, met him at the door. An unfamiliar smell caught his attention.

"Come in, Rube. Welcome to our home in progress. I was just brewing some camomile tea. Would you care for some?" Millie smiled over her shoulder as she led him toward the kitchen.

"Sure," said Rube, never having tasted it before.

Millie's naturally curly, red hair was combed back on each side. She wore a form fitting knit top which accentuated her ample breasts. Her matching shorts were covered by an apron which she used for a hand towel.

"Wally's getting his things together. He'll be down in a minute. Come on in and have a seat. I'll pour our tea," as she got cups from the cupboard.

Rube noticed that when Millie wasn't smiling, she was waiting to smile. This was the first time he had had a chance to talk to her, although he met her briefly at Pretty Boy's wedding performance.

"Millie, I appreciate you and Wally coming to our wedding. I'm sorry it was such a disaster."

"Oh. That's okay. It was one of the best weddings we've ever been to. Wally and I still talk and laugh about it all the time. He always threatens to buy me a parrot for my birthday. By the way, how's Kristy doing? We heard she was in a bad accident, but the baby was okay."

"Yes, Sam was fine. He's a big, healthy boy. I never knew that I could love someone so much. As for Kristy, she never got over the accident. It changed her personality. She was never the same. She turned inward, and any love that she had for me was destroyed in that accident. I guess I didn't tell Wally yet, but Kristy and I were divorced this spring."

"Oh, Rube. I'm so sorry. She seemed like such a nice person. I can't believe it. I know that you've been through a lot. I wish we had known. Maybe there was something we could have done."

"I don't think so, Millie. There was nothing anyone could do, really. I tried everything I could, to keep it together, but it didn't do any good. Her mind was made up. I'm just thankful I was able to get Moochie to take care of her and the baby. You remember Moochie, Moochie Dunlop? She's the one that Pretty Boy pooped on. Remember?"

Millie grinned as she passed the honey for Rube's tea. "Yes, of course. How could anyone forget Moochie? I'm surprised the walls of that beautiful old church didn't crumble after what she said. You'll have to ask Wally to do his imitation of her after the bombing."

Wally, wearing a yellow golf shirt and Bermuda Shorts, overheard her comment as he came down the steps, and entered the dining room shaking his fist and saying, "You dirty bird! You s.o.b.! If I get my hands on you, I'm going to kill your feathery ass!"

Rube rose from his chair, and bent double in laughter.

Wally grabbed him by the shoulders, straightened him up and hugged him, almost, but not quite as hard as Moochie.

"Hey, Old Buddy! How's everything over in Athens?" boomed Wally.

"Hey, Wally! It's good to see you again, my old friend! Things are fine, I guess, but I miss the good times we had back in college. I'll tell you about the rest of my sorry life as we drive to Savannah."

"I'm ready to go, Pal! Just let me gulp my tea, and kiss my 'mother' goodbye," he laughed as he grabbed Millie and hugged the protest out of her.

She handed them each an apple as they went out the front door, "Here's a snack for you crazy things! Have fun. I love you."

Wally threw his suitcase into the back seat of Rube's car and piled into the front. They left Millie standing on the steps smiling and waving.

"Look at her, Rube. What a great girl I married!"

"I know what you mean," said Rube. "I've only seen her twice and already I'm smitten."

"Watch it, Buddy!" grinned Wally as he settled into his seat and reached across to adjust the air conditioner.

Rube told his friend about the accident, the breakup, finding Amy again and their present situation. Moving on, he asked, "How's your practice goin'?" For the rest of the trip it was only a matter of nodding, laughing and enjoying the stories that poured out of Wally.

"Did I ever tell you about what happened to me during my first week in practice?" asked Wally.

"No. What happened?"

"Well, my X-ray room and exam room were the same. I had a new girl that I was training to be my chiropractic assistant. She was supposed to take the patients to the room and say, 'Please take off all your cloths, and put on this gown. It opens in the back. Dr. Thomas will be right in. He will knock, and you let him know when to enter.'

"On Wednesday of that week, a new female patient was scheduled. Jane, the assistant, took her to the X-ray/exam room and gave her instructions. Either the assistant forgot to tell her to put the gown on or she didn't hear her. Anyway, I knocked on the door, and she said, 'Come in.' I opened the door and there she stood in the middle of the floor with no threads on. I grabbed my heart and shielded my eyes. Still, the image of those well rounded breasts, thin waist and well, you know, was burned into my memory forever. Finally, I said, 'Oh, here, let me help you with your gown.' She didn't seem that embarrassed. You know, since I've gotten to know that patient, it wouldn't surprise me at all if she did that on purpose. What do you think?"

"Could be," said Rube. "You know, Wally, sometimes women do things that we just don't understand, maybe we never will."

Wally removed the stem from his apple and laid it on the dash. Then, he bit into his apple, and immediately launched into his next story. "You know there are a lot of farmers around Washington, and I treat quite a few of them. There was this farmer who came in one day with severe pain in his low back. I did an exam and X-rays, and treated him the same day because he was in so much pain. Then, I didn't see him for several months. One day he called and came into the office. I said, Well, Jaybird (that's his nickname), where have you been? It's been such a long time, I figured the adjustment must have done you a lot of good.

"He said, 'No, Doc. The adjustment didn't help at all. But, the next day I was out loading some hogs onto my truck, running them up a narrow chute, when this big ole boar ran into me, knocked me into the fence and down on the ground, and two or three other hogs ran over me. I finally got under the fence and outta the way. When I got up, course I was sore, but, you know my back didn't hurt me at all. Yesterday it started aching a little, so I decided I'd better come on in to see my choirpractor.'

"That's what he always calls me, his choirpractor. So, I said, Well, Jaybird, do you mind if I send a few of my patients out to be trampled by your hogs? Just the difficult ones?

"He laughed. 'Sure, Doc. Send 'em on out, but I can't guarantee you what they'll smell like when they get back!' Every time he comes in, we get a big laugh about that incident."

By this time, they were both about finished with their apple, at least that's what Rube thought. Rube laid what was left of his in the empty ashtray and expected his friend to do the same. Instead, Wally kept right on eating until the core, seeds and all were gone. Then, he took the stem from the dash and began to massage his gums with it, finally popping it into his mouth so he could chew it up.

By that time, Rube couldn't stand it any longer and blurted out, "Wally, what in the hell are you doing? I'm becoming a little concerned that my gearshift knob might be next!"

He laughed, "Oh, no! Don't worry, Rube. I only eat cars made by American companies, not Nissans. No, I just believe that we should try to get as much nutrition out of our food as possible."

"Okay," said Rube. "Well, from now on I guess I'll have to start eating my watermelon, rind, seeds, and all."

Wally launched into yet another story and one followed another all the way to Savannah. Soon they pulled into the circular drive of the Bay Street entrance to the Hyatt, unloaded their luggage and checked in at the valet parking station. Rube had been to the Hyatt before, and always enjoyed going back. Everything about this beautiful, historical city was exciting to him. It was like stepping back into a special time and place, a feeling of suddenly being removed from the problems of the modern world. He liked to walk to one of the parks and sit on a bench among the live oak trees. There was a feeling of unconditional love and peace that he had never experienced in any other place.

He enjoyed wandering in and out of the small shops, especially the antique stores. The faint smell of shellac and polish on the old furniture gave him a sense of timelessness, and at the same time made him realize how many generations had passed into history since the furniture was made. At times like that, he thought about how brief our time on earth is, and how much there is to learn.

They walked into the expansive lobby and registered. A piano player was in the center of the raised lounge area with small groups of people sitting around, talking and casually listening to the strains of *Fools Rush In*, a Johnny Mercer tune.

"Would you care to dance?" asked Wally.

Rube laughed, "No thanks, you're not my type."

The escalator took them to the second floor where they checked in and got name tags, each choosing to take the X-ray classes taught by Dr. Russell Erhardt.

Rube enjoyed these gatherings. It was a chance to meet old friends from college, and the speakers were usually very good, although it was tiresome sitting all day. On Saturday evening, he and Wally ate at the Boar's Head Restaurant on River Street, then moved along the famous thoroughfare with the crowd, wandering in and out of shops. Turning back, they walked along the river, stopping at times to watch individual performers: a unicyclist/juggler, a one man band, a folk singer with his guitar, and a trumpet player. Rube was thankful that everything, so far, was going smoothly.

On Sunday morning, he and Wally ran into Andy McKay in the lobby.

Rube said, "Hey, Andy, how's that extremity adjusting class?"

"Fine," said Andy, "I've always been good at pulling someone's leg, now I can do it the right way."

Wally smiled broadly, remembering that Andy had originally planned to be a veterinarian. "Do you think that technique will work on a Chihuahua?"

"I don't see why not," said Andy, "but, I'd hate to try it on a jackass."

They laughed heartily, and talked of other happenings at college, as they moved into the hotel restaurant for breakfast.

They sat down and ordered their food, Wally asking for, "a bowl of fruit, two scrambled eggs, biscuits and gravy, and plenty of hot java."

Rube smiled, "Andy, I have to warn you, don't be surprised if Wally eats the flowers out of the vase, or even a cup and saucer, depending on his nutritional needs for the day."

"Okay, wise guy, see if I offer you one of my biscuits," said Wally.

Rube asked Andy, "Have you seen or heard anything about Dr. Wilkins? I think of him often, and just wondered what happened to him."

"Yes. I talked to Dr. Gooch not long ago. He told me that Dr. Wilkins is semi-retired. He lives near Hiawassee in North Georgia, limits his practice to only one day a week, and studies the rest of the time. You know, he was always the scholarly type. Dr. Gooch says he's obsessed with finding the meaning of life."

"Hell," said Wally, "I already know the meaning of life. It's for livin' and lovin' and eatin'!"

They laughed, turning their attention to other people and things of mutual interest. Rube stored the information about Dr. Wilkins in the back of his brain. He secretly wondered if his favorite professor might have some explanation for his own dilemma.

As they talked and drank their coffee, Rube noticed an unusual trait Andy had apparently developed since he left college. He could tell by the amused twinkle in Wally's eye that he had noticed the same thing. Every time Andy took a sip of coffee, he ran his lips along the edge of the cup in a swooping motion to catch any aberrant drop with the mistaken notion that it could escape to the relative freedom offered by the saucer.

Rube watched in fascination, but said nothing, not wanting to hurt his friend's feelings.

Wally had no such inhibition. "What the hell are you doin', my friend? There's plenty of hot java, so don't worry about spillin' any of it. I'll see that you get more if you run out. You're makin' me nervous, runnin' your lips along the cup like that."

"Oh, I'm not worried about losing the coffee, I just don't want to make a mess. It keeps the coffee from running into the saucer. My wife, Weymanda, is lazy as hell. She says if I can keep from getting coffee into the saucer, she won't have to wash it, and can put it right back into the cabinet. I guess I just got into the habit."

"Well, what the hell, Old Buddy, Weymanda's not here. So, drink up and don't worry about the spills. They've got plenty of help back there in the kitchen," said Wally.

Rube said, "Andy, I'm sorry, I never met your wife. Did you say her name is Weymanda?"

Andy took a sip of coffee, carelessly letting a drop roll down the cup. "Yep, that's what I said, Weymanda."

Wally said, "Damn, Man, where'd they come up with a name like that?"

"Well," said Andy, "It's a name that's been handed down through their family for generations. The first born daughter gets the name. I always call her Mandy when I'm not around the family. She's expecting right now, so I'm hoping and praying it's a boy."

Rube and Wally assured him they would be praying along with him.

As they paid their bill and left the restaurant, Rube suddenly felt like he needed to go sit on the park bench and commune with the oak trees.

"Listen fellas, I hate to deprive you of my company, even for a short time, but I think I'll take a little walk over to the park and back. Okay? I'll meet you in class, Wally."

"Okay, Pal, but don't be surprised if I've given up your seat to that good lookin' chiropractic assistant who sits in front of us."

"See you later," said Rube as he headed for the front door of the hotel. He was thinking about Amy, Sam, Kristy, and wondering if his life would ever get straightened out as he stepped from between two cars along the curb. He turned his head left just in time to see the horrified look on the parking attendant's face as the car struck Rube on the left side. Fortunately, his left foot was not planted. The blow knocked him onto the hood, rolling him over the top of the car. His left shoulder and head slammed into the trunk, then he bounced onto the pavement behind the 1989 Cadillac Seville.

He was stunned and motionless for what seemed like an eternity, but not unconscious. He was able to move his right hand, lifting it to his face where he began the search to see what damage had been done. His head hurt and was already swollen, but there was no open wound or blood that he could find. He was able to move his left shoulder, although it hurt. Rube thought, how could I be so careless and stupid? The young, Mexican driver was devastated. He ran to Rube, holding his face in his hands, sobbing, "Lo Sinto! I'm sorry! Are you all right? I'm sorry!"

Rube was so concerned about the driver that he gradually pushed himself to a sitting position, gasping, "I'm okay. Don't worry, I'll be just fine!" As he sat up he winced with pain in his left hip and right knee. In the distance he could hear a siren, someone must have called 911, he thought.

By this time, a crowd had gathered. "Are you okay? Are you hurt bad? Maybe you should lie back down. Can I get you anything?"

"No. I'll be fine," he lied. Now, the curse is getting serious, he thought.

He placed his hand over his increasingly painful left hip. "Could someone go get my friend, Wally Thomas, from the chiropractic seminar?"

A lady who was apparently attending the same seminar said, "I'll go. I know where it is. I'll get him," as she ran off.

By the time the emergency medical technicians arrived, Rube was standing with his arm around the driver, trying to console him. The young Mexican had managed to move them both to the side of the car and away from the noxious fumes of the still running automobile.

The medics moved quickly thru the crowd, asking, "Where's the injured? Please step aside!"

Someone pointed to Rube who lifted his good hand with his arm still around the driver.

"Are you okay, Sir?"

"Yes, I think I'll be fine. But, this poor man needs some help. He may need a sedative to calm him down." Rube's knees buckled slightly as the driver moved away.

"Okay, Sir, we'll check him too, but first we want to make sure you're okay?" He led Rube to the ambulance and ask him to lie down, so they could check his vital signs. They did, apparently to their satisfaction.

The lead technician said, "Sir, I think you ought to go with us to the hospital so you can be examined more thoroughly to make sure there are no broken bones, or other damage that might cause a problem."

Wally arrived just as Rube was saying, "I appreciate your concern, but I think I'll be fine. I'm sore all over, and I expect that to get worse before it gets better, but other than that, I'm okay."

"Are you sure? We'd be glad to take you to the hospital."

"No. I'm okay. My friend here will drive me back to Athens. I promise you, when I get home, I'll go to my doctor and have him examine me thoroughly."

"Well, okay. But, if you have any problem, get to an emergency room immediately."

"I'll do that. Thanks for your help."

Wally said, "Rube, are you really okay? I'm going to have them bring the car around right now. You sit on this bench over here while I check us out, and go to the room and get our luggage. Now, stay there. Don't move."

As soon as Wally left, two policemen arrived with lights flashing. One came over and sat with Rube, gathering the basic information, then finally asking for his version of what happened. Rube told him everything he could remember, eventually having to reassure the officer that he was all right. He told Rube that if he wished, they could mail him a copy of the report.

While waiting, Rube noticed a young man wearing an Atlanta Braves cap sitting across the circle drive, near Bay Street. He had sideburns to his lower jaw which pointed to his chin. He wore a trench coat and tennis shoes which struck Rube as odd. Sunglasses covered his eyes, but Rube could feel the stare.

Wally drove and talked all the way back to Washington.

Rube reclined his seat as much as possible, and although there was pain, it was not unbearable. He assured Wally that he would be able to drive home, but Wally wouldn't hear of it. He went inside and came back with Millie, keys in hand, to follow them to Athens. Rube didn't like people making a fuss over him. It was embarrassing. But he knew they meant well. He would do the same if Wally got hurt.

By the time they got to Athens, Rube was as stiff as starched underwear. They managed to get him inside and on his bed. They wanted to stay with him, but he assured them that he would call Amy who was a nurse, to come over and take care of him. Wally made sure by handing him the phone. "Here, Pal, call her up. We want to make sure someone's here before we leave. Besides, we want to meet this cute little nurse of yours."

"Amy, this is Rube, I called to let you know I'm back. I was in a little accident down in Savannah, and hurt my shoulder and legs. No! No! I'll be fine. I'm just very sore. But, please bring a suitcase with enough clothes for tomorrow. Okay? I love you too. See you in a few minutes."

He hung up the phone, "She'll be here shortly."

When she arrived, suitcase in hand, she rushed into the house, "Rube! Where are you?"

"In here, Amy. Come on in and meet my friends."

"Amy Buchanan, these are my good friends, Millie and Wally Thomas. They're concerned about my welfare, and wanted to make sure I'm in good hands. I told them you're the best."

Rube could tell that Amy and Millie liked each other immediately. They sat and talked as though they had been friends forever.

Finally, Wally said, "Well, Amy, we hate to drop this sorry, wounded chiropractor on you like this, but I know you'll take good care of him. You may need to have one of those "real" doctors look at him to make sure he's okay."

"Thanks for bringing him home to me. He's lucky to have true friends like you. I'll make sure he gets the best care possible. It was so nice to meet both of you. I hope we can get together soon, under better circumstances."

Wally patted Rube on the shoulder, "Bye, Pal. Take care of yourself. Let us know if there is any way we can help."

Millie brushed his cheek with a kiss, they waved goodbye, and Amy saw them to the car.

When she came back in, she sat on the edge of the bed, giving Rube a long, welcome home kiss. "Okay, Mister. Now tell me everything that happened."

He told her all the gory details. Then realized, "Amy! I've got to call Sara right now, so she can call and cancel all of my appointments for tomorrow!"

After he hung up the phone, Amy said, "I'll call Dr. Slocum's office first thing in the morning so they can arrange to have X-rays, a CT scan or whatever else they might need. As for right now, I'm going to draw a bath for you and get you settled into bed so you can rest."

Amy helped support Rube as he hobbled into the bathroom, then helped him get undressed. He climbed into the warm, steamy bath and sat down carefully.

Amy said, "You just relax and I'll give you your bath."

"Amy, I appreciate that and there's nothing I would enjoy more. But, I don't think that's a good idea right now. Just make sure the soap and towel is close enough to reach."

"Don't be shy. I'm a nurse. I can do this without any problem."

"It's not you that I'm worried about."

"Okay, well at least let me wash your back."

"All right, if you insist."

The next morning Amy called Dr. Slocum's office, and her supervisor so she could have the morning off to take Rube to the doctor.

After all of the tests were done and analyzed, Doctor Slocum came in to talk to them.

"Dr. Winters, I thought I recognized your name. How's your wife doing?"

"Oh, she's doing just fine. All of her wounds healed very well. But, she was never the same after the accident. It definitely changed her personality. We weren't able to keep it together, and divorced."

"The baby?"

"He's doing very well, as healthy as can be. Thanks for asking."

"Rube, I have a little bad news for you. Let me show you the X-rays. See this crack on the neck of the femur where it fits into the acetabulum?"

"Yes. I see that."

"This is your left hip, the one that hurts so badly. The fracture goes about half way through the bone. It's good that it didn't go all the way through, but the bad news is that you won't be able to bear weight on it for about six weeks. If you do, there might be a complete fracture, in which case we would have to do surgery and insert a pin in your hip to hold the bones together. Also, your knee is badly sprained. So, for right now, at least, you're going to have to be in a wheelchair."

"Oh, no!" said Rube. "What in the world will I do about my patients?"

Amy said, "It'll be okay. We'll think of something."

"I'm sorry to be the bearer of bad news," said Dr. Slocum.

"That's okay, Doc," said Rube. "I'll just have to find someone to take my place."

Dr. Slocum stood up, "We'll lend you one of our wheelchairs until you can pick one up. Do you need a prescription for pain?"

"No thanks, I'll be fine."

After Amy got Rube loaded into the car with the wheelchair in the trunk, they drove to Rube's office. He called Dr. Austin at Life, and asked him if he knew of a recent graduate who might be interested in filling in for six weeks.

"The only one that I can think of that might be able to do it would be Dr. Reese McCord. He has a Georgia license, but is waiting to take the state board exam in Alabama. He has decided to go back to his home state to practice. I'll look up his number for you. Just a minute."

Rube wrote the number down and called him immediately. Dr.McCord sounded interested and they arranged to meet the next day.

As soon as Dr. McCord walked into the room and they shook hands, Rube knew he was the man for the job. He was about Rube's height, but weighed considerably more. He was not fat, he was just a big man. His short hair was reddish brown, and his face had an outdoorsy glow. He smiled easily and told Rube of his background, explaining why he had decided to become a doctor of chiropractic.

When the interview was over, Rube offered him the job which Reese was happy to accept because he could make some money while waiting for the Alabama exam.

Amy had taken a leave of absence from her job to take care of Rube against his objections. He didn't think it was fair to Amy because she had to give up her income. At the same time he didn't know how he would get by without someone to help. It was a low point in his life, and he wondered what else could possibly happen to him.

CHAPTER NINETEEN

The walls of the apartment began to close in on Rube. He had never been confined, always busy with school or work, and daytime television only made him more depressed. The only positive about the whole situation was that he had more time to read. For the first time, he could read the professional journals cover to cover, and he discovered *Healing Field* by M.T. Morter, Jr. That was the beginning of his 'real' education about health and healing.

One evening after dinner, as Rube was telling Amy how boring it was to sit around all day, he flipped through the mail and noticed a brochure from a company in Florida selling time share condominiums.

"Amy, have you ever been on a vacation?"

She looked surprised. She thought for a minute, then said, "No. Come to think of it, I've never been on a trip of any kind. My parents never had the money to travel. Why?"

"I was thinking, since we have nothing else to do, that we might take a trip?"

"Rube! I can't leave the hospital. They depend on me."

"But, you have two weeks vacation coming."

"Yes, but I've already taken a leave when you first got hurt. I've never had reason to take vacation time. They just pay me at the end of the year."

"Well, now you do. We could go down to Destin, Florida. I spent a vacation there with my parents once, and have always wanted to go back. After a couple of days we could drive over to Biloxi, Mississippi and see the casinos. What do you think?"

"I don't know, Rube, I hate to leave the patients, but that sounds fun. I'll ask my boss, and see what she says."

"Great!" said Rube with growing excitement. "It might be hard with me in a wheelchair, but at least we'll enjoy the beach. It's a beautiful place."

Amy could hardly wait to get home the next day. "Rube!" she said, running in breathlessly, "Guess what? She said this would be a good time for me to take a vacation." She ran to where Rube was on the couch and gave him a big kiss and hug. There were tears in her eyes.

Rube suddenly realized what this would mean to Amy.

Her first vacation. Now he knew it was the right thing for both of them. He pulled her to him, and they held each other for a while. Rube hoped he could leave the recurring disasters behind in Athens and a shudder rippled through his body at the thought.

"What's wrong?" said Amy.

"Oh nothing," said Rube. "I just got a sudden chill."

Rube called the next day and made reservations at the Hilton Hotel on the beach.

They found the room overlooking the ocean tastefully decorated in bright colors. There was a small deck outside the sliding doors. By this time, Rube could put a little weight on his left leg, and had become proficient at moving himself from the wheelchair to the car seat, the bed, etc. And, Amy was an accomplished wheelchair "driver," as Rube called her.

"Come on, Rube. Let's go exploring!"

Amy had spotted a large outlet mall on the way to the hotel, and Rube, suspecting she would like to go there, said, "Why don't we get something to eat, then go to the mall?"

"That's a great idea!" said Amy, as she released the brake, twirled him around and out the door.

Amy whipped him in and out of the stores, buying small items which she placed in a bag slung over the handle on the wheelchair, but mostly looking. Amy asked Rube if he could fend for himself in the *Bugle Boy* store while she looked in the ladies store next door.

"Sure," said Rube. "No problem."

While Rube was aimlessly pushing himself through the store, he noticed a pair of sunglasses on the floor. Since he had forgotten to bring his, he picked them up and tried them on. Good fit. He thought, I know I should turn these in, but if I do, they'll only be thrown in a box and forgotten. I think I'll keep them.

When he got outside Amy immediately said, "Where'd you get the sunglasses?"

"Oh, I found them in the store. They don't sell sunglasses, so I figure someone lost them."

"Why didn't you turn them in?"

"Well, I just decided that the person was not likely to return, looking for them. How do they look?"

"Rube, you know that's not right."

"Yes, I know, but it's only a cheap pair anyway. The person will probably never miss them."

When they got back to the hotel, Amy said, "Let's go to the beach."

"Amy, I can't walk around and it would be too hard to push the chair in the sand. You go ahead. I'll sit by the pool."

"Great! Let's go change into our swim suits."

When they got to the room, Rube shifted to the side of the bed, and got undressed. While watching Amy get undressed, he got a brilliant idea.

"Amy, come over here a minute, I have a secret to tell you."

"Rube, can't it wait? I'm about to put my suit on."

"No. It's very important. I don't want to forget it."

She came over and sat next to him. He leaned over and whispered in her ear, "I love you."

"Rube, you tricked me! I love you too." They kissed.

Then, she stood up and moved between his legs, first pulling him to her, then, pushing him back onto the bed.

A wooden walkway led from the pool about a third of the way to the beach.

"Push me as far as you can, and I'll sit and watch while you walk on the beach."

"Okay, Honey. Do you still love me?"

"Oh, I sure do," said Rube. Adding, "Even more now than I did an hour ago." He looked back and smiled.

"Okay, wise guy, next time I might not fall for your trick," as she pinched him on the shoulder.

Amy pushed Rube onto a wider part of the walkway next to the shower where people washed the sand off when returning from the beach. It was a perfect day, and the beach was as beautiful as Rube remembered. There were two colorful sailboats on the horizon, and a speedboat raced horizontally, leaving its ever rising plume of spray. Seagulls gathered in groups, competing for small scraps of food left behind. Rube could see, hear and even feel the pulse of the waves as they rhythmically made their last rushing then whispering protest at having to leave mother ocean. He had the same sensation as when he sat amongst the vast live oaks in Savannah, of being a part of something much greater than himself, as though he was only a step away from being in touch with the great I Am. Rube thought, if you were looking for the earth's pulse, this is where you would find it.

Rube was jarred back to the earth plane by the laughter of two small boys racing to see who could get to the shower first. Glancing past them to a bench a few feet away, he noticed a pair of sunglasses, and wondered why he hadn't seen them before. He instinctively felt for his own "found" pair, then rolled over beside the bench. Looking out at the ocean, trying to get "the feeling" back, he glanced fleetingly at the silver glazed lens, hoping their owner would return and pick them up. It won't hurt to look at them, he thought, as his hand shot out to retrieve the obviously "lost" glasses. His left hand automatically removed his current shades, as his right hand deftly set the new ones on his nose and pushed them into place. They fit perfectly, curving around and covering his peripheral vision as well. Wow, he thought, it's as though they were made especially for me. He slipped the other pair into his shirt pocket, and sat there feeling "cool."

When Amy returned, she said, "Hey, where'd you get the new shades?"

Rube, a little embarrassed, said, "I found them on the bench. Someone just left them lying there. How do they look?"

"They look fine, but I hope you're not thinking of keeping them."

"Why not? Really, there's no place to turn them in. If I leave them here, someone else will pick them up. Besides, they fit me perfectly, and this would give me an extra pair."

"Okay," said Amy, "But, don't say I didn't warn you."

As she pushed Rube back up the wooden walkway, she reached up and slapped her cheek, "Ouch! A bug just bit me."

"What kind of bug?"

"I have no idea, but it's okay now."

That evening, they went to downtown Destin and had dinner at the seafood restaurant, on the beach. Rube parked next to the walkway which ran parallel to the beach and led up to the restaurant. It was a struggle for Amy because it was a steep incline, and she was wearing high heels to accentuate her shapely legs. Working together, they powered the wheelchair to the top and went in to eat. They were fortunate enough to sit next to the plate glass windows overlooking the Gulf with all the beautiful yachts tied neatly in their slips along the dock. Rube noticed Amy rubbing her cheek.

"What's wrong? Is that where the bug bit you?"

"Yeah, it's beginning to itch and ache a little. But, I think it'll be okay."

Rube ordered Chardonnay for Amy and a Merlot for himself which they sipped until dinner arrived. For a long time he had wanted to discuss the troubling plague which seemed to follow him around. She was an important part of his life now, and had the right to know.

"Amy, I want to talk to you about something that's been bothering me."

"Oh, did I do something wrong?"

"No, not at all. You've been wonderful. I know you remember our first date, the slippery mud, and your father shooting at me. And, you know what happened at your parents' funeral. Well, things like that have been happening to me all my life----my wedding which I never told you about, Kristy's accident, my accident, et cetera. I call it 'The Curse.' The trouble, and the reason I'm bringing it up again, is that things seem to happen to people around me too. I just want you to understand."

"Rube, you can't be serious. Are you kidding me?"

"No, no, I'm very serious! No one ever listens to me when I talk about it, but it's true." He took Amy's hand, "And, there's something else. I think someone is following me. I don't know if he has something to do with the curse or if he's been hired by someone like Kristy."

Amy reached up and felt her now swollen and red jaw. "I can't believe what you're saying. This is the twentieth century. There is no such thing as a curse. What makes you think someone's following you?"

"There's a man who looks familiar even though he wears different disguises. I saw him in Savannah, and he was at the cemetery when your parents were buried, driving a dark green Jaguar. Remember the old man?"

"Old man? I didn't see any old man."

Rube shrugged and decided to drop it. "How's your jaw?"

"Oh, it's a little swollen and sore, but it'll be fine."

"Good," said Rube as their food arrived, "Just think about what I told you."

After dinner Amy pushed Rube along the dock where all the boats were moored. It was a pleasant night as they strolled along waving to the few people they saw. There was a faint mixture of salt water, dead fish and grilled steak in the air. They sat at the end of the dock for a few minutes, each caught up in thought.

Finally, Amy said, "It's getting a little chilly out here. Do you mind if we go back to the hotel?"

"No. I don't mind at all. It's been a long day. Besides, we need to get up early and head over to Biloxi."

When they got back to the restaurant, they turned right to descend the long, steep walkway to the car. They had gone only a few steps when Amy's right heel caught in a crack. Her ankle turned, and her foot dropped off the shoe, landing hard on the wooden plank. Her knee buckled to the right causing tremendous pain.

Amy screamed, "Rube, my knee!" and fell across his right shoulder. He caught her with his right hand and held on to keep her from falling to the walkway. Amy tried to put her right foot down, but screamed in pain, and the wheelchair began to pick up speed.

Amy kept screaming, "Oh, Rube, it hurts so bad! I think I broke my leg!"

By this time the wheelchair was moving pretty fast. Rube thought, I've got to do something to slow us down. He reached with his left hand to grab the wheel and caught two of his fingers in the spokes, yelling, "Ouch! Damn!"

Amy's weight on his right shoulder and arm was pulling them both to the right as he desperately tried to hold on to her.

"Rube! Do something! Stop us! Help! My leg is killing me!"

Rube looked up and saw a young couple, both with long hair and tie-died shirts, coming up the walkway. He yelled, "Watch it! Get out of the way! We can't stop!"

As they whizzed by, the kid yelled, "Cool man! Rev it up, Dude!"

Rube moved his right foot off to the side of the chair and dragged it to help slow them down. He thought of the wheel brake and reached for it with his hurt fingers, knowing he must be very careful not to pull too hard, or it would jerk the chair around, causing them to crash.

"Hold on Amy!" he yelled as he began to apply pressure to the rubber wheel. It began to smoke and Rube had to let up to keep it from stripping away. This managed to slow them down about the time they reached the level part of the walkway.

They came to a halt two feet from the right, front fender of their car.

"Amy, I'm going to slip out from under you. You can rest across the wheelchair while I open the car and get you inside. Okay? Use your right hand to hold onto the arm."

"Okay, but be careful!"

"Don't worry. We'll make it."

He hopped on one leg over to the car, unlocked the doors, then, the trunk. As he made his way back to Amy, he said, "Now, you just hold onto the wheelchair and I'll pull you over next to the door."

"Okay. The pain is better now. I can push with my good foot. Go slow!"

Just then the hippie couple came running up, "Hey, Dude, are these yours? I think you dropped them."

"Yes---I mean no. What I mean is, I just found them."

"Hey, Man, I lost a pair just like this on the beach today. They might be mine!"

"Okay, Dude, I mean young man. Maybe they are yours. Why don't you go ahead and keep them?"

"All right, Man, if you're sure it's okay---."

"Oh, that'll be fine. I've got another pair in my pocket." He caught Amy's eye as she glanced sharply at him when he took the other pair out and slipped them on.

As Amy's pain subsided she was able to stand on one foot, and even put some weight on the injured knee. She worked her way to a sitting position on the passenger side. Rube rolled the chair to the back of the car, folded it, and put it into the trunk. Then, he hopped to the driver's side, got into the car and said, "We'd better get you to the hospital." Amy moved her leg around, saying, "No, .I can move it around, so I don't think it's broken. It's probably just sprained, but my shoe is ruined."

Rube smiled, "Well, we could take your shoe in, but I'm pretty sure your insurance won't cover it." Amy slapped him on the shoulder.

As Rube backed the car out, he noticed a green Jaguar moving slowly down the street. "Amy! Look to your left. See it? That's the car I was talking about."

"Hmmmm. Yes, I see it, but that doesn't prove anything."

"I know, but just wanted you to see it."

Rube drove them back to the hotel. In the parking lot, they were struggling to get out of the car when an older couple walked by. They stopped and the lady said, "Hello, there. It looks like you all are having trouble. Is there anyway we can help?"

Rube said, "Yes Ma'am, we just had an accident with the wheelchair and my friend hurt her knee. We're trying to get to our room."

The man said, "We'll be glad to help. Just get the wheelchair set up and I'll roll your friend to the room and then come back and get you. Love, you just point me in the right direction."

As Rube sat in the car waiting, it dawned on him that the old man was almost blind.

When they got back with the chair, Rube hopped over and sat down, "I hate to put you to all this trouble, but we've had a run of bad luck lately."

The old man said, "Oh, it's no trouble at all. We're always looking for someone to help. Aren't we, Love?"

"We sure are. It makes us feel so much better when we help another person. By the way, Mr.---. I'm sorry I didn't catch your name. Our names are Ollie and Jeb Weatherford."

"Rube---Rube Winters."

"Well, Mr. Winters, I was just going to compliment you on your glasses. They look just like a pair my husband had until he lost them. They were to protect his eyes from the sun until he got inside and put his prescription glasses back on."

Oh no, thought Rube. He was afraid to ask, but knew that he must. "Oh, where did he lose them?"

"We were at the outlet mall, looking around, and he must have laid them down or dropped them. We went back to the mall to see if we could find them, but no such luck. We were just returning from there when we saw you."

Rube took off the glasses and put his other hand over his eyes. Lord, forgive me, he thought.

"Mr. and Mrs. Weatherford, I'm embarrassed. I guess a better word would be humiliated. I must say, these are probably your glasses. I found them at the mall early this afternoon in the 'Bugle Boy' store. I should have turned them in, but I decided to keep them. I'm so sorry."

"Jeb, we were in the *Bugle Boy* Store, weren't we?"

"Yes, I think so, Love, but I can't be sure since I don't see too well."

Rube said, "Here are your glasses, Mr. Weatherford. There is no doubt in my mind that they are yours. All I can do is ask you to please forgive me."

"Why, of course we forgive you, Son. We learned a long time ago that it does no good to hold a grudge. God taught us to love one another, and that's what we try to do."

Rube was speechless as they opened the hotel door and rolled him inside. He managed to mumble "Thank you," as they left.

Rube sat there, looking straight ahead.

Amy said, "Rube, what's wrong?"

He said, "You're not going to believe what just happened." When he finished telling her the story he said, "You were right. I promise to never again take something that doesn't belong to me."

It was an ordeal, but they finally got ready for bed. They turned out the light and both lay there thinking, wondering and hurting. Finally, Rube reached over and took Amy's hand, "Sweetie, there must be some lesson in all of this that I'm just not getting. I was raised in a family with strong religious beliefs. I've always believed in God. Maybe that's where the answer lies."

Amy rolled on her side and put her hand on his chest. "Don't worry, Rube. It'll all work out. I just know it will."

CHAPTER TWENTY

The next morning when Amy awoke, the right side of her face was so swollen that her eye was closed tightly. Startled, she cried, "Rube, help me. I can't open my eye!"

Rube sprang up and examined her face, "Let's get dressed. I'm taking you to a doctor."

They found an independent, medical emergency clinic and were able to see the doctor right away. He prescribed Benadryl and antibiotics.

As they drove to the drugstore to get the prescriptions filled, Rube said, "Sweetie, we may as well forget about this trip and go on home while we're still in one piece."

"No, no, Rube! I'll be okay. The Benadryl will take affect shortly. My leg is already better. Let's continue our trip."

When they arrived in Biloxi, Rube pulled up in front of the hotel/casino and motioned a porter over. Handing him the keys, "Could you please get my wheelchair out of the trunk, and bring us one more from the hotel. You do have a loner don't you?"

"Yes, Sir. Don't worry. I'll take care of everything."

Rube slid out and hopped to his chair, then came around to where the boy was helping Amy out. The young man's face went from a very pleasant look when he saw her leg emerge, to one of shock when he glanced at her grotesquely swollen face.

Rube called room service for lunch, rolled down the hall for ice, and using a hand towel, made an ice pack for Amy's face. After lunch, she lay in bed with the ice pack while Rube sat up, halfheartedly watching a basketball game. At one point he leaned over her, looking into her good eye, and said, "I'm so sorry all of this happened. I love you, and I don't want to hurt you."

"I know. I love you too, Rube. I'll be just fine. It's not your fault." She did not seem as convinced as she had been before.

By four o'clock the swelling had gone down, and Amy felt better about her appearance. They decided to go down to the casino in spite of both being in wheelchairs.

The casino was a vast, carpeted cavern with hundreds of people walking among the flashing lights of the one armed bandits, roulette wheels and blackjack tables. They stood for a moment, fascinated by the scene and anxious because neither of them had gambled before. Rube bought two buckets of tokens, and they set out to find just the right machines. They pulled up beside a woman in her fifties with bleached blond hair and a mini-skirt that ended at the middle of her thighs. She was turned slightly away from them with one leg propped up on the stool next to her. There was a large bucket of tokens on her right. When they entered her space, she slowly turned and looked down from her stool, flashing a bright red and white smile that revealed one gold tooth on the left. "Well, hello there, Handsome," she said to Rube.

"Hi," said Rube, "I hope we're not disturbing you. We could move to another machine."

"No, No, don't be silly, Goodlookin'. You're not botherin' me at all. What in the world happened to you two?"

Rube, not wanting to be rude, gave her a brief description of their woes, then turned and began playing his machine.

Charlene, their new found friend from Decatur, Alabama continued to glance at Rube and flash a smile every now and then. Finally, she turned toward Rube, re-crossing her legs in front of him, "Why, you all are such a sweet couple, and I feel so sorry for you. I'll tell you what I'm gonna do. I've won a lot of money here today, and I'm gonna buy your dinner tonight. In fact, I'm gonna buy your dinner and your breakfast tomorrow morning. Amy, you stay here and watch our spots while I take Rube up to the third floor so we can pick up the tickets."

"Well, that's very nice of you Miss Charlene. We appreciate it. Will you be okay for a few minutes, Amy?"

"Sure, I'll be right here losing my tokens."

Thelma wheeled Rube over to the elevators and pushed the button. She waited until an empty elevator arrived, then pushed the chair on board. As soon as she pressed the third floor, she leaned over in front of Rube's face and said, "You are the most handsome man I've ever seen." Then, she kissed him long and hard. He could feel her gold tooth pressing against his lip. He was stunned at first, then began to struggle free. "Miss Charlene, please don't do that!" He grabbed her wrist and pushed her away.

"Sugar, I've got a room on the sixth floor. Would you like to see it?"

"No, no, Miss Charlene! I can't do that! I don't want to be rude, but, I just can't do that!"

"Okay, Sugar. Relax. I was just checking to see if you're loyal to your friend downstairs."

As the door opened, Charlene said, "Come on, let's go get your tickets."

On the way back, Rube was hoping and praying that there would be more people around. As they approached the elevator, he saw a young couple standing there, and relaxed.

A short time after they got back to the machines, Rube complained of not winning and suggested to Amy that they try another section. They thanked Charlene profusely and moved on. As soon as they were a safe distance away, he told Amy what had happened. All she could say was, "Unbelievable. Unbelievable."

While feeding the new machines Rube glanced to his right and back one row. The man on the end machine was wearing a black coat with a rounded white collar, and Rube assumed he was a priest. Strangely, he had on an Atlanta Braves baseball cap and black, high top tennis shoes. Rube tapped Amy on the arm and flipped his thumb toward the man. When they looked his way, the man turned away and crossed his legs on the other side.

"Come on, let's go meet the 'father' and get a better look," said Rube as he grabbed Amy's hand and helped her off the stool and into her wheelchair.

"But----," protested Amy.

They rolled over beside the man until he glanced over his shoulder and slowly turned around.

Rube said, "Hello, Father. We couldn't help but notice your cap. Are you a Braves fan?"

"Yes. I live near Atlanta and see them every chance I get. Looks like you folks are having a hard time."

Amy stood dumbfounded as Rube said, "Yep. We sure are. It seems like someone out there is trying to make our lives miserable. I don't know if they're holding a grudge or just harboring hate. Anyway, it doesn't seem like a Christian thing to do. What do you think?"

Anger flicked in the man's eyes for an instant, then, "Well, my children, hate can be a very powerful motivating force. Sometimes hate takes on its' own face, even after the reason for hate is gone. Have mercy upon those who hate, for they suffer too." He turned back to his machine.

As they rolled away, Rube said, "That s.o.b. I know he has something to do with what's happening to us."

"Maybe so, but did you notice his blond hair and dark blue eyes? Why, he's a spittin' image of you. He could be your brother." Amy looked confused.

Rube hadn't noticed the similarity, but said, "Hmmmm. I wonder what his real name is."

In spite of all that had happened, they had a good meal at the hotel restaurant, then sat in the main bar for awhile, listening to a jazz combo, sipping a glass of Pinot Grigio.

Amy said, "Rube, maybe you're right. Maybe we do need to go home. But, I want you to promise me that we'll go on another vacation some time."

Rube sank into his seat, feeling terrible that he had ruined Amy's first vacation. "I'm sorry about all of this. I promise you that I'll find out the truth about my problem. When I do, we'll go on the most wonderful vacation that you can imagine."

They retired early, helped each other with their shower, slipped into bed, and held each other tight for a long time.

Finally, they made love like two people who just got their first disability check.

Rube lay awake for a long time trying to sort things out as his mind jumped around like a wild monkey. Finally, he decided that something had to be done. He had to get to the bottom of his problem.

By the next morning Amy was much better, the swelling in her face was gone, and she was able to walk with a limp and some pain.

The drive to Athens was uneventful. When they entered the apartment, Rube noticed a sheet of paper taped to the television screen. He yanked it off. "Amy, take a look at this."

To solve the curse you must find a vortex with
a receptive mind. It will be higher than the
ancient pyramids, but simple if you listen with
your heart. Do not judge, but wait upon the truth.
There is only one truth and one source to seek.
Open your heart and listen quietly. It will come.
It can not be found with boundless energy, drive
and determination, but only with pure, unconditional
love, even for those you hate.

They read the message together. Amy said, "I don't understand."

"Neither do I, but there may be clues that will help us find answers. Right now, I'm concerned about how they got in here." A thorough search was made, but there was no sign of forced entry. That worried Rube even more. Do they have a key? He wondered.

While Amy put things away, Rube called to check on Sam and Moochie.

"Hello, Moochie speaking."

"Hi, Moochie Speaking. How are you?"

"I'm doin' just fine, Honey. How was your vacation? You weren't gone very long."

"No. Amy hurt her leg, and we decided to come on home. How's that big boy?"

"Why, you wouldn't believe it, Honey. He's walking all over the place---into everything. I have to watch him like a hawk."

"I can't wait to see him. I don't know how much longer I can stand this court order not to see my own son."

"I understand. I'd sneak him over to see you, but I'm afraid she'd find out and have you put in jail."

"How's she doing, Moochie?" It always made him sad, and lonely, deep down inside when he thought of Kristy.

"Oh, she's doin' okay physically, I guess. She'll still snap your head off, if you're not careful. I worry about her, though. I hear her crying at night, so I know she's not happy."

"I'm sorry about that. I'd give anything if there was some way I could help her. How's Coach Seifert doing?"

"I don't really know. He stays clear of me since I put the squeeze on his link to the next generation. Remember, I told you about our little chat?"

"I do, and I'm thankful you're there to watch out for Sam. If it had been me, I might have killed him."

"By the way, Bud and I have been seein' each other right regular. I'm tryin' to think of some way to ask him to marry me, and make him think he asked me. You know what I mean?"

"That's wonderful, Moochie! I'm glad you all found each other, and I'm sure you'll find a way. You might suggest that he take you out to dinner. When he does, say 'Since you asked me out to dinner, I assume you have something special to ask me.' If that doesn't work, you might have to knock him in the head and carry him off to the preacher."

Moochie laughed out loud, then cackled 'til she got her breath. "Lord-a-mercy, Honey, you're as crazy as I am."

He rested the phone on the cradle only for a minute before making a second call.

"Hello. Yep, 'is here's Dr. Gooch. Who's speakin'?"

"Dr. Gooch, this is Rube Winters, one of your old students. I doubt if you would remember me."

"Why hell yes, I remember you, Boy! Ain't you the one that spit your gum down that dummy's throat?"

"Yes, Sir, I hate to admit it, but that's me."

"Well, what can I do fer you? You didn't get one of your patients caught in the adjustin' table again, did ye?"

Rube laughed. "No, Sir. I just need to ask you if you know how I might get in touch with Dr. Wilkins?"

"Why I shore do. I jest talked to him last week. Ye know, it's kinda weird, he asked me if I'd seen you lately. Said he's a wantin' to talk to you about somethin'. Hell, he's a smart feller, but he's way out yonder, ye know what I mean?"

"Yes, Sir."

"Well, here's his number. Ye got a pencil or sharp stick to write it down with?"

"Yes, Sir."

"It's area code 706, 546-8520. Ye got it?"

Rube felt the urge to say, "Yes, Sir, I've got it rat cheer," but instead said, "Yes, sir. I've got it. Thank you so much for your help."

"Okay, Rube, when you talk to him, say howdy for me."

As soon as he hung up the phone, he dialed the number given. It rang several times before he heard a distracted sounding "Hello."

"Dr. Wilkins, is that you?"

"Yes. May I ask who's calling?"

"This is Rube Winters, one of your students. I hope I didn't disturb you."

"Oh, no. I was just meditating. It takes me a while to come out of it. I'm glad you called. I've been meaning to talk to you for a long time."

"Dr. Wilkins, this may sound strange, but I've been needing to talk to you also. I've been having problems in my personal life, and somehow I feel that you might be able to help me. I wondered if I could arrange a meeting with you?"

"Of course you can. When would you like to come?"

"Would Thursday afternoon be okay? Also, is it all right if I bring my girlfriend to meet you?"

"Sure, and Thursday afternoon would work out quite nicely. I'll look forward to seeing you both. Before you hang up, let me give you directions to my place from Hiawassee. It's a little difficult to get to *The Source*, as I call it."

Rube wrote the directions down in detail, then leaned back and closed his eyes. A feeling of peace and serenity filled his head, then flooded the rest of his body. Somehow he knew that everything would be all right. It was like a new door had been opened.

Inside Information

Whoops! I apologize. I had the impression from the author that Ned Blankenschipf, III was a master of disguise.

Wrong! Who ever heard of wearing a priest collar with a baseball cap and black tennis shoes, or a trench coat with fake sideburns in warm weather. Why, it's enough to make a real P.I. bow his head in shame.

Anyway, I get the impression that Ned is getting weary of trying to enforce the curse. Now, he's got to school his own son about all this mess.

I got a call from Cousin Herschel, the printer's assistant. Says they're getting close to printing the book. He doesn't know who will look at and give the final okay. He's very nervous as you can imagine. Having trouble sleeping. I told him not to worry. I think I may be able to get him a job at the bowling alley, mopping floors, dusting and carrying out the trash. He got all excited when I mentioned that. I think he'll be all right.

It's a struggle for me. The political writer I work for is a little peeved at me. I keep slipping in little bits of truth into his speeches, and it makes him uncomfortable. He says if you give the voters some of the truth, they might expect more, and before you know it they want the whole truth. He thinks that would put his candidate on the skids, take him off the public payroll. He might even have to work for a living.

I don't know if I told you that Cousin Caresse is remarried. Yep. He was a strong man, a farmer's son from Mississippi. Now, he looks like a dried up pine cone. I don't know how much longer he can last. Reuben is ten. Things keep happening to the boy and he can't figure out why. But, you and I know.

Caresse's first husband is also remarried and works for the mob back in New York.

Narrator

CHAPTER TWENTY ONE

It's a good thing he had Amy with him to help navigate. The Source was about ten miles north of Hiawassee on one of the smaller mountains that sprang from the Appalachian range which begins in Eastern Quebec and extends into Alabama. Amy read the directions while Rube drove and reset the trip odometer after each turn. They left the pavement when they came to a road that circled the mountain. Rhododendron and laurel, still green, were scattered among the trees. They crossed a small stream which hurried along, anxious to fulfill its destiny. Finally they turned onto a small trail with room only for one car and a space to pull off to the side every now and then. The trail dead-ended into a huge formation of solid rock which jutted out of the mountain. Off to the left was an old Jeep and room for two more cars to park.

The chill of fall was in the air as they got out and looked across the valley below. Rube was comfortable with his long sleeved shirt. Amy grabbed a light jacket from the back seat. It was a clear day except for a few wispy clouds which drifted slowly to the east. Most of the leaves were off the trees by now, and Rube and Amy's view was uninhibited. Amy said, "Oh, Rube. This is breathtaking. I've never seen anything like it. It's so beautiful, it makes me want to cry." Rube put his hand on her shoulder and pulled her close.

Engulfed by the smell of the mountain flora, they turned and looked at the large, moss covered rock formation with its weeping cracks.

"Now I know why the road builder stopped here," Rube remarked.

To the left of the rock, on the other side of the Jeep was a sign with *The Source* carved into the wood. Straight up the hill about a hundred and fifty yards was the outline of a small clapboard house with smoke curling from the stone chimney. Rube caught the smell of burning wood.

The path wandered back and forth between the trees on its way up the steep incline. Rube had been given permission by his doctor to start walking again, but his wheelchair time had left his legs weak. Amy's knee was much better, but she still wore an elastic support just to be safe. Three squirrels chattered among themselves and scurried off as Rube and Amy approached. Stopping several times to rest and catch their breath, they turned to more fully take in the panorama of blue sky and the contrasting shades and colors of the valley below. They were exhausted and exhilarated at the same time when they reached the back yard of the small house.

The building sat on a large plateau which ran off a ways to the north. It was located in the southwest corner of the lot and appeared to rest precariously on the edge of a shear cliff. It looked like a strong breeze would blow it over. Fifty yards northeast of the house was a large, pyramid shaped, wooden structure with a single chair in the middle.

Suddenly, Amy grabbed onto Rube like she was trying to keep from falling. "Hold me," she whispered. "Don't let me go."

"What's wrong?"

"I'm fine now. I just had an overwhelming feeling of awe, a feeling of peace, and yet like something special was about to happen. It's hard to explain. This is a sacred place, like a church. Do you feel it?"

"I do. There's a powerful force here. I wonder if we're standing on a magnetic field or something. Anyway, let's go find Dr. Wilkins."

They stepped onto the rickety back porch and knocked on the crooked screen door. Two large bowls, one filled with food pellets and the other with water, sat on the warped pine floor. As the inside door jerked open, Rube saw the smiling face of his old professor. They stepped back as Dr. Wilkins pushed the screen door wider and drew them into the small kitchen.

He appeared a little older than Rube remembered with wrinkle lines radiating from the corners of his eyes. But, there was something different, a glow about him that caught Rube by surprise. He had heard of auras before, but this was the first time he had ever been able to see one, and even feel its presence. Love and peace seemed to float around Dr. Wilkins and reach out to anyone or thing close by.

"Welcome to *The Source*. Thanks for coming," said Dr. Wilkins, giving them each a long hug. Rube was overwhelmed by the pure love that radiated throughout his body. Amy stepped back from her embrace with astonished eyes, filled with tears of joy. Her body trembled as she grabbed Rube's arm. Rube heard Mozart's "Overture to The Marriage of Figaro" playing in the background, recognizing it only because he had seen the opera.

Rube and Amy were startled when a huge cat suddenly appeared in the doorway. Rube thought at first it might be a bobcat, but after seeing its tail realized it was only the largest housecat he had ever laid eyes on.

Dr. Wilkins saw the frightened look in their eyes, and reassured them, "Don't worry, it's only Tiger, my Maine Coon cat. His breed is very large and his tail is as long as his body." Rube reached cautiously to pat Tiger on the neck as he wove and pressed his way through their legs, purring like a young tiger cub.

Dr. Wilkins paused to light a fire under the tea kettle, "You all come on into the living room, or maybe you would prefer to sit on the front porch, that's where I spend most of my time when the weather is nice."

"I think I would like to see your front porch," said Rube. "Is that all right with you, Amy?"

"That's fine," she said, still clinging to his arm.

They passed through the small living room with a stone fireplace to the right. A big oak log still smoldered with red hot coals underneath. Above the thick wooden mantle was a large, carved out image of a bald eagle, clutching arrows in one foot and an olive branch in the other. The dark, wooden walls were decorated with what appeared to be original oil seascapes ranging from port scenes to a full-blown storm on the high seas. Heavy wooden and upholstered furniture was arranged around an oriental rug in front of the fireplace. The multi colored pillows and Afghans invited one to sit down and curl up with a good book. To the left was a door which Rube presumed led to the bedroom.

Dr. Wilkins led them onto the front porch and invited them to sit in a weathered swing angled so you could see the view and still carry on a conversation with the person sitting in the rocking chair to the right of a small wooden table.

As always, Dr. Wilkins combed his light brown hair straight back, but now there was graying at the temples. He wore wire rimmed glasses which did not distract from his pale blue eyes. He appeared to be at peace with the world and serene in his slim, well conditioned body.

He smiled, "Thank you both for coming. I'm glad you called, it saved me a call to you. I have something I want to talk to you about. Before I get to that, you mentioned a need to see me about something. How can I help?"

"Dr. Wilkins, all my life things have been happening to me and people with me, unexplainable things which ordinary people don't seem to experience. When I was in high school, my Uncle Billy told me of a curse that had been placed on the first born son in each generation of my family. During the past two years these events have become more serious. Frankly, Dr. Wilkins, I'm worried about the future. I love Amy very much and I don't want her to get caught up in this. I'd appreciate your advice."

Suddenly, a sharp whistle from the kitchen pierced the screen door. "Excuse me. I'll go fix our tea. I hope green tea is okay. It's all I keep around the house. Do you all take honey or cream? I'm sorry, I don't have sugar. Amy?"

"I'll try honey in mine, thank you."

"A spoon full of honey will be fine for me too," said Rube.

"I'll be right back," said Dr. Wilkins as he scurried inside.

After he left, Amy said, "Rube, I can't believe this place. If I couldn't see the porch, I would swear we were sitting on a cloud, talking to an angel. He is such a nice man! Is he for real?"

"Yes, I think so. He was always a nice man, but there's something different about him now. He's more spiritual somehow. I can't explain it. Are you scared?"

"A little, but not from fear. It's like being in a place far removed from the normal, every day life. It's so quiet, spiritually as well as physically."

"Yes, It's as though everything has slowed down. You can see and feel things more clearly. The last time I felt this peaceful and content was when I was nestled in my mother's arms as a small child. I thought I was relaxed before we came here, now I realize what a bundle of nerves I was, afraid to let go, fearful of what might happen if I gave in for one second. Here, there is perfect peace, love and security." Rube touched Amy's chin and turned her face so he could look into her dark blue eyes. "I love you Amy, I mean I really love you. I don't know why, but I suddenly have an urge to tell you that. In the past I have felt that showing love was a sign of weakness. Now, I know that it's the most powerful feeling you can have and its' power is multiplied when expressed." Rube was proud of what he had just said, but also startled by it. It was not like him to be so open. Amy, her eyes a stream of tears by now, leaned into Rube and told him with her lips how deeply she loved him.

Dr. Wilkins backed through the screen door with a tray loaded with cups of tea and bowls of fruit. "I hope you like fruit, something I picked up at the local market. Oops, I'm sorry, I didn't mean to interrupt."

"Oh, that's okay, Amy and I were just discussing our wedding plans," said Rube. Amy's glace expressed approval.

Settling back in their seats, Dr. Wilkins said, "Rube, give me an example of these things that have happened to you." Tiger was curled up at his feet.

Rube gave a brief summary of his wedding, Kristy's accident, his injury in Savannah and their disastrous trip to

Destin. He also mentioned sightings of the strange man driving the dark green Jaguar.

Hearing him out, Dr. Wilkins nodded, "I understand. Before you leave I'm going to give you some information that will explain what's happening in your life and why. But, for now, I will simply say that things happen for us, not to us. This allows us to learn the lessons that we need, to grow spiritually. I ask you to consider the possibility that the things that have happened in your life brought you to this place. Also, before you leave, I will balance your body, mind and spirit using a new, non-force technique that I have learned."

"First, though, let me explain how I found this place and why I wanted you to come here." He leaned back in his rocker and took a deep breath. "Milli and I stumbled on it about five years ago when we were trying to decide where to retire. I doubt if you ever met Milli. She was my wife for thirty five years." His eyes misted over. "Anyway, we loved it here and decided to make it our retirement home. Three days after we signed the contract, she had a serious stroke and was in the hospital for two months, then in a nursing home for two years. She died three years ago. I missed her so terribly, I almost gave up on life. I felt so alone it was a struggle to keep going. We had no children and I had no one to turn to. I continued to teach at the college, but not very well I'm afraid. One evening I walked into my bedroom to get ready for bed, and was overcome by an urgent need to pray. I fell to my knees and pressed my forehead into the carpet. I prayed out loud, 'Lord, have mercy on me. You have promised to be with me always. If I've ever needed you, I need you now. Is my mission finished on this Earth? If so, please take me home. If there is more for me to do, I need your guidance. Please help me." He leaned to his right, resting his elbow on the arm of the chair. "Shortly after that, I went to bed, and the next morning awoke with His clear answer running through my mind: 'You must make yourself a channel for healing." He drank the last of the tea and set his cup on the table.

"Is that when you came back to *The Source*?" asked Rube.

"Yes, I retired at the end of that year and spent the summer returning this place to a livable condition. I found a local handyman to help me with the hard stuff. He helped me build the pyramid structure in the middle of the field. That's where I do most of my meditating because I find it to be the most receptive location on the mountain. Information from the universe flows freely at that spot." He paused and looked into their eyes, saying, "Amy and Rube, I know all of this may sound strange to you, but I'm speaking from my heart and telling you what I have experienced. I meditate and pray two hours in the morning and two hours in the afternoon everyday except Wednesday, or if I have to make a trip back to civilization. I decided to practice one day a week, so I opened a small office in Hiawassee. I want to help the people of this area, and it gives me a chance to use some of the information I'm receiving. I charged only a small fee, just enough to pay the cost of the office. After a short time I was flooded with patients and working until nine o'clock at night. There was a long waiting list. So I finally hired another doctor to help out.

"A young doctor by the name of Randy Marks, called one day, looking for a place to practice. I brought him and his wife here, taught him my technique and how to teach his patients. He's in the office four days a week. Of course I had to raise the fees to pay him a reasonable salary, but, he does a good job."

Rube thought, oh no, he's going to ask me to move up here and practice. He said, "Well, Dr. Wilkins, it sounds like things are going fine. I don't see why you would want me up here."

"No. No, Rube, I don't want you up here, unless, of course, you want to come. I have something else in mind." He reached down and brought Tiger up to his lap. "The information about healing that I'm receiving needs to be made available to as many people as possible. I asked you here because your name was given to me by the Universal Source."

Rube sat there in disbelief until Amy touched his arm. "Why Dr. Wilkins, I would love to learn your method of healing and use it in my office. It sounds like it's very effective." The soft drone of an airliner, miles away on the horizon, intervened into the peacefulness of the valley below.

"That would be fine, Rube, but it will take more than that. What I'm talking about is spreading this information to mankind, worldwide. It's what God wants to give his people. He is very concerned about the increase of chronic diseases throughout the World, and the lack of progress in dealing with them. We're looking for our healing in the wrong places. We must look within ourselves, the God power that He has given each one of us, that part of us that is in His image." Tiger licked Dr. Wilkins' hand, then preened his own right ear with a large paw.

"Rube and Amy, let me make it very clear that I can't prove that the information is coming from God. That's just my belief, and Rube, if you become involved in this, we are both likely to be ridiculed or even persecuted for our beliefs.

"I have been using my word processor as a journal, entering all of the information I receive. I do this after each session so it's as pure as possible, and not mixed with my own belief system. But, my Source tells me there must be a way for this information to reach the people. Otherwise, it's like a vessel with no outlet. It will fill up and the flow of information will have to stop."

"That makes sense, Dr. Wilkins, and I would like to see the information you've received, but I still don't see where I fit into the picture. I'm just one chiropractic doctor with little training outside my profession. It sounds like you're looking for someone who can write, teach, promote and distribute this information throughout the world. That's way beyond my capabilities. It would be much better if you could do it." He took Amy's hand for moral support.

"My dear Rube, all of those things have been considered. I have learned not to question what I'm told. I was made a channel for this information, just as I asked. That's all I am, and all I am allowed to be. I am not allowed to take part in any organization or business arrangement, nor to make a dime of profit that has anything to do with this information. Mind you,

I'm not comparing myself to Moses, but it reminds me of his situation." For the first time, Rube noticed that Dr. Wilkins was not sniffing when he talked, as he did in college. He attributed that to the clean mountain air.

Dr. Wilkins continued. "You, on the other hand, could function freely, and even be facilitated in your actions in the business world. Your job would be to build an organization that would spread this information to the people. All profits from that organization, other than your salary and expenses, would be directed toward the health of mankind, primarily by teaching them how to live a healthy and happy life. What do you think?"

"I really don't know what to think. It's all a bit overwhelming. I mean, I'm honored by your confidence in me. But, I just don't see how I could ever accomplish what you're asking. I wouldn't even know where to start!" said Rube.

"I understand how you feel. It's frightening to think about such an endeavor. We both must remember who's walking beside us, then, we will not be afraid. For right now, would you be willing to come here each week on Monday to help me organize and re-write the information I have received?"

"Well, I guess I could rearrange my schedule and make Monday my day off, instead of Thursday. Still, it's a long drive. What do you think, Amy?"

"If you're being called to do something for the health of mankind, and we both know how many sick people there are out there, we'll find a way to do it," said Amy.

Dr. Wilkins smiled reassuringly. "What He's asking us to do is much greater than we are. It's not about us, but God's work through us. Our abilities and knowledge would be like one grain of sand compared to universal knowledge represented by every grain of sand on every beach in the world. He never asks us to do something without giving us the resources to accomplish it. Do you see what I mean?"

"Yes," said Rube, "I understand, but what you're talking about is such a large task. I can't even comprehend it, much less know where to start."

"Do not be afraid, Rube. Always remember The Source. The path will be made clear as we begin the journey. From this time on, you must do more than believe, you must <u>know</u> that our mission will be accomplished."

"Dr. Wilkins, I have faith in God, and I believe you're sincere. For those reasons, I will say yes, but, both of you have your work cut out to make me into the kind of person you're talking about."

"Don't worry. Your transformation begins today, from within. I'm going to give you a copy of what I have received so far. But, first let me adjust you and Amy." He led them into his surprisingly large bedroom where there was a small adjusting table under the window overlooking the valley below.

"This is a 'no force' technique that is used to balance the body, mind, spirit and memory so they are all working together without interference. There is nothing the God power within us can not heal if we allow it to be expressed freely. All of that will become clear as you read the material that I will be giving you before you leave."

After Amy and Rube were balanced, Dr. Wilkins said, "Don't worry about the, so called, curse. As you read the information, it will become clear why things happen to you and others. You will find that the solution is simple, and yet not so easy to accomplish."

He led them back into the living room and picked up a folder from his desk, handing it to Rube. "Please read this with an open mind over the next few days. Call me if you have questions. We can discuss it in more detail the next time I see you."

"Okay," said Rube, "I can't wait to get started."

"There will be time for that when you get home. For now, please come with me and I'll show you the rest of *The Source*."

They walked along a path of carefully laid stones, bordered by dogwood trees about ten feet apart on both sides. Interspersed between the trees was an array of shrubs, plants and flowers that were asleep for now, dreaming and planning for the time when they could once again show their glory. Tiger left his sign on a few of the trees to make sure all creatures understood whose territory they were entering.

The pyramid shaped structure was more substantial than it appeared from a distance. There were six by six posts rising three feet above the foundation at each corner. Four by four posts connected the corners and provided support for the floor joists and exterior plywood floor. From each corner of the floor rose more four by fours reaching an apex twenty four feet above the ground. Eight feet above the floor more boards tied the risers together and formed an open ceiling. Everything was held together by angle irons and bolts which helped support the plywood, felt paper and shake shingle roof. The four sides were open up to the eight foot level.

Dr. Wilkins pointed out that the pyramid "Was built so that each side faces either north, south, east or west."

"Does the pyramid shape have anything to do with the energy of this place?" asked Rube.

Dr. Wilkins shook his head, "I don't think so. The energy was already here. It's just something I wanted to build."

The path led them to the south side of the pyramid which faced the spectacular valley below. They went up two steps onto the platform, and Rube immediately noticed a difference. It was as though he was floating two inches above the floor. Dr. Wilkins gently guided them to the center and moved the chair to the side. They stood, holding hands, eyes closed.

There was no need to speak or even think. This was a place to receive, not to give. Rube felt an energy flowing into his whole being, like a breeze blowing from all directions. He sensed a gentle electric current rushing between him, Amy and Dr. Wilkins. They were as one for the moment.

Rube had no sensation of time or place. Those things did not matter to him as he experienced a peace that he had never known before. He was reluctant to move when Dr. Wilkins pulled them from the center.

They stood off to the side, breathing deeply, still holding hands. Dr. Wilkins broke the silence, "Thank you, God, for your presence in our lives."

Rube blew out a breath, took in another and released it slowly before speaking. "I don't know what to say, how to explain what just happened. It was as though we were part of the entire universe and it was part of us. Does that make sense?"

As Amy slowly opened her eyes, Dr. Wilkins said, "You are exactly right. That is what happened. We were in a spiritual state of being which makes up about ninety-eight to ninety-nine percent of reality. Our physical lives account for one to two percent, but receive most of our attention."

Tiger purred his agreement as he wove his way through their legs.

Amy bent over and picked up a white feather from the deck. "Now I know that I no longer have to worry," she sighed. "God will take care of us, just as he does all living creatures." Rube glanced at Amy whom he knew had little or no religious training, and thought, at this moment she could be mistaken for Mother Teresa.

The wind picked up behind them and pushed them along as they walked back to the edge of the plateau.

Rube spoke first, "Dr. Wilkins, thank you for allowing us to come here, to talk to you and to experience this place. My brain is still trying to comprehend exactly what has taken place. Hopefully, it will become clear with time. I am ready now to take the next step, to read this material and see where we go from here."

"Thank you both for coming. There's a sense of relief now that I have been able to share this information with you. Even a burden of such joy and promise needs to be shared. It is meant to be shared, and must be spread to all people. Only then will the fullness of its meaning be felt and the promise kept. May God bless and keep you until we meet again."

The three of them shared a long embrace before Rube and Amy descended the path which had brought them to *The Source*, many spiritual years ago, or so it seemed.

CHAPTER TWENTY TWO

As they retraced their route along the narrow trail, Rube said, "Do you realize that we just stood in a pyramid higher than the ones in Egypt, if you count the mountain?"

"That's right," said Amy. "And the mountain certainly felt like a vortex. What else did the note say?"

"An open mind. That must be Dr. Wilkins. I would say we were in the right place."

They rounded a curve and came face to face with the pinched in nose of the Jaguar. Rube slammed on the brake, tires sliding on the loose gravel and dirt. There was not a pull off and no way to get around. They sat silently for a moment, squinting to see through the tinted glass of the other car, wondering if he had a gun, and what he planned to do.

Rube, with no weapon himself, realized there was only one thing to do. "Lock your door, and when I get out, lock my door. I'm going to have a talk with the mystery man."

"No! Don't. He might have a gun. Stay here."

"No choice, Angel. We're sitting ducks. If anything happens to me, get out and run back to Dr. Wilkins' place. I want to try and settle this now."

Rube walked in front of the Jaguar and stood facing the driver, making sure his hands were seen. The door cracked, and the man got out and stood behind the door. He slowly raised his hands and rested them on top. It was obviously "the priest," but he was wearing a full beard, black leather hat and jacket.

"We need to talk," said the man.

"Fine," said Rube. "What's your name?"

"That's not important. I want to talk to you about something that happened a long time ago."

"Okay, Mr. Blankenschipf. I agree that we need to talk. What did you have in mind?"

"I don't know about you, but I'm sick and tired of the curse thing. Sometimes I think it's just as hard on the ones carrying out the curse as it is the cursed. Now I've got to turn around and teach my son to do the same. I dread that. And, for what? Because my great, great grandmother was offended by your relative. I don't even remember what it was about."

"Your great, great grandmother twirled on the dance floor when her lover, my great, great grandfather didn't mean for her too, so he walked off the floor. Then, he married her best friend, my great, great grandmother. I'd be happy to apologize for that even though I wasn't around at the time."

"That won't be necessary. My wife does that to me all the time. But, I've learned to live with it. A woman's scorn can burn long and deep. My great, great grandmother is proof of that. I don't know about you, but I'm not anxious to go to war over a miscreant twirl."

Rube grinned and shuffled his feet. "I couldn't agree more."

Ned scratched his false beard and it came loose on the left side. "The only problem is, I gave my word to my daddy that I would carry this thing out. I don't want to break my word. So, it's important to me that you find the secret to breaking the curse."

"I worry about my son, Sam. I don't want him caught up in this thing," said Rube.

"Have no concern about Sam. He is not part of the curse.

"By the way, I want you to know that I had nothing to do with the accident involving your wife and unborn child. I would never do that. Also, I felt bad when you got hit by the car. That young man just panicked and hit the gas pedal."

"Thanks for telling me. I'm just as anxious to break the curse as you are. Are you working for my ex-wife?"

"I can't reveal information about my clients, Mr. Winters. That's how I make my living." He pushed the fallen beard back up, just as the part over his lip came loose.

"Now, I'm going to back up to the next pull off spot and let you by. Be sure to read Dr. Wilkins paper all the way to the end. I will know if you find the secret."

"What was that all about?" asked Amy when he got in the car.

"You can relax, Angel. It was just some unfinished family business." Then, he told her about the conversation.

When they got back on the main highway, Rube saw a scenic view sign and pulled off the road. "Let's stop here for a few minutes and talk about this."

"Good idea," said Amy. "Sounds like we've got a good chance to break the curse. Sometime you'll have to tell me about the unintended twirl."

"I will, but right now let's talk about Dr. Wilkins. What do you think?"

"I don't know. I can't believe we just committed to something like that without thinking or even talking about it."

They got out of the car, walked to the edge of the cliff, looked into the distance for a moment, then turned and faced each other.

"Amy, I must admit to you that I'm afraid. I have a feeling that all of this will change our lives forever. You're right, it's a big commitment, and I've agreed to at least come and help him re-write the material. After that we'll have to see what happens."

"I just don't understand all of this, the spirituality, the messages from God or whoever. I believe in God even though I rarely went to church. But, if this is real, it's much more than just believing, it's like being close to the Almighty. I just don't know."

Rube took Amy's hand and led her to a wooden fence next to the telescope. Propping one foot up, he said "I don't know either. I do know that Dr. Wilkins is an honest and sincere man, and that he believes what he's telling us. Based on that alone, I'm going to follow up to see where it leads."

"That's fine with me, Rube. It won't hurt to look into it. If it does bring about changes in our lives, we'll just have to deal with it. One of my nursing instructors once said that we are here on this earth for two reasons, to grow spiritually and to help other people. If that's the case, it sounds like you're being asked to do both."

"You're right. Knowing that you're with me makes things easier." He turned to see Amy smiling and his mood softened. "By the way, you never said you would marry me."

"Well, I don't know," she teased. "Maybe I need some time to think about that."

"Okay, you have two seconds. If you don't answer by then, I'm going to squeeze it out of you," he said, grabbing her in a bear hug.

"All right, you beast, I'll marry you. But, remember, Didhe is part of the package."

Rube laughed, "It's a deal, but you have to promise to keep him out of our bedroom and off my leg."

They kissed and then embraced, each thinking about their future together.

He kissed her again. Then said, "Come on, let's head back to Athens. Would you mind reading the material while I drive? Then, we can talk about it."

As Rube started the car, Amy opened the folder and found a cover letter from Dr. Wilkins. She began to read, *"To whom it may concern: Two years ago I began receiving information from a universal source which I choose to call God. This knowledge comes to me as I meditate, staying centered on the God Spirit within me, just as it is within all of us.*

"I am not special, nor do I have extraordinary gifts which allow me to receive this information. I am all too human, and have my faults, but for whatever reason, I have been given this mission, and I intend to carry it out to the best of my ability. I have promised to pass on the information I have received, and will receive, to as many people as possible. I will do that by keeping my own belief system neutral, and recording this message truthfully. Please take into account that I record the

thoughts that have been given to me after each session, and must rely on my memory until I can record them on my word processor. Also, remember that my choice of words when I sit down to record the thoughts might be different than you or someone else might use. I am not qualified to speak for God, and do not intend to do so. I will be telling you in my own words what my mind has received from the Universal Source, and I take full responsibility for it. Any in-accuracies, or misinterpretations are entirely my own, because I believe The Source to be true.

"It was made clear to me that this information is intended to bring better health and healing to the people, and is not to be used to create another religion or affect the existing religions in any way.

"One of the most striking revelations is that there is nothing new since the beginning of time. The truth was there and has been revealed to us in the past through our life experiences, philosophers, prophets and especially Jesus. God is dismayed by the fact that His people hear, but don't listen. In recent decades, He has become alarmed by the dangerous drift into chronic diseases. Once again, He wants to re-iterate the important principles of health and healing. I have no idea why He has chosen to do so through me. Perhaps it has something to do with speaking through the least of His people.

"Following is a synopsis of the most important information I have received and recorded in my journal."

Amy turned the page and continued to read. **"Synopsis of information received between May 14, 1990 and August 15, 1991.**

"I began meditating in May of this year seeking peace of mind, knowing that Milli was gone and that it was entirely up to me to decide how I would spend the rest of my life. Also, it was the only way I knew to make myself a channel of healing as I had been instructed.

"When Jesus said to us, 'I am with you always,' He was speaking of God as well, and meant that literally. His power is within each one of us, just as it is in all things in

233

this universe. That power never changes. It was there in the sperm and egg before we were conceived, and upon conception, it provided the knowledge to develop our bodies and cause them to grow and function. If there is no interference with the power, our bodies will grow and function in a perfect way. His light (power) was there before our heart and blood vessels or any other organs were formed. It was there before our brain and nervous system existed. And, that same power is still with us today. It has not changed, it has not weakened and never will. God wonders why we, His people, are always looking in other places for healing. Do we not realize that the power that made the body can heal the body?"

Amy paused to take a deep breath and Rube said, "Would you like to stop up ahead for lunch?"

"Sure. Let's take a break."

Rube had always liked small, chainless restaurants. The people who frequent them seem more real, and the waiters have not been trained to say just the right thing. They pulled into the gravel parking lot, joining a couple of cars and four or five pickup trucks. The wooden sign between the two windows on the right said "Woody's Place." A neon "OPEN" sign lit the front door that opened into one large room. A bar along the back wall was interrupted only by a space and swinging doors into the kitchen.

A voice boomed from the kitchen, "Have a seat, Mates. I'll be with ye shortly!"

Not wanting to interrupt the regulars at the counter, they chose a small table on the far right, next to the windows. The napkin holder, and salt and pepper shakers sat in the middle of a red, vinyl tablecloth. The chairs were wooden and slid easily across the once white tiles on the floor.

Rube was fascinated by the colorful jukebox in the corner. "Amy, I think we must have just walked through a time warp. This has got to be the 1950's that my Daddy and Uncle Billy always talk about. Look at the R.C. Cola sign on the other wall."

Just then a burly, red faced man with thinning white hair burst thru the swinging doors, "Howdy, Mates! What can I get ye to drink---coffee, sweet tea, lemonade or coke?"

"Amy, what would you like?"

"Coke, please."

"I'll have sweet tea."

"Thank ye, Mates. I'll see to it straight away. While I'm gone, make up yer minds about what ye want to eat. Welda, my former waitress, called up this mornin', said she's quittin'. Outa the blue. No warnin', mind ye. Nothin'. Just like that," he said with a snap of his fingers, then headed for the counter, yelling into the kitchen as he went by, "Cora, is that cornbread ready yet?"

"I like this place," Amy grinned as they opened the plastic covered menus. "We should have invited Ned to have lunch with us."

"Maybe, but I don't think his false beard could have withstood the rigors of lunch."

Woody set their drinks in front of them, "I don't mind it none with Welda gone, fact I kinda like waitin' on my own customers, gettin' to know people like yourselves. Where are you all from?"

"Athens," replied Rube.

"Athens, is it?" said Woody. "Well, now, I'm from good old England, myself. 'Course, I been up here in the mountains so long, I speak what I call English hillbilly. Welcome to the mountains, Mates."

"Thank you, Sir," said Rube, "Are you goin' to fill the vacancy?"

"Hell no. She didn't leave no vacancy. I found out this mornin' that I'd rather do it my self. All she did was stand around most of the time, smokin cigarettes, drinkin' coffee and yappin' at the customers. I can do that as good as she can, 'cept I ain't gonna smoke none o' them nasty old weeds. What'll ye have, Mates? I'll tell ye right now, Cora's cookin' up some good, fresh vegetables back there."

They both ordered the vegetable plate.

While they were waiting, a tall, lanky man with a battered cowboy hat pushed back on his head ambled toward the jukebox, fishing change from his pocket as he went. He touched his hat and smiled, "Howdy, folks," as he went by. After putting his money in, he quickly punched two numbers. Then, he turned to Amy, "Ma'am, would you like to choose a song or two?"

Amy, surprised, said, "Sure," and jumped to her feet. She walked over, studied the list and chose two songs that sounded familiar, even though they were before her time. Sitting down, she said, "What a nice man."

Rube smiled, "Yes. But, I really think he was just trying to get a better look at you. It was love at first sight." Amy blushed.

Rube leaned forward and put his hand on hers, "Amy, I don't know what your training taught you about how the body functions, but mine says the most important system in the body is the brain and nervous system. Dr. Wilkins journal says there is another, unseen power, God or God's Spirit in each one of us. What do you think?"

"I don't know, Rube. It's so hard to believe in something you can't see. But, it does make sense in a way. How else would the cells know to divide and make each organ and gland?"

Their food arrived and they ate to the strains of *I Didn't Know God Made Honky Tonk Angels*, and *The Tennessee Waltz*.

Finally, Rube said, "Well, my Honky Tonk Angel, I'd like to sit here all afternoon, but we'd better be on our way." They walked to the antique cash register on the counter and paid Woody, also the cashier.

Woody grabbed their ticket, punched some numbers and slammed it onto a spindle next to the register. "Well, Mates, how was them vegetables?"

"They were great, Woody, the best I ever ate," said Rube as Amy smiled and nodded.

Woody yelled over his shoulder, "You hear that, Cora? Best they ever ate."

Amy and Rube took one last look at the Juke-box, waved to Woody and stepped back into the nineties.

As soon as they pulled onto the road, Amy picked up the journal and began reading.

"His light (some call it the God power, superconsciousness, subconsciousness) resides within each one of us. That power is perfect in every way. It is the part of us that is in His image, the Holy Spirit. The external part of the Spirit is sometimes called the aura or an electromagnetic field. It surrounds us and is through every part of our bodies, around each cell. What happens in our bodies is determined through the Spirit. Whatever happens in our Spirit will also happen in our bodies whether it's health or disease."

Rube broke in, "It just hit me, he's saying that whatever we're putting into our spiritual field, whether it's love, hate or fear, we will attract."

"Yeah, or those things will affect our health," said Amy.

"Don't you see, Angel? This is the answer I've been looking for. I've been putting fear of the so-called 'curse' into my field all the time, and that's what I've attracted. Does that make sense?"

"Maybe. Let's see what else we find," as her eyes returned to Dr. Wilkins writing.

"If His power within us was allowed to flow freely, we would be perfect in every way. But, we were born with a conscious mind and given a free will so we can grow spiritually and find our way back to Him from whence we came. It concerns God greatly that most of us are making little progress. And, it makes Him sad that so many of His people are suffering from chronic diseases and looking everywhere but the right place for healing. That is why He wishes to make this information available to all of His people.

"Some of us believe that we are physical beings undergoing a spiritual or mental experience. Actually, we are spiritual beings seeking our way back to Him. That is

why there is a general feeling of loneliness, restlessness and uncertainty among us. We are homesick for the spiritual realm and searching for our way back to that place. Unfortunately, most of us seek answers only in the physical world, even when we go to church and read the Bible, it's a rote thing, something we go through in a physical way, hoping we will be suddenly enlightened by His grace. That's not likely to happen.

"Others do the same thing, secretly hoping they will not be enlightened or saved. It would be too much of a burden and would interfere with their compulsive addiction to the physical world."

Amy dropped the notes into her lap and propped her left leg on the seat, "Rube, you've gone to church all your life. Is that true? Is that the way people are?"

Rube glanced at Amy, then back to the road. He sat silently sorting out the people he knew in the church.

"Well?" said Amy.

"I never thought about it, Honky Tonk Angel, but that's very possible. I hate to admit it, but I probably fit into the second category."

Amy picked up the journal.

"When we are first born, the subconscious mind, conscious mind, body and spirit work in perfect harmony (assuming the mother has done nothing to directly affect the baby). When we are exposed to other people and worldly things, we begin to make choices in life and form beliefs. These beliefs become the basis for our soul. They can change throughout our lifetimes. These values determine how we react to the world."

"That makes sense," commented Amy. "I've never understood just what the soul was or how it was formed."

Rube was in thought and only nodded his assent.

"The things that we are really in search of: God's love, joy, wisdom, healing and peace lie within and can never be found in the physical. That is why there is still a restless seeking, even among those who are highly successful.

"The physical world, that is, those things we perceive through our five senses (hear, see, smell, taste and feel) make up only about one to two percent of reality. That is where most of the people find themselves, and that is a conscious choice we have made, so we must accept the responsibility. The other ninety-eight percent of reality, the spiritual world, is ignored and pushed as far into our subconscious mind as possible. If our subconscious tries to remind us of a problem, we spend a restless night, and suppress it once again, instead of dealing with it.

"The God power within our subconscious minds, along with the Holy Spirit that surrounds, and is in our bodies, runs our bodies in a perfect way for survival. We must realize we were not made to be healthy or sick, but to survive."

Amy paused, "Hmm, this is new, I always thought we were supposed to be healthy."

"Yeah, me too," said Rube, "I guess he'll tell us what determines that."

Amy continued to read.

"The choices that we make with our conscious minds determines our state of health. Remember, we have a free will, and God does not force us to do things. It's our choice. He does not bring sickness upon his people to punish them, as some believe. The power to heal is always there, inside of us, but we can interfere with that power by our conscious thoughts, as well as the negative things that are stored in our memories.

"The negative memories must be dealt with so they do not interfere with the free flow of God's light throughout our bodies, minds (conscious and subconscious) and spirits. As we grow, we will learn how to prevent the negative thoughts from being stored in memory in the first place.

"The conscious choices that we make in the six essentials of life determine whether we are healthy or sick. The essentials of life are the air we breathe, what we drink, the food we eat, the amount and quality of rest that we get, the amount and type of exercise we get and what we think. Each individual is made differently (different genetic codes, etc.) as God intended. So, it's impossible to apply specifics to all of the people, but there are things that we all have in common, and general guidelines that we should all follow, if we wish to be healthy. It's our choice as individuals or groups up to and including the entire world population.

"The amount of oxygen in the air has dramatically decreased over the last one hundred years and is getting worse. We already know the things that can be done to improve this, but so far we have not chosen to do them, at least not to the degree we should. As individuals we must make wise choices in the air we breathe: a job that allows us to breathe clean, fresh air, a home that is not so tight the air can not circulate normally, a location where the air is free of industrial pollution, and using products in and around the home that do not pollute our immediate space. These choices are not always easy. For example, a person might not wish to quit a job where they have worked for 20 years. That's an understandable choice, but one which they have made and are responsible for."

Rube exclaimed, "Man, what about the poor guys who spray pesticides and herbicides, or clean homes all day? Finding another job might not be that easy."

"Yeah," said Amy, "and they might not even know they are endangering their health."

"What else does he say?" asked Rube.

Amy searched for her place. "Let's see-------."

"Another essential of life is water. Again, we find ourselves in the same situation. We have polluted the rivers, lakes, streams and oceans to a dangerous degree. Our group choices are gradually decreasing our parameters of choice as individuals. Of course, our bodies can not function in a healthy way unless we drink a sufficient amount of water. So, we must find (or produce) a source of pure water, free of chemical additives, toxic materials, bacteria and viruses.

"The food that we eat is vital, because if the nutrients that the cells need to grow and function are not there, we can not maintain a state of health. Make sure the food that you eat is clean and free of chemicals that have been injected or sprayed. Organically grown food, when properly done, is best. Do not overeat. Many people are starving to death while others are eating themselves into an early grave. Eat in moderation, and make sure seventy five to eighty percent is fruits and vegetables. That is best for most individuals, because our bodies are essentially alkaline by design and acid by function. The metabolism of protein in the body creates acid, and when we eat too much meat, the amount of acid created overwhelms the body's ability to deal with it, leading to exhaustion of the organs and eventually disease.

"Quality rest is the time when our bodies rebuild themselves, and if we fail to get the amount of rest that we need, our body will gradually degenerate and become sick. As I said before, individuals are different, but the generally accepted amount of eight hours, is best for most people. We will be able to tell if we need a little more or less. Eight hours of restless, wakeful sleep does not count, nor does eight hours of drug induced slumber. Sometimes other areas of our life must be put in order so that we can get the rest we need.

"Our bodies were not made to run on idle, anymore than our brains can be idle. There must be an appropriate amount of exercise to aid our digestive, metabolic, circulatory and all other systems of our bodies. We must take into account our present state of health and how we're doing on the other five essentials (especially what we eat and think because this determines the amount of acid in our bodies) before we decide on an exercise program. Once we decide, it is usually better to start slowly and gradually increase the amount that we do."

Rube interrupted, "Let's take a break. I'm going to stop here, get some gas and look at their antiques."

"Good idea. My eyes are tired, plus I'm thirsty. Hey, look, there goes the Green Jag. Ned must have shaved his beard."

"Yep. Still wearing his leather coat though, even in this heat. You know, I'm beginning to like Ned, now that I've met him," said Rube.

As Rube approached the country store, the eyes of the old man with his chair leaned against the building, popped open. "Hot. Yes sir, mighty hot today. But, there's a touch of winter in the air. I can feel it in my bones. Yes, sir, in my bones." His toothless mouth closed and his eyes shut again under the floppy, brimmed hat.

Rube walked on into the store and antique shop. Amy followed. When she passed, the old man's eyes popped open again. "Legs. Yes, sir, mighty pretty legs." Amy smiled broadly.

CHAPTER TWENTY THREE

Amy and Rube wanted to have an RC Cola or Coke, but finally settled on bottled water for health reasons. As they stepped out the door, the old timer came to life again. His eyes blinked twice, his head raised up and his jaw dropped down. He flapped his jaw a couple of times to get it back on track. "Bye, folks. Come back to see us real soon, hear?"

"Will do," said Rube. "I hear we're gonna have a bad winter this year."

"Yep. Reckon we will. Hot right now, but you'll notice a little nip in the air when the wind blows. 'Sides, my right hip's startin' to ache. Sure sign of cold weather."

Rube and Amy waved goodbye and walked toward the car. The old man settled back in his chair and closed his eyes. He mumbled, "Yep. Cold weather. Pretty legs, though."

As soon as they were on the road, Amy grabbed the journal and began reading.

"The last, and most important essential of life, is what we think. Thoughts are actually things and affect all aspects of our being at the sub-atomic level. God knows that these are difficult concepts for His people to grasp, but it must be done if we are to make progress against the chronic diseases that bring suffering and death to our bodies, minds and spirits. For too long we have been treating the body at the atomic and larger level. That level obeys a different set of laws (sometimes called Newtonian physics). These laws which have been revealed to us over time apply very well to non-living things, but not to living organisms which have the ability to grow and systematically replace damaged or dying cells. It is time for our scientists to recognize this, and concentrate on quantum physics or the study of things smaller than atoms.

Our entire being was designed to survive. Whether we are sick or healthy is determined by our choices in life. Our bodies will deal with whatever choices we make in a perfect way for survival. For example, if we choose to smoke, our bodies will do everything they can to protect us from the harmful effects and keep us alive as long as possible. He has given us a free will. If He imposed His will upon us, everyone would be perfect, and this would deprive us of the opportunity to grow spiritually closer to Him. He will not do that. We must make our own choices which will lead to sickness and sadness or health and happiness."

Amy paused, tilted her seat back and rested her bare feet on the dash. "Rube, isn't it possible for our choices to affect other, innocent people?"

"Yes. Certainly, a smoker can affect the health of others, or if a cocaine user plows into an oncoming car head on," said Rube.

Tears welled up in Amy's eyes as she said, "My father's choices, especially the loss of my mother, will affect my life from now on."

Rube winced and thought how much her father's decision to drink and drive on the night he ran Kristy off the road had affected her life. My God, he thought, how can I ever forgive that man. And, how can I ever tell Amy that he was responsible. Maybe some day.

"Yes, and his father's choices affected his life, et cetera, back through time," said Rube.

Amy sighed, "How can we ever overcome those things?"

Rube reached over and took her hand, "Don't worry, we'll find an answer as we go along. Why don't you rest your eyes for a few minutes, take a nap?"

"Good idea," she sighed as she laid the manuscript on her chest and closed her eyes. She dozed restlessly with visions of her dead mother and father sprawled on the living room floor.

Her mumbling became crying until, finally, Rube woke her, "Amy, Honey, wake up. You're having a bad dream."

"Oh, I'm sorry. I was dreaming about Mama and Daddy. I miss them, and I get sad knowing that I'll never see them again, at least not in this world." She moved over and rested her head on his shoulder.

"It's okay, Sweetie. I understand. I'm sorry all of this is bothering you. If you feel like reading on, maybe we'll find some answers."

"Sure," said Amy as she picked up the papers and found her place.

"Many of our health problems today are blamed on stress which should be defined as anything which changes our response to life. As far as our health is concerned, the stressful events that we experience can be good or bad. Basically, it depends on how we react to the stressors. As Shakespeare said, 'Nothing is good or bad, but my thinking makes it so.' If we are proactive, seeing each incident as a learning experience, and finding the good lesson in everything, we will continue to grow and experience a healthy and happy life. If we are reactive to the inevitable things that happen to all of us, blaming everyone else or even ourselves, and seeing only the bad, our being will be filled with negativity, causing hate, fear, anger, envy, dread, regret, et cetera. If there is enough emotion involved, the events will be stored in our subconscious memory, and our body systems will continue to react the same way each time we think of that incident. The same chemicals will be produced and our glands and organs must deal with them. Continual response to such incidents stored in memory will eventually lead to exhaustion and failure in some part of our bodies. That is when disease begins."

Amy looked out the window at a young boy walking on the opposite side of the road, head down, hands in pockets.

She waved, but there was no response. "How will we ever get this message to the people who need it most?"

"I don't know, Angel. All we can do is try." He reached over and turned her face to him. He grinned. "Now, don't get down on me. We're going to do this proactively and enjoy every minute of it."

She laughed, "Okay, Wise Guy, we'll try it your way. Just remember it's a new way of thinking, and takes some getting used to." She resumed reading.

"The best way to look at life is that things happen for us and not to us. Remember, we are spiritual beings undergoing a physical experience. Most of the events that happen and the people that we meet provide an opportunity for us to learn and grow spiritually. If we recognize and accept the positive lesson in each event, we can continue to grow and move on with our lives instead of suffering the damage to our health that we impose on ourselves. If we do not accept the lesson, we will continue to attract similar incidents until the lesson is learned."

"That makes sense," said Rube. "But, what about the things that have already happened, and are stored in our memories?"

"Maybe he'll tell us that in the next section," said Amy. "Rube, can we stop here in Helen for a short break? I love this little town."

"Sure," said Rube, spotting a small church on the right. "Why don't we pull in here and park? It may be too crowded if we go farther."

There was a coolness in the air even though the clear blue sky reflected its light off the church facade and stained glass windows giving it a peaceful glow. Rube turned and put his hand on Amy's shoulder, looking into her dark blue eyes, "Amy, why don't we get married here? You love this town, and this is a perfect setting. I can see you now with your beautiful body wrapped in a flowing, white gown walking down the aisle to me. What do you think?"

Amy's happy eyes filled with tears. "I think that's the best idea I've ever heard. Let's go see if we can arrange to use the church and set a date."

There was no one in the church, but they found a sheet of information about who to call to make arrangements to use the facility. "I'll do that tomorrow morning from my office," said Rube.

They walked down the south side of the street, looking at all the colorful decorations, sliding in and out of the small shops, until they reached the small bridge in the middle of town. Crossing the street, they made their way back toward the church. Along the way, they found a children's shop, and bought a "Helen, GA" jacket for Sam. Thinking of Sam made Rube sad. He had an urge to be with his son, to hold him. Amy sensed this and put her arm around him.

Back in the car, they moved with the flow of tourist traffic through Helen, holding hands and discussing plans for their wedding.

Out of the congestion and headed south on Highway 17, Amy picked up the manuscript, "Shall we continue?"

"Go for it," said Rube.

Amy read on, **"As long as these memories are stored in our subconscious memory, and have not been reprocessed, they will be stressful on our bodies. I'm sure you know people who are still reacting to events that happened twenty or thirty years ago, and the other person may already be dead.**

"Often times we are told to forget those things, and move on with our lives, but that never works. Those things must be reprocessed by the four steps of forgiveness, and this must be done with as much emotion as when it was originally stored. God has already told us that we must forgive our brothers and sisters seventy times seven times.

"We must forgive the other person or persons involved. This may be difficult to do, some would even say impossible in their case. I say to you that even the most despicable acts must be forgiven for our own sake. The other person will be judged, along with the rest of us. But, it is not our job to judge others. If we never judge, we never have to forgive.

"The other person may be dead, or perhaps we haven't seen them for years, but we're still their slave if we hate them. We are doing this for ourselves, not for them.

"By taking this step we are giving up any chance for revenge. We must understand and accept that. We were given directions about this matter in Colossians 3:13-14: 'Bear with each other and forgive whatever grievances you may have against one another. Forgive as the Lord forgave you. And over all these virtues put on love, which binds them all together in perfect unity.'

"The second step in the process is to give the other person permission to forgive us. Interaction between people is a two way street, and it is rare when there is no blame to be placed on one side. They may have judged us, even if wrongfully, and their forgiveness of us may be facilitated by this step. They don't have to be told of our decision, but it must be put into our field.

"Perhaps the most difficult step is to forgive ourselves for the things we have done to others and to ourselves. Many times we continue to punish ourselves long after the event is over. The other person may have forgotten the event, or not even know we were hurt. And yet, when that thought returns to us, we put ourselves under the same stress that was originally created, and produce the same chemicals that must be dealt with by our organs and glands, causing exhaustion. And, who is causing this damage to our bodies? We are, by our negative reaction and lack of forgiveness.

"Finally, we must learn the positive lesson in each occurrence, even if it's only that we choose to act differently than they did in the same situation. I know that it's difficult to find a positive lesson in some events, but it must be done so that we can move on with our lives without suffering the consequences of living in the past.

"Does forgiveness mean that we have forgotten the past? No, only that we have reprocessed and neutralized those things so that they no longer affect us in a negative way. God tells me that if there was one thing that he could tell us to do that would have the greatest impact on our health, it would be, 'Learn to forgive...replace your hatred with love.'

"Lastly, as it says in Matthew five, 'Love your enemies and pray for those who persecute you, so that you may be children of your Father in heaven."

Amy closed the manuscript and stared into the distance.

Rubes eyes got bigger and bigger, "Amy! Read that last part over!"

"All he said was, 'Love your enemies and pray for those who persecute you."

"That's it, Angel! That's it! Don't you see? It's easy enough to say I forgive, give them permission to forgive and forgive yourself. But what you just said seals the contract. If you can truly love your enemies and pray for them, then it's over---finished. That's what I've never been able to do. See?"

"Amazing," said Amy. "I read that part without seeing or hearing. It's like I was blind and deaf. That's scary. I wonder how often we do that in what we read, hear, or even life itself. Is it because we don't want to know certain things?"

"Maybe. Having a free will is nice, but it can get us in a lot of trouble." Rube glanced out the window at the declining light of the sun as it danced over the brown, green and grey landscape, turning the sky to shades of gold and lilac. "When you think about it, we already love our friends and family. So, who needs our love the most? I guess it would have to be our enemies."

Amy laid her hand on top of Rube's, "It's so simple. Why can't we learn to forgive and love all people? What's wrong with us as a people, Rube? Why do we continue to punish ourselves with sickness, war and death?"

"That's a good question, Angel. Hopefully, the Universal Source will supply the answers to those questions and many more. If we're going to be successful in our mission, we'll need all the help we can get."

As they drove back to Athens, the string of mountains to the west dropped long shadows across the road in the blue fall evening. Amy fell into a restless sleep with her head propped on her hand.

Rube's mind was a beehive. Had he found the secret to unlock the curse? What needed to be done to get the messages from The Source to all people? Finally, he decided to be patient and take one step at a time. He thought about the coming wedding and smiled, knowing that he had always loved Amy and always would.

Rube saw a set of headlights coming up behind them, fast. He slowed a bit. When the lights got closer, they flashed on and off rapidly. As the dark green Jaguar passed, Rube saw an Atlanta Braves cap and a thumbs up sign.

Rube smiled and waved. Then, returned the thumbs up. He said softly to himself so as not to wake Amy, "Okay, Ned Blankenschipf, and Imogene Blankenschipf and all the Blankenschipfs in between, I love you. Yes, unconditionally, and I'll be praying for you." He thought, after all, you were almost family, in fact, you are family in a way.

As Ned's taillights faded into the distance, Rube thought of Uncle Billy, his kindred spirit. He couldn't wait to share his new knowledge about why things happen to or for people, knowing that Uncle Billy would understand. Then, he would put his arm around him and tell him that the curse had been lifted.

Rube knew this was a new beginning. He looked ahead into the falling curtain of darkness with hope and love in his heart.

Inside Information

I'm sorry to jump in here, but there are a few things we need to talk about.

Can you believe that the author still wouldn't let Rube even mention his affair with Cousin Caresse, much less the fact that he had a son by the name of Reuben. When Ned told Rube that Sam was not part of the curse, I just about dropped my Palm Pilot. Surely, you saw that as an obvious clue. Yet, Rube said nothing about it.

Ned Blankenschipf turned out to be a nice guy, but how he ever passed private investigator school, I'll never know. Especially disguise class. Why, my fourth grade son does better than that on Halloween.

Herschel's getting a little edgy. So am I, for that matter. I've been thinking that maybe I can hook up with one of these college professors around here. They're always writing stuff. Some of them write textbooks about mites and monkeys. I sure as hell don't want to narrate textbooks. Maybe I can find a professor who's writing about a friendship that develops between a Hispanic bricklayer and George W. Bush. That would be interesting, don't you think? Some people write romance novels. Hey, there's an idea. I'm pretty good at narrating love stories. Remember the scenes between Amy and Rube?

Don't worry about me. I'll find something.

Narrator

EPILOGUE

Rube and Amy were married in Helen the following spring. Rube chuckled when he thought of asking Reverend Ralph Lee to marry them. Reverend Lee had been there during some of the most trying times in Rube's life, the latest being the fall in the grave affair while presiding over the funeral for Amy's parents. He hadn't met the new Rube.

The church secretary buzzed Rube's call into Reverend Lee's office. "Hello, Preacher Lee speaking."

"Hello, Reverend Lee. This is Rube Winters."

"Rube, I haven't heard from you in a long time. What's wrong?"

"What makes you think something is wrong, Reverend Lee?"

"Oh, I don't know. I'm sorry, Rube. I guess it must be from our past experiences together," he stammered.

"I know what you mean. I've put you through a lot in the past, but I am a new man now. You can take my word for that. Sometime I'll share the lessons I've learned with you. Right now, I want to ask a favor of you. Amy and I are getting married, and we want you to be the referee."

There was a long pause, a couple of coughs and a sniffing noise, "Rube, my boy, I would be honored. Just don't invite any birds, or set any traps that I might fall into," he laughed. "Now give me the when and where details."

The wedding went well to Reverend Lee's surprise.

Although Rube's life was extremely busy during these years, Amy's presence was always a stabilizing factor. After a few years, she consented to come and work at Health from The Source, eventually becoming office manager of the corporation.

Moochie Dunlop and Bud Arrington were soul mates. They bought a small house near the large new home Kristy's parents helped her buy, so Moochie could be near "My Boy," as she called Sam. Bud learned how to survive Moochie's massive hugs. He gave up drinking and was now in charge of the shipping department at Rube's headquarters, and doing a good job.

Uncle Billy retired from the meat packing plant in Dallas, and moved back home to Winder, Georgia. Rube talked him into coming to work three days a week as head of the Public Relations Department. Garcia Rose and Amy actually ran the department from day to day. But, when there was a meeting, Uncle Billy always sat at the head of the table, kicked back in his swivel chair with his straw hat cocked to one side. There was always a fruit jar of sweet tea with a spoon in it next to him.

He usually stopped in the shipping department and had a cup of coffee with the boys, telling his war stories which seemed to grow in magnitude each time. Bud kidded Uncle Billy about winning *World War Two* single-handedly.

Within two years Kristy was divorced from the coach, and not wanting to be in the same school system, accepted a job in Oconee County. After that, she and Rube were on speaking terms, and able to discuss Sam's future in a civil manner.

Time could not erase the impact of that first visit with Dr. Wilkins. In some ways it seemed like a lifetime ago, in others only yesterday. He had visited his old professor and dear friend every Monday since then, except for a few days when the weather was bad, or one of his flights was delayed. At first, the trips to The Source were a chore. It was a long drive so he had to leave very early in the morning, work at reorganizing the notes and planning the strategy of how to get this information to all people, worldwide, then drive back to Athens. It became easier as time went on, especially when he began to grasp, not only in his brain, but in his heart and soul, what this could mean to mankind.

The business started by Rube, called *Health from The Source*, was a tremendous success. They taught seminars all over the world, published a monthly newsletter and sold nutritional products. Rube refused to take credit.

As the business became even more successful, grants were made from *The Source Foundation* to colleges and other education and research organizations throughout the country. The latest and largest contribution was recently pledged to the *University of Georgia* for a new quantum physics building unequaled anywhere in the world. This philanthropic work was important to Rube and Dr. Wilkins.

But, even more important was getting the information to people so they could live healthy, happy and successful lives, accomplish their missions, and make their way back to *The Source* and unconditional love which heals all.

Surprise! I'm still here. I know you think I'm crazy for risking my job as a narrator, but now it turns out I am crazy like a fox. Herschel was able to sneak our last comments into the final printing, and they printed one thousand books. Mailed them out to all the book stores. Then, the editor discovered what had happened. Needless to say, the whole waste disposal system in this town hit the fan. The editor was so upset with the printer that he threatened to sue what he called his "ink stained heart" all the way to the Supreme Court. The printer threw poor Herschel up on the table and tried to run his head through the printing machine until the other employees pulled him off. I went into hiding for a few days. When I re-surfaced, the author wouldn't even speak to me. Said I was lower than whale droppings on the bottom of the ocean. He had a change of heart after I reminded him of what he said about forgiveness in the book. He said he would try very hard to forgive my double-crossing hide, and even pray for me. I promised to do the same for him.

After a while the editor called the publisher and begged him to recall all of the books. "Can't do that," said the publisher. "It wouldn't be prudent. I've got too much money tied up. See if they won't sell. Maybe readers won't be too offended by that loony narrator."

Well, Sir. A few weeks went by and they began to get feedback from readers and bookstores. Guess what. They loved me. Said it was the first time an author found a way to keep them informed about what was goin' on under the surface. Said it made them feel like an insider.

The author took credit for everything. Said it was all his idea. That prune face! Oops! Sorry. I did forgive him and told him so. I even wished him well on his next novel. He patted me on the back and apologized for all the bad names he called me. The printer went looking for Herschel and offered his job back. Herschel respectfully declined. Said he was having too much fun sweeping and mopping. The fact is, the bowling alley allows him to do all the "Glow in the dark" bowling he wants. That's what kept him there.

As for me, I'm working on the next novel. I can't wait for you to read that one. I don't know for sure yet, but Tony Colosimo and Rube might show up in the new book. Of course, I can't reveal anything to you since I've been signed to an ironclad contract to keep my big mouth shut unless the author gives me permission.

I quit narrating for the political writer. You know how I am about telling the truth. The writer resigned too. Had an idea for a new business. Said he was gonna start writing "Rent a Sermon" for preachers on the internet.

Narrator

P.S. All of my comments about this book will be included in all future printings.